COINCID

Brian Fearon

For someone who spent his life avoiding decisions, relationships and conflict, George McNeill, suddenly encountered all three. A decision would lead to conflicts and the conflicts would threaten newly formed relationship and some old ones as well. In life, he adopted a conciliatory path, but when he succeeded in antagonising some very dangerous people this resulted in, his friends, family, and colleagues being placed at risk. It may be events shaped George, not the other way around, right up to the final conclave.

Foreword

Where does a story come from? For me the idea I had nurtured for almost sixty years was prompted by a spoof on April Fool's Day in the 1960s by BBC Northern Ireland news. They showed a man walking through Shaftsbury Square in Belfast beside the old Edwardian public conveniences, long since gone. As he reached the steps there was a sound of an underground, subway train pulling in at the foot of the steps. Belfast has never had a subway. The little prank tickled me and stayed in my head.

When I began writing it popped out and at the foot of those steps the drama contained in 'Coincidences' began. The story emerged in layers with the plot of a violent crime and then a cast of characters emerging. Each layer prompted another twist in the plot.

I wish to acknowledge the support of my wife Katy and my daughter Roisin who read and reread the story and the work put in on proofreading by Bobbie Dickie and Lyn McLean.

Brian Fearon

Table of Contents

Chapter 1

The Calm Before the Storm

Inspector Walker (PSNI) speculated on whether George was an innocent passer-by, a banker for the drugs cartel, an MI5 agent, a dissident IRA man, a combination of some or even all of these. What did he know? Who had he killed?

George drummed his fingers on his desk. The sound was oddly comforting. He put his hand on his forehead and asked himself again, '*Why did I do it? If I just close my eyes, it will all turn out to be a dream. I can just go back.*' He opened them. Nothing was different. George glanced at the bottom drawer, the one where the gun had been. He knew it was no longer there, but he looked anyway. He opened the drawer. There were a few old file covers, a discarded broken stapler, an old desk-tidy the kids bought for him years ago for Christmas. There was no gun. How could there be? Surely other cities: London, Glasgow, Dublin were not as violent as Belfast. It is a legacy of the Troubles. George would soon find out.

A week earlier George got up from behind his computer and stretched. Each member of staff in the Accounts section was based in a tiny cubicle behind a perspex screen. Company policy decreed staff worked better in a private space if they could see colleagues. Baileys was a large finance and accountancy firm based in Belfast City Centre which arranged loans for medium and small businesses. There was also a personal loan section that provided finance to individuals. A recent initiative led to them acquiring property. They audited firms, medium or small-sized enterprises and provided tax and investment advice.

Gus and Dan rose from their computers just sufficiently to look at each other.

"It'll be 12.30 then," whispered Dan. Gus nodded.

They waited until George walked out of the office to the lifts before shutting down their computers and heading off for lunch. Nothing against George, but he was an old guy, forty, and not exactly scintillating company. Anyway, it was common knowledge he preferred to be on his own. Nobody who encountered George in his work or personal life considered him a complex character. More senior people in Baileys who had known him for over twenty years were quick to point out,

"The thing about George is you can read him like a book. He is totally reliable, regular in his habits to the point almost of obsession, avoids conflict and relationships. He just wants to live quietly."

Tall, a shade under six feet, he tended to stoop as he walked, giving the impression of being smaller and spoke slowly and deliberately.

How would George describe himself? Much the same, a meticulous employee; he would acknowledge he avoided conflict. Deep down he had dreams such as owning a performance car and he fantasised about strutting his stuff, if only he could find the confidence. The old saying springs to mind: "the meek shall inherit the earth... if no one minds awfully."

His parents were quiet folk, his older brother was quiet, but when George was young, his shyness suggested he may be on the spectrum. His mother took him to Child Psychiatry. The consultant saw him as a normal wee boy apart from coming over as 'afraid', although she could not fathom of what. She identified that his mother was ill when he was born and for several years thereafter.

George was on friendly terms with five of Baileys' partners. The sixth, Cyril Gallagher, had not worked his way up through Baileys, the firm's preferred option. He entered as a partner. To get a partnership, it was necessary to purchase the shares of a retiring partner. The partners operated effectively as a Board of Directors. Usually, an existing employee at senior level purchased the shareholding of a retiring partner. When the last partner left, there was no obvious choice and the other partners either purchased the shares themselves or invited an outsider, in this case Cyril.

Cyril tried to persuade his fellow partners to diversify and broaden their business. He produced ambitious plans to take over smaller accountancy firms in other UK cities and put a 'Baileys' brand on them. Cyril became Baileys 'hard man.' If a difficult or unpleasant task was necessary, Cyril did it. He was brought in because he was intellectually and emotionally suitable for the tough role and, in fact, relished it. Not all the partners were enamoured by the change. The senior partner, an older man who held a large shareholding was a 'silent partner' these days but influential. Alliances were brokered and lost as the major players circled each other. Peter Donald, the partner most respected by both camps, worked to prevent total conflict.

George's lunchtime routine began as he left the office. In the lift were a young woman from HR and two guys from IT and Peter Donald, the partner. The lift was quiet until George got in and Peter said, "Hi George."

"Hello Peter, how's the family?" asked George.

"Fine," responded Peter," How's.... (Just stopped in time, George separated from his wife two years previously) ...things with you?" finished Peter. He was a grey man, silver, grey hair, grey suit, grey pallor. Quietly spoken he possessed a calm, reassuring presentation and more than a hint of gravitas. Small talk followed between them, and the younger employees maintained a discreet silence.

George walked by the reception desk where Mandy, a recent employee, stared aggressively at him. He just ignored her; they all went out into Bedford Street. Mandy had joined the firm 4 months previously. She moved from a similar post in an engineering firm where she got into a relationship with a manager.

This led to complaints when Mandy got an undeserved promotion, and someone told the Manager's wife about his involvement with Mandy. She lost her job as a result with a minor payoff. Mandy came to Baileys through her previous paramour's links with a manager there. When she joined the firm, she was briefed that there were six partners, all male, one in his late seventies, another in his sixties and the others in their forties. She must ensure any matters they needed resolved were dealt with immediately: "Most of the staff here are nice but be wary of the partners, they are conscious of their position."

Mandy cut a bit of a character. She favoured low-cut blouses and dresses which got the attention of a fair number of the male employees. She saw George exit the lift frequently, chatting with partners, the only one who responded to her smile. Over the next few weeks, the new receptionist smiled at him each time he passed the reception desk and, being affable, he responded.

On a Tuesday, five weeks after starting, Mandy was with a colleague, Patsy, who acted as relief receptionist when she was on a break. Patsy spoke to George. Mandy joined in the conversation thinking, "Well he isn't stuck up." A little later she spoke to Patsy,

"He," meaning George, "seems more human than the other partners."

"Goodness, George isn't a partner, he is an accountant, and a junior one at that, on the second floor, deals mostly with pay day loans. He has been here for years."

The four younger partners started within a year of George. They all worked alongside him before becoming managers and, ultimately, partners. Most of the other managers here also worked with him. They all know George, a loaner and so quiet."

Mandy was furious. George let her down with his friendly smile and wearing a suit and talking familiarly to partners, acting important. She glowered at him whenever he appeared. Poor George, oblivious to his 'failure' to be what Mandy wanted, continued to smile at her for a few days, receiving the 'dirty looks' then just ignored her. Patsy never could figure out what made Mandy so angry at George. Mandy's own scheming caught up with her, so Patsy just nodded and moved the conversations on.

George's daily lunch routine was set in stone. Each day between 12.30 and 1.30 pm he enjoyed a break from the computer. Four years previously, the firm's office canteen, which George liked, went by the wayside in 'cuts'. He used a nearby sandwich shop instead. He would purchase a ham salad sandwich, a carton of orange juice and an apple. The staff in the shop were bemused by his unchanging diet. Over time, they got to know George by name. He would be greeted affably. George would smile back, agree,' the weather was nice or awful, cold, or wet,' take his place in the queue and exit as quickly as possible. The women speculated about George. When they discovered his single status, they dropped hints concerning sisters or friends who were single who would love a 'blind date' with him. These suggestions made George quite apprehensive. Once, a recently divorced woman who just started in the shop asked George if he could help her with her garden and George explained he had a bad back.

"He wouldn't be much use for anything else then," Doreen, the assistant manager observed, and they all laughed.

And George, well, George just returned to the background, attracting a friendly greeting daily but no expectations. The only exception to his daily routine was each month he purchased a glossy car magazine. He might own a battered old Escort, but George fancied an Aston Martin or a racy BMW 7 series. If he ever got the opportunity, he wanted to buy an upmarket car.

George joined Baileys, aged 17, as a message boy. His job was to deliver mail around the city and around the office. He collected documents from the printers back in the traditional days of bulk printing and photocopying. Gradually he became absorbed into the clerical workforce moving from the General Office, as the business grew and modernised, eventually to Accounts. At first, he dealt with loans to people, someone else approved them and George chased up payments and knocked on doors all over the city.

He then moved into the approval side of personal loans and proved quite competent. A few years later a colleague he started at Baileys with got promoted to a senior manager's post and, aware of George's young family, encouraged him to be involved with small businesses to see if he could make the jump to that demanding, but more prestigious task. It did not work. George proved not assertive or effective enough, and he was allowed to slip back to personal loans. Three businesses that liked George were keen he stayed with them. That was agreed, a face-saving exercise, really. Despite this setback, George was much happier at work than at school.

George did not care for school. His older brother was two years ahead of him, and a teacher commented, "David McNeill's a quiet lad but, in comparison, his young brother is practically mute."

Towards the end of his first year, he was confronted by a fellow pupil, Keith Davis. Keith's big brother and David McNeill previously fought. David came off in marginally better shape. Keith decided to redress the family honour. He punched George on the nose. Blood flowed; "Fight, fight" went the cry. Keith waited for George to retaliate and when he didn't, knocked him down. "Kick him, kick him" the crowd urged, but a fourth form girl, Mary Fox, heard the commotion and brought peace to the scene by clipping Keith on the ear and taking George to the school nurse.

In the fifth year, studying for O grades, the pupils were divided into smaller mixed groups and brief relationships emerged among different pupils. He got friendly with the three who were most often in his subject group, Michael, Catherine, and Irene. Michael and Catherine began to 'go steady' and George and Irene tagged along.

They drifted into a relationship. A relationship pitifully slow in developing, much to Irene's frustration, "He doesn't even try anything," Irene bewailed to Catherine.

"He is just a nice quiet boy" said Catherine, "either make a move on him or dump him."

Irene a plump and not fashionably dressed girl did not decide either way. She stayed with the flow, perhaps because no other offers happened. They all passed their O grades; George's were just mediocre grades. The other three stayed on to do A levels, while George began an apprenticeship at Baileys.

He had more money, which Irene welcomed, and they could go out more than most eighteen-year-olds in those days and this pattern continued for three years. As Irene often pointed out, George never proposed. She sort of said, "Maybe we should get married." and George sort of agreed. Irene chose a ring and three years after they were engaged, she, with the help of George's mother, made all the preparations. A low-key wedding followed, they could not afford a honeymoon, after which they rented a modest house on the Castlereagh Road.

By the time Irene reached her final year of teacher training at Stranmillis College she entered into a brief relationship with another student on the course, but it fizzled out. Irene was quite stimulated by the experience and quite down when it finished. She lost weight, dressed more fashionably, and appeared a more attractive prospect, which did wonders for her self-image. When the affair ended, she was deflated and moody. George put it down to her being under pressure on the course and was supportive, in a George way.

They bought a semi-detached house in the Upper Knockbreda area of South Belfast, and Irene, now teaching, became the major breadwinner in the family. All went well for several years. Then Terry, followed by Melissa, came along, quite different children. George wasn't a 'hands on' dad, but he got on well with his son, a quiet wee boy. Father and son walked a lot, or Terry cycled with a tricycle, or stabilisers and spent time with his dad, like George's experience with his own father. George experienced a measure of sadness when his parents died. Odd experiences drifted to back to him such as his father smoking his pipe. Sometimes, if George closed his eyes, he could smell the pipe tobacco. Each Christmas a relative bought his father an overly sweet pungent foreign tobacco that she believed was fashionable in an 'arty' way. George's father never bought it for himself, "far too expensive," but, for a month around Christmas, that sweet pungent aroma pervaded the house.

Melissa was a demanding child, a poor sleeper and feeder, always crying. George was patient but helpless when left with her. They did not bond, and gradually, Irene's parents, especially her mother, were more involved. When Irene's maternity leave finished, Melissa's care came mostly from her maternal grandparents. She and George did have a relationship, but never as close as father and son.

Irene continually badgered George to get a promotion at his work. He became an Accountancy Assistant, which meant more money, and studied for his Articles which he eventually struggled through. The firm designated him an accountant, but, in fact, it proved the end of the line for any prospects. Work for George was more routine, and he was content.

Almost invisible in the workplace, when colleagues who drifted to other employers met up over the years and discussed 'the old days,' as they remembered work mates, George's was the name they forgot. Like Brad Dexter in his favourite movie, "The Magnificent Seven,' every fan remembers Brynner, McQueen, Bronson, Coburn, Vaughan, and Buchholz.

"Oh yes, now I remember George. Nice enough bloke, but so quiet."

Irene spoke to him one evening. She brought up her previous affairs. She stuck it out for as long as she could, as she declared later, because no better offer happened. She explained she was unhappy in the marriage. All of it was a disappointment to her. That included their sex life, which she described as boring and lacking any passion or stimulation.

This surprised George given the little intimacy between them in recent years. Also, George initiated the little intimacy left in their relationship. She waited until Terry was 14 and Melissa 11, when she said that they should split up.

"The thing is George, you live here but you do nothing, you say little, you wait for me to decide, you agree with everything, and you leave it all to me."

She added she would partially re-mortgage the house, George could have a third of the balance of the equity and she and the children would keep the house with Irene, in effect using the re-mortgage to buy George out. She estimated his portion would realise £7,000 and George could use that as a deposit on a flat for himself. Irene worked out all the details of how she and the children would fare but wasn't clear on George's future arrangements. If some practical arrangements did not materialise the matter would drag out as George would not be capable of organising himself.

George initially panicked. He had no problems with Irene's perspective on their relationship. He found out that she engaged in two further brief relationships with colleagues, one was married, the other divorced. He knew because a 'well meaning' acquaintance phoned him to alert him to the affair with the divorced man. The married man's wife visited the house when Irene was away on a 'special education course' organised over a weekend. George ignored what he assumed was a first brief encounter, but this was altogether more serious. He regarded the young wife who appeared that weekend at his house with astonishment. She presented as devastated; her husband suggested he might leave her for Irene. He described Irene as a sexy woman, a description George could not for the life of him recognise. The young woman wavered between wanting to stab them both to begging George to get his wife to see sense.

Eventually, George calmed her down and promised to speak to Irene which he did. She retorted, "It's none of your business,"

Perhaps the education course proved less special, but the man agreed to try again in his marriage and he and Irene parted, although George guessed an odd encounter took place over the next year. However, faced with this ultimatum, George did not know what to do, so he went to visit his brother David. Moira, his sister-in -law, sat in on the discussion. Strangely, neither she nor David expressed surprised or were the slightest bit critical of either party or Irene's previous relationships. Given the nature of Belfast George guessed they were aware of what was going on. Irene did little to hide herself away, almost trying to provoke George into a reaction.

His sister-in-law came up with a helpful suggestion. She knew of a couple called Barrow, who lived on the Beersbridge Road who took in long term, 'respectable' lodgers. One of her colleagues lived there for three years, it would give George breathing space to plan his next move.

George moved in with the Barrows. It proved an agreeable experience all round. For a consideration Mrs Barrow dealt with his washing and ironing, he got an evening meal seven days a week and somewhere to park his old Ford Escort. It was a simple bus run to and from work. George roamed on his weekends, went for a walk in the evenings in dry weather and met Terry for a burger tea or the cinema at the weekend. Melissa came at first but often pronounced herself 'bored', so it tended to be father and son.

He and Irene divorced a year after they separated. In the end, it was a relief to call time on their marriage. On weekday nights when football was on the TV, (with European nights that could be three or four times a week), George and Mr Barrow watched the games together while Mrs B headed out to join her cronies at the bingo. George's room might be described as the master bedroom with its comfortable armchair, and a sink though not a toilet. He installed his own TV. George intended to stay only a year to get on his feet, but after three years, he remained comfortably ensconced. He was not allowed female guests, an unlikely prospect for George. If he had been gay would that have been alright? No, he could not imagine Mrs Barrow recognising the concept. Initially, George was content, but his brother and sister-in-law continually harped on at him to invest in his own place.

Even with the financial support he had to give Irene, he saved a reasonable amount each month in a building society account which, with his share of the house, could provide a deposit on a flat.

Two months previously, Mr Barrow had a health scare, and this brought home to George that his comfortable existence could be disturbed by events outside his control.

He became involved in a couple of relationships at work. Firstly, with a new accountant recently divorced who took a shine to George when she joined Baileys. They pursued a short-lived, initially passionate encounter, mostly in her home. The second was with Pauline, the mother of a boy who played in Terry's football team. Terry found out about the romance, through comments from his teammate. Both boys were unhappy, and Terry told George straight out that there must not be any 'messing around' when team members were in earshot.

He continued to faithfully attend his son's football matches each Saturday. George transported some of the players in his car. He didn't attempt any coaching like other dads, nor was he vocal from the side-lines. He refused to do any refereeing even if Terry's team or their opponents were desperate. He and Terry went out to tea afterwards, sometimes bringing Terry's friends from the team. Pauline and George met every other week for a year. They were both lonely, but it was never likely to be a permanent relationship.

As for work, well, his immediate manager changed from time to time as people in the company moved up. George, acted as the reliable 'Mr Go to' if s small problem needed fixed quickly, provided no major decision or action was required, and above all, no confrontations.

Of the three businesses which were keen to stay with George Mrs Abernethy's Tea House caused concern. It was well known in South Belfast, sitting on the front of the Lisburn Road on a corner site with one of those winding avenues that went through to the Malone Road. Old Mrs Abernethy opened it in 1935, in 1965 her daughter, Mrs Canning, took it over. Mrs Canning herself was now in her late seventies. The plan was for her daughter Eleanor, in her turn, to take over but sadly Eleanor died of breast cancer at the age of 44. Eleanor and her husband had kept the business side of the tea house afloat with able management and financial inputs unbeknownst to Mrs Canning.

One Sunday evening at a church service Mrs Canning mentioned to a Baileys partner that she was worried her business might be 'struggling a little. 'It seemed ideal for Baileys' Community Business Model. George agreed to assess the situation and see if the firm could help with a grant. Mrs Canning surveyed the man sitting before her in her simple drawing room. She hoped for an older person, a person she knew from the church. This man appeared as quiet, almost diffident.

"Mrs Canning what do you think the current loss might be?"

She responded, "It could be as high as £20,000."

"Have you submitted any accounts for the last two years?"

The old lady gravely shook he head. "In recent years my daughter and son- in -law have dealt with that side but she died…." Her voice trailed off; her eyes moistened.

George felt genuinely sad for her, caught between maintaining her own mother's legacy and the tragic death of her daughter.

"Well, if you are happy a colleague and I will work through the books, identify issues, and ideally come up with a solution."

He tried not to be too bright and upbeat; Mrs Canning wasn't in the mood for that, but he wanted her to be reassured that they possessed an expertise that would see her through this problem. A fortnight later they sat again in an austere room with its hint of pre-war furnishings. Mrs Canning was not one for material trappings. He rehearsed his next sentence many times since they concluded their examination of the business. No matter how he tried he couldn't soften the blow enough.

"Mrs Canning, I am afraid the new is worse than we thought. The business's debts amount to almost £70,000." Mrs Canning gasped, she paled, and George fetched her a glass of water. By then she regained her composure.

"What can we do?" she stated softly almost thinking aloud rather than expecting George to come up with a solution.

George surprised her. "I have a rescue plan in mind."

Part of the plan meant a reduction in wages for staff. Of the seven employees, four were friends of Eleanor's who drifted into the cafe for pin money as they raised their young families. Their only concern was to save the business. Two of the women were dependent on their wages and an informal arrangement around tips might enable them to stay. A member of staff used this as an excuse to leave, helping reduce overheads further. Baileys would provide a lengthy loan with a low interest rate. It was feasible. The café would stay above water, only just. George also had a plan for some Belgian high-quality baking to improve footfall combined with basic marketing.

Mrs Canning tempered her gratitude; she wasn't an emotional person, but she told the Baileys partner after church, 'What a pleasant, kind young man George was and how lucky they are to have him.'

One other business George kept on was a bakery run by a Belgian man, Jan Tieleman and his daughter, Elena. Jan had been a chef in the merchant navy, fell in love with a Belfast girl, jumped ship, set up home with her and they had a daughter.

He was of average height, balding, with a moustache and an anxious demeanour The mother died when Elena was 12 and her father brought her up on his own. European Union regulations helped him move from an illegal to a legal residency, but he remained nervous of authority.

Jan contacted George in 2001, something he was to do over the next few years, because his business slowed from September. It would pick up near Christmas, but he needed a loan to keep it ticking over. George went out to the bakery in North Belfast for a chat about how Baileys could help Jan. Over the years his friendship with Jan and Elena. Jan would phone George from time to time looking for advice on a range of matters when he believed he was being taken advantage of this ranged from disputes over tax payments to arguments with neighbouring businesses over parking and deliveries. All he asked in return was a preferential arrangement to supply Mrs Abernethy's Tea Room.

George would reassure Jan that his adversary was behaving normally for Northern Ireland's culture, or that the tax authorities could do what they said they could do. On occasional weekends, he and Jan attended motor bike racing or any car-based events. Jan was desperate for a friend, someone supportive and George ended up in the unlikely position of being propelled into responding warmly, acting with decisiveness, and even developing a relationship. Since she was little, Elena had been told George McNeill would help them and he usually came up trumps. She admitted to a crush on George since she was 13, although as an attractive young woman, a string of boys pursued her, much to Jan's discomfort.

"I don't know what to do, George," he complained on George's latest visit. "She brings these shaven headed yobs or bizarre looking punks to the house, and I want to chase them all away. Will you speak to her, please?" Jan begged.

Elena and George's relationship was on an of 'uncle and niece' basis. He spoke with her more than anyone, even Terry. He saw himself as an uncle to Elena and was not clear exactly what Jan wanted him to say. To stop the pleading, he agreed. He made a special visit. Elena's eighteenth birthday approached, and George bought her a birthday gift.

Jan ushered him into their lounge and shouted, "Elena, George needs a word with you" and made himself scarce.

George was not equipped to deal with matters of teenage relationships any more than he could deal with any other relationship. He spoke to Patsy, the relief receptionist, concerning a suitable present for an eighteen-year-old girl, and she recommended a fashionable bracelet. She stood beside Mandy when George walked over to speak to her, and Mandy stomped off.

George muttered, "She's a strange girl" and Patsy rolled her eyes musing: *"George's daughter can't bet eighteen already."*

For his heart-to-heart with Elena, George made the unwise decision just to 'wing' it. Elena came into the room and kissed George on both cheeks as she always did, in the manner her aunts taught her, the European way.

"Here is a birthday gift for your big day."

There followed small talk on the bakery, customers, invoices, sales, employees. Despite her age, Elena was involved in the running of the business. She left school to be her father's right hand. She knew as much as he did about the bakery's inner workings. She attended college at night to sit her A levels as she wanted to go to university to study Law. Jan felt both proud and apprehensive, pleased with her ambition but certain that she would leave home. When they finished the bakery chit-chat George sat on uneasily, aware he promised his friend he would speak to Elena regarding her 'social life' but not knowing where to start. Elena sat on the settee a little self-consciously, glancing at her watch. "I don't know where Dad is. I am afraid I need to go. I am meeting friends in town."

George saw an opening, "Well Elena" he said stirring uncomfortably in the chair and realising that Elena was a day off reaching the age of legal responsibility, she was intelligent mature now a young adult not the wee girl of years gone by.

"It's just this, your Dad asked me.... as an old family friend to, er em, speak to you because he is worried about you and your relationships."

Elena glared at him for a second. "Oh, he wants you to give me sex education, how cool." she declared, "It's just I want to get pregnant, but I have no idea what to do, please advise me George. A man of the world like you will know a lot. Should I do this?" and she adopted a provocative pose across the settee. "If I have a boy, I am going to call him George."

George blushed and stammered again, but Elena jumped up, "George, I am almost 18. Since the age of fifteen, I've been going out with boys. I have heaps of girlfriends and we have talked little else except boys, well, boys and bands, for the last six years. I promise you I will be careful; tell my dad he has a level-headed daughter and not to worry so. The wildest looking boys are often the nicest." With that, she got up, gave him a big hug, a kiss, and she was gone.

George assured Jan his daughter could be trusted to behave in a responsible manner. Jan wasn't sure George was direct enough but at least Elena got advice, though about what, he had no idea.

A new manager called in the papers on the Tieleman's account. He resented George's links with more senior people in Baileys, though George tried not to emphasise them. He noticed George approved a loan for Jan; they discussed it and the manager, Alan Carson, said it was not to be approved.

There were issues for George: he was invariably left to make his own decisions given his experience and his reputation for being a safe pair of hands; secondly, George understood without the cash injection

Jan would have to go to a less scrupulous source of financial loans or wind up his business.

In the end George raised it with Carson's predecessor, the senior manager for the entire section. He summoned both men in, listened to their arguments, and approved the loan. Carson was furious and vowed to get his own back on George.

In business terms, Carson was right. Although the Tieleman's always paid back their loan, given the staff time involved and the small interest rate, it was not a productive account. It started as part of Baileys 'Support Local Businesses Initiatives' that bit the dust when the economy tightened. George suspected the senior manager who supported him did so on a personal level and as Alan Carson also believed this, it did nothing to cement any relationship between the two men.

George made an enemy and the next months would result in a bumpy ride at work. The outcome of the dispute of course spread all over the Accounts sections. The other staff were interested to learn what would transpire. Like many new managers, Carson stood on a few toes and not just in his section. As a new broom, he changed practices and scrutinised existing performances. Staff felt the dispute between George and Carson reduced tension between him and them, and they were fascinated at how George would handle the undoubted pressure that lay ahead. 'Badly' is how most believed that question would be answered. It was a slight but petty-minded thing for Carson to do. He scrutinised George's decisions, never acting against them but just making George feel undermined, less appreciated and created a tension in his working day. If this hostile approach continued, George might have to rethink his future. But a lucky break came George's way.

Years earlier, a rising young politician, Thomas Whyte MP, got into financial difficulty. The firm were aware that since so many senior people moved in similar social and, shall we say, organisational circles to the politician, it would be better if a discreet junior member of staff handled the matter. Someone who could understand the sensitivities and would not exploit them. George was the natural choice.

As the years passed, the politician's star rose but his combination of alcohol and gambling problems grew. George was called on to bail him out.

'Bailed out by Baileys', as inquisitive local journalists called it.

They could never get the entire story, although twice George was approached as journalists got a whiff of a scandal and offered him cash for the inside story. George reported this up his chain of command, increasing the general respect he was held in by senior people in the firm. Rumours continued to circulate within the media about Whyte with no printable evidence.

Two months after the loan was issued to the Tielemans, George received a phone call from Thomas Whyte. He behaved with an odd mixture of charm and desperation.

"We are all men of the world," "We have known each other a long time," "You have been so helpful to me in the past," "I tell, X partner and Y partner what a terrific job you are doing."

George had been on the receiving end of similar opening lines, but never as effusive as this. He detected a heightened sense of stress from his client. The politician's alcohol problems led to his gambling addiction, the more severe of his two conditions.

He was married with two children and his wife devoted herself to ensuring his reputation was kept clean in the public eye; she worked assiduously for his re-election. He inherited his seat from her father, and she policed the drinking as best she could because it led to spiralling debt. George cared little for the politician and his particular brand of politics that sought to demonise in quite a personal way his political opponents. Whyte created no problems for him beyond faintly patronising conversations. Baileys, as an important part of the Northern Ireland economic wheel, held a Christmas event when key civic figures, the Lord Mayor of Belfast, members of the Northern Ireland Executive from a range of political parties, and well-known media and sports stars were invited. George was issued with a three-line whip to go. He dreaded the prospect, but his politician 'friend' was going. The man more or less blanked him with only a limp handshake and a fleeting insincere smile. This present contact was different, bordering on the desperate, the sum requested over thirty thousand pounds.

"George, I have other irons in the fire but if Baileys could manage thirty thousand, that would be a big help."

George guessed he told a rival firm, 'I have thirty thousand, so I only need twenty from you.'

None of the usual mention of horses he received 'dead certs' tips from friends inside the horse racing fraternity emerged. He did not mention gambling at all, though usually he spoke openly about his fall, one that "would never happen again."

The thirty thousand sum was above George's pay grade, so he went to see Alan Carson.

A busy Carson did not even use the request to humiliate George. "You know who he is, you know who he knows, phone him and send him a letter tonight, first class, approving it."

George left the brief meeting at late on Friday evening certain that something was out of kilter in the politician's life and this decision was a mistake. He told Whyte he would confirm the decision on Monday morning.

The Sunday papers proclaimed "Tragedy: leading politician Thomas Whyte MP, found hanged in his own garage." Not only had he killed himself, but two letters he left were also found. The first related to an alleged drunken encounter with a gay prostitute in London, in which Whyte claimed he was being blackmailed for a sum of fifty thousand pounds. This letter was not leaked, but a portion of its contents was divulged, no doubt at a price. However, a second document became public, a letter from a major rival of Baileys, refusing him a loan for twenty thousand pounds, Alan Carson read the report with horror. Carson phoned his boss on the Sunday evening to warn Baileys had an outstanding issue. He left a message, as his boss was at church.

The latter consulted with the partners. Alan was told to come to an emergency meeting first thing Monday morning and bring George. The Partner Peter Donald phoned George:

"George, the partners are meeting first thing on Monday morning. You will need to brief us."

George did not get the Sunday papers, but he tried to explain to Peter that the matter was fine. Peter cut him short, so stressed was he by the tragedy. A friend of Whyte's, he couldn't take in George's information.

Alan insisted a letter was sent out on Friday night. Of course, the letter's contents would not have been bad news, but it would have drawn Baileys into the affair, which the firm would be desperate to avoid. If they wrote, like their rivals, to turn him down, they would have been implicated in factors that led to the tragedy. If they wrote to approve the loan to pay blackmail, their professionalism would have been frowned upon by other customers and shareholders. A lose, lose situation.

Next morning Alan joined the meeting a fraction late. This added insult to injury when the blame game started, as it would. He sat down as unobtrusively as possible; George was in full flow.

"Normally we, (You the Partners) would want to help Mr Whyte but this was a very large sum and we were more than a little apprehensive about taking it forward, so we decided to hold back."

"Clever," thought Alan. *"Drawing the partners in."*

From the exchanged glances between partners, they knew they would have approved the loan without hesitation and Baileys would have been involved. Alan also noted that George protected him in his explanation.

The partners were relieved with the briefing, almost forgetting to record, until George suggested it, the tragedy of the event and agreeing a letter should be sent to the late Mr Whyte's widow, expressing the firm's sympathy.

Peter Donald sensed it was George who held back though he said 'we' and noted how competent George performed in this tricky situation. Since he first worked with George, he recognised the potential, if only George pushed himself instead of holding back. He could have risen in the firm, if not to partner then at least to a more senior role. It might have helped keep his marriage together, too.

On the way down in the lift, George kept his counsel. Carson said to him, "I appreciate what you did in there, George."

The first time in ages he used his colleague's first name. George bowed his head in acknowledgement and the relief flooded through

Carson. As the lift halted at their floor, he grabbed George's hand and shook it.

Two weeks later, George met with Peter Donald.

"Thomas Whyte's widow, Aileen, wants one of us to visit her concerning an unresolved business issue. It is a sensitive matter, but we can rely on you." He did not enlarge on the 'sensitive.'

George telephoned Aileen Whyte and arranged, reluctantly, to call at her home on Belfast's Malone Road. To him an unattractive prospect, since he was neither by nature curious or interested in other people nor on widening his social circle. Still, Aileen Whyte had been a celebrity for years. The passionate advocate of her father's political campaigns, regularly pictured on the stump during a campaign exhorting doubtful voters to back 'the man they could depend on, Edmund Proctor.' She, often to the chagrin of Party bosses and rising political stars, was pushed forward by her father to do TV and radio interviews. His forte was rural church halls and fervent audiences the length and breadth of the constituency. Many considered he intended Aileen succeed him.

Aileen graduated from Queens University with a First in Economics and Business Law, worked for the Belfast Chamber of Commerce, and then round the corner for the Northern Ireland Chamber of Commerce. Regularly called on by the media, especially TV, to comment on Chancellors' budgets, closures of major employers, and other finance related issues, Aileen's profile grew. Then to everyone's surprise, she had a quick romance with Thomas Whyte. They got married and two daughters soon followed, which took her out of the political reckoning.

After her father's stroke, Thomas Whyte, already an Assembly member at Stormont, stepped into his father-in-law's vacated Westminster seat.

George phoned and spoke to the very cool Mrs Whyte to arrange the appointment. She did not elaborate on why she needed to meet him, but he agreed to call the following Tuesday after work. He would miss his evening meal, which irritated George somewhat.

He arrived at the large double fronted Malone Road villa. There was a pebble driveway that curved up to the front door with a large turning circle. The house was recently painted. Aileen Whyte was brought up here, it was her parents' home. They downsized to a bungalow after her eldest daughter, Abbi, was born, and Aileen and Thomas moved into the bigger house. George parked his car down the drive. A police officer stood guard. The Whyte's had police protection, like many other senior politicians in Northern Ireland, and removal of this perk was in the 'sensitive' category. Also, the papers were rife with rumours that the Party would choose Aileen Whyte as her husband's successor. The circumstances around Thomas's death meant in a by election she was a shoe in,

He rang the bell, and Mrs Whyte ushered him to a large hall with a curved staircase and black and white patterned tiles. From there she brought him into a large front drawing room with an enormous fireplace, mantelpiece, chandelier and offered him coffee. On the strength of having been deprived of his evening meal, George acquiesced. The room was furnished tastefully and expensively, the wallpaper struck the right balance between being modern and yet fitted the grandeur of the house. The furniture was expensive rather than comfortable, not much family life happened here. Meeting a person, you have seen often on TV is odd. They appear heavier or thinner or younger or less striking than their TV persona suggests.

George considered Aileen Whyte more attractive, and smaller than he expected. She was the same age as himself, just shy of forty. She wore a colourful sweater and a plain, quite short, navy skirt. 'Nice legs too,' he noted. She had a fuller figure than he expected from her TV appearances, where she just seemed plump.

Her skin was flawless, the dewy skin of a female a third her age. A perfect oval face was framed with brown hair worn long below her shoulders. What stood out were her big brown eyes. Even on television they were a striking and an attractive feature. He could not believe he was thinking along these lines, it just wasn't his suit. Much less of the downtrodden, grieving widow than he expected. George was surprised at himself. He rarely noticed what people were wearing or their appearance.

George only ever had crushes on two people in his life: a fourth form girl at school who was kind to him. He couldn't remember her name, but it might have been Mary and a young trainee accountant called Evie who started at Baileys, straight out of college, more than ten years before. George was asked to mentor her. He made excuses to have coffee and lunch with the young woman. George invested effort in his mentoring role because he liked to be in Evie's company but did not admit to himself, he was attracted to her. In the office toilets, he overheard three colleagues discussing George and Evie and saying, "How sad George is pursuing someone so much younger" and how "He needed to be careful it didn't veer into harassment."

George was horrified and drew back, although the Evie fantasy stayed with him. She left Baileys and four years later George met her and her husband in Royal Avenue and he was introduced as her first mentor and a senior colleague who helped her as a young recruit. George considered Evie less negative in her opinion of him than his gossipy colleagues. The experience made him wary of contact with women at work. He recognised he was attracted to his younger colleague, but he couldn't bear ridicule of any kind.

He was drawn to Aileen Whyte as she unfolded the reason for her meeting with him.

"Mr McNeill, my husband described you as a discreet, trustworthy person" then she added as an afterthought, "I don't know why he didn't like you."

George thought it best to ignore this, it irritated him, he remembered Whyte's attitude towards him at the Baileys' Christmas reception.

He liked me well enough when he needed me to sort out the problems his drinking created. But he didn't say it aloud.

"My husband told me after our second daughter's birth that he was bi-sexual, attracted to men and women. It was a particularly vulnerable time for me because I just had a baby. My religious commitment meant I had reservations concerning homosexual acts and my father's first heart problems occurred at the same time"

She paused and looked quite wistful. George wondered was it the recollection of a younger Aileen losing the dream of an idealistic marriage, the strain of coping with children and this added dimension to her life, or the memory of her father to whom she was especially close. She became aware she of her silence and that George was staring at her.

"Don't worry, Mr McNeill, I will not be emotional; I have shed all the tears that Thomas deserved a while ago. I did not realise that he was as disturbed as he must have been to take his life. That will always impact on the girls and," she added, as an afterthought, "on me, I suppose." Then she adopted her business-like tone again. "As far as I know, my husband did not have longstanding relationships, but he was involved, or so he claimed, in the gay club scene in London.

Some English tabloids were alerted, but their Belfast counterparts were reluctant to touch the story, especially with limited evidence and the likelihood of repercussions. You know Northern Ireland…" George nodded.

"However," she continued, "almost three weeks after his death I received a letter, then two more." She crossed to a bureau and brought out three letters.

"They are from a person called Hamish Campbell. He claimed that Thomas and he were in a relationship, and that Thomas promised him they would set up home and Thomas would look after him."

Politicians make promises, always have. Campbell's expectations were a lot to expect of a figure in the public eye, with two daughters and a wife who was the cornerstone of his electoral power base.

Aileen went on, "He has asked for fifty thousand pounds to be paid to him, but then you know that. I ignored his first letter; I was still in shock at the events around Thomas's death, but his next letters were more desperate. He has threatened to approach the media. The story they think they have is not correct, and they have been made aware of that. They are delving around to get more information while Thomas is still a figure of public interest. I need someone to go to Campbell, bring him money, warn him there will be no more, and try to get him to drop the newspaper interest."

George observed, "You know, if he agrees, as soon as that money is done, he will demand more. He will do that even if you gave him the fifty thousand."

Aileen Whyte sighed, more in exasperation than sadness. "Look, Mr McNeill, I have been involved in politics since I the age of fifteen. I know how these games are played. I intend to ask you to make three trips to London over a two-month period, giving Campbell money with the promise of more. All I need is two months, after that he can do what he likes. You will receive a thousand pounds for each trip, plus your expenses." she added.

George pondered on this. A sum of three thousand pounds would be handy for his plan for his own flat. He could not work out why, with her contacts, a couple of' 'heavies' were not sent to give Campbell a warning or a hiding or both.

As Aileen said, "Will you do this for me please? "the penny dropped. She only wanted this out of the road until she was chosen as the Party's candidate. The by election would be held soon; two months being a likely timescale. Then Campbell could say whatever he liked about Thomas Whyte, it would only create more sympathy for that "poor woman and her wee girls."

"OK," said George and Aileen Whyte sprang across the room and gave him a kiss on the cheek then, shocked by her emotional reaction, she apologised profusely. George was startled but quite flattered by this attention.

"Right George, is it ok if I call you George? You are my knight in shining armour," said Aileen. "We will speak soon."

Aileen stood at the landing window, watching George drive off, feeling confused. What on earth made her kiss a perfect stranger? A nice enough guy, but oh he took ages to get things out. Life has been so tough for such a long, long time.

Daddy dying, though they knew he was in poor health and Thomas's admission about his sexuality coupled with her own feelings and mood after Rosemary's birth. She was proud of her new daughter, though exhausted and tearful, which, as a strong woman, she hated in herself. Then, the ongoing worrying of how her parents and her daughters would react if Thomas's 'coming out' became public. Neither of her parents liked Thomas. Her father recognised his ambition and her mother said, “It’s always got to be about Thomas, hasn’t it?”

Her father’s political rallies were more like religious revival meetings. In a typically Northern Irish way, he combined religion and politics. He was an instinctive politician and Aileen believed the politics led the faith rather than the faith leading the politics. She drifted away from church attendance but didn’t know if that was because of her father’s death, or Thomas, or another reason.

She fell in love with the dashing young politician from County Armagh. Even her father’s reservations did not impinge on that. The disapproval acted as an aphrodisiac. But the reality of the marriage was much less than she dreamed.

She had few boyfriends before Thomas. At university, she wanted to be ‘one of the boys,’ (almost all those involved in politics were male), a passionate debater, an energetic political champion of her cause. She was conscious everyone knew who her father was and was determined not to live in his shadow.

A ‘friend’ confided in her that half the guys in the Students Union thought she was a lesbian and the others saw her as boring and ‘up herself.’ Aileen played up to that, determined to stand and fight. Then one term with no exams, she grew her hair long, dressed in a feminine and fashionable way; soft pastoral summer dresses cut lower at the neck and the knees than she would normally wear. She used more makeup and took a back seat in the Students Union during political debates.

A comment was made, “It is as if Aileen’s twin sister, a very girly person, has appeared instead.” But it was a game. Could she reinvent herself for her own amusement? She wasn’t short of dates that spring and she played the game until term ended. She then went off to spend the summer at a Bible College in South Carolina. It was a mixture of a summer camp for the off springs of Bible Belt worthies and deprived kids from small town Tennessee. It included periods of Bible Study and how to run and manage religious rallies. A good grounding for campaigning in Northern Ireland. All the children and staff were white, and it was here she lost her virginity to a young man from Arizona called Jay, who was set on being a pastor. She hoped he would propose; he didn't, but they stayed in touch for a year while she did her final exams at Queens and then they drifted apart.

As a busy young mum before her father's last illness, she enjoyed the mother and toddler groups, the playgroups, and still acted as a helper to her father in elections or when the constituency office got too busy. With Parent Teacher Councils and more advice centre work on behalf of her dad, she was constantly busy.

The physical side of the marriage tailed off more and more. Rosemary's birth might have been an attempt to rekindle family life but if Aileen's father was not around Thomas became more and more negative towards her, After Edmund's death, the double life, and the stress, made Thomas more of an unpleasant person than he wanted to be.

She didn't miss the physical side of marriage. Occasionally they would make love or have a cuddle, but he was away most of the week and, if out late, slept in a spare bedroom. He tried to be involved with his daughters; Rosemary was grateful for any hint of attention and affection from her father, Abbi less so.

George was so different to most men she met, quiet, diffident, if that was the real George. She only met him once, but some instinct led to her liking him, and trusting him. There was something - she was not sure what, that made her want to know him better. Had he a sad back story like her? Were they kindred spirits?

"Now Aileen don't be ridiculous, just because this guy is going to resolve a problem doesn't mean he would be interested in you or that you should be interested in him, how silly and how unlike you of all people."

Fedor's eyes narrowed in the gloom. The little Irishman, always chattering, always smiling, was irritating him. He didn't like this rendezvous. Dark, cold, and narrow, with only one way in and out. His uncle said this gang was to be trusted. They knew there was a new show in town and wouldn't try any double cross.

Patrick Quinn eased closer. He touched the briefcase with the money and surveyed the bag with the drugs the Eastern European carried and then lightly touched his Glock pistol with its silencer. He would have the money, take the drugs to contacts in Liverpool and head to Madrid and then to South America. He had it all worked out.

An instinct led Fedor to grasp the knife he carried. He turned to Quinn. They both heard footsteps getting closer to the entrance, and then Fedor heard the click. He recognised a gun being cocked, he struck.

Chapter 2

The Event

I suppose that Tuesday early in August 2004, was the day it all began, or was it the day it all ended? George was to think about 'that' day over the next months, toying with which of the scenarios captured the event. It began familiarly. He rose and stretched at 12.30, quite aware of the amusement his routine gave to Dan and Gus, but eager not to discuss it with them lest they felt obliged to join him for his lunchtime sojourn. George was affable in the lift towards Peter. He got his sandwich, apple and juice and went to the City Hall, and as there were no seats available on that nice summer's day, he sat on the grass people watching until he finished, disposing of the sandwich wrapping, empty carton and apple core in a bin.

Then he began the walk he took every day: back past the office, up Bedford Street, through Shaftsbury Square, down Great Victoria Street and back to Baileys. Sun, rain, or snow, this was George's pattern. He followed the same routine. He became barely visible. People who might have seen him years ago never saw him anymore. Like the street furniture he was ignored. That suited George fine. The sandwich shop was already too much of a social obstacle. He needed no more. On his walk he fantasised about being 'someone,' a person looked up to, with power and influence. Same old, same old.

His equilibrium had been disturbed a little while ago and he was no longer as comfortable with his daily walk. In mid-July, as he entered Shaftsbury Square, a figure launched himself, grabbing his hand and shaking it. "George, George McNeill, my old school mate," said the figure. His assailant, because that's how it felt, was a tubby character with glasses wearing a black sweatshirt sporting the remnants of a meal by the look of it and emblazoned by the slogan CCTV in capitals and below it, Your City Centre Safety Partner.

"It's me George, Matt Robb, you old son of a gun."

It was just George's luck that when pupils were paired with someone on school trips, or at assemblies or PE, George and Matt had no natural partners and were thrust together. George was considered an odd bod at school, but when he started going out with Irene and her crowd, he faded from view as an oddity. Robb remained the least popular person. It is no mean achievement to be 'seedy' at 13, but Robb managed it. He got into trouble when he was caught with graphic pornographic magazines in the boys' toilets and that incident went around the school. Now, he wouldn't be the first, but being on his own and with the general intolerance youngsters have for someone different, he was ostracised. At a school disco, when he was 15, he had tried to fondle an older girl pupil, and only the fact that she had too much to drink prevented her from making a formal complaint. The female population of the school were briefed, and they steered well clear of Matt Robb.

Robb had left school at 16 and George had heard, via Irene, that he had gone to Birmingham.

"George, this is great, I am living back home. I have spent twenty years in Birmingham, and I thought I would look up the old gang and have a few drinks, catch up on happy days."

George nodded. Matt said that he headed up a Belfast City Centre CCTV project and said he had seen George on the CCTV in Shaftsbury Square and had come out to meet him, he asked about Irene and sympathised. "Worn that tee shirt," he talked about that "wee bitch," the mother of his two children who had thrown him out because of his drinking.

He suggested they meet for a drink. George agreed, took his business card promising to get in touch and rushed off, saying he had an important meeting back at work.

A fine August day, he walked up Bedford Street and paused near Shaftsbury Square. The sky was blue, there was a breeze and occasionally patchy clouds appeared chasing each other across the sky. A couple of showers happened earlier, but it was dry now though puddles lay on the pavement. '*I can't believe I need a pee*,' he thought and couldn't believe it. George decided to 'tough' it out. As he walked, he focussed on Aileen Whyte. She came into his mind every day, several times a day and last thing at night. Usually his fantasies involved performance cars, but Aileen was now there all the time. Since their meeting, every time George closed his eyes, he saw Aileen's face.

It was no good he was at the Square turning towards Great Victoria Street where he always felt conscious Matt Robb would see him and charge out to arrange their drink. Then he remembered the old Edwardian public conveniences that the Belfast Historical Society had refurbished. There was a piece on the news saying they were a tourist attraction. Loos as a tourist attraction, only Belfast. Still a city that headlined its prominence by boasting about building the Titanic, 'It was all right when it left us,' was capable of anything. He turned back into Shaftsbury Square and went down the stone steps. He wondered if the toilets were functioning or just a replica. The tiled floor, stalls to the right, cubicles to the left. The need for relief was incredible. He walked part way along; the urinals gave a hiss and water fell from a pipe across the top. They were working, brilliant. Halfway along meant that if anyone else came in, they both could observe social distance.

George relieved himself and felt much more comfortable, but, as he was almost finished, he heard a grunt, and then another one from behind him. He glanced over his shoulder. There was a man lying face down on the toilet in the cubicle. Just then, there was a scraping noise and the man's legs slid out a little. Another groan. George turned away and then, fascinated, glanced around again. Even worse, there was a second man lying under the first. Once more George turned back as he prepared to zip up his fly and although he saw himself as broad-minded, he thought, "*how disgusting, I mean fine if they want to have gay sex, go into the cubicle, and close the door. It's 1.00 pm for God's sake.*"

As he zipped up, George turned to walk out, but he couldn't resist a last look into the cubicle behind him. His eye was caught by a red liquid that was oozing over towards the urinal. He looked at the man with his back to the ceiling and saw a large silver, partly red blade protruding from his back. George peered in, gazing into the lifeless eyes of the man underneath, with only his head visible. There was a neat hole right in the centre of his forehead, with tiny black marks around it and blood as well. In addition, he saw a black bag full of plastic pouches with white powder inside them. George stepped back and kicked against an object. He looked down and picked up the gun. It was a black automatic pistol with what was a silencer fixed to the end. As he lifted the gun, he saw a large briefcase wedged between the cubicle door and the toilet, so he picked it up as well. It felt heavy. He went up the steps and walked down Great Victoria Street.

George walked down the pavement, a path he trod every day. A very observant person could think "There is the man you see every day but there is something different. I know, today he is carrying a briefcase." George, with his capacity to leave no 'footsteps in the snow,' did not attract a comment or glance.

He stopped, he felt faint, so he moved over beside an office building and supported himself against a wall, putting the briefcase down, praying no one would notice or come over to see if he was OK. No one did, and he stood there taking deep breaths. He took out his mobile phone and pretended to be talking on it.

"What am I going to do about this?" At first, the thought occurred that he should just leave the briefcase there and make his escape. But what if someone noticed and chased him down the street with it? Also, what did he do about the gun in his pocket? At any minute he knew the police would be in the Square in force and with all the surrounding CCTV he would be identified. Matt Robb would see to that. George suspected that he had stumbled on a drug deal that had gone wrong. *Why oh why had he lifted the briefcase and the gun?* He had no recollection of any thought processes prior to doing what he did.

It came to his mind many times later, and he did not know why he had, as a reflex, lifted the two items. His dilemmas increased by the minute; he would be charged with leaving the scene of a serious crime without calling the police. He told himself this means the end of my career at Baileys, my job, and pension. No firm could keep an employee who acted like me. Worse; I have a gun in my pocket that killed a man. I could be charged with murder. The briefcase, likely as not, contained money, so I would also be charged with theft. If I hurried back to the office, I could phone the police and say I took the briefcase for safekeeping, but then why had I lifted the gun? A prison sentence beckoned. His job and pension were down the tubes. Even if he reported in now, his subsequent behaviour would have dire consequences. George lifted the briefcase, walked back to Baileys, analysing the situation, and rehearsing possible plausible explanations that showed he was not involved in a drug deal and had not tried to steal the proceeds. He went into his cubicle and placed the briefcase on a chair in the corner, draping his coat over it. He took the gun and put it in his bottom desk drawer.

Alan Carson came in to speak to him soon after he got back, lifted the coat and the briefcase from the chair and sat down, observing "That's some briefcase George, more like a small suitcase." He followed that with, "I hope you are not taking the company's earnings home night by night."

"Are you OK George?" said Carson at one point, "you don't look well, can I get you a glass of water?"

"No, I am fine." mumbled George. "It's just the heat in here today."

At 5.30 pm, the Accounts section emptied, and George remained behind, a rare occurrence. About 5.50, he went for a wander around the office. Everyone had gone. He went back into his cubicle, brought the briefcase onto his desk, and opened it.

There was row upon row of 200 Euro notes in one half of the briefcase and rows of 100 Euro notes alongside. He did a quick estimate, half a million Euros. George sat there for about ten minutes trying to work out what he should do.

He balanced the loss of his job, pension and liberty with an alternative, any alternative. George had always relied on avoidance, so did nothing and caught the bus home to Mrs Barrow's, complete with briefcase.

"Bringing work home now, George." Mrs Barrow said as he came into the house. "I hope they are paying you overtime."

"Baileys don't do that," replied George.

He didn't want his rent going up on the strength of him getting overtime. The irony that he was carrying a briefcase stuffed with half a million euros was lost on him. He put the briefcase and the gun at the bottom of his wardrobe and piled sweaters on top. He knew it was unlikely Mrs Barrow would delve into the bottom of his wardrobe in one of her rare cleaning sprees.

George knew how important it was that he should not change his routine. If he were identified on the CCTV, then the police would already be on their way to the house.

He sat and picked at his meal with the TV news on in the background. It moved from the national news to the local news. George concentrated, there was no mention of the incident in Shaftsbury Square. "Strange", he thought.

He went out for a long walk, expecting the police to be waiting for him upon his return. He kept asking himself why he had taken the briefcase and how could he get rid of it without bringing everything down upon his head. Then he remembered he had left the gun in his desk drawer. He panicked. What happens if a nosy cleaner opens his desk drawers?

George decided to tough it out. He had no other choice. There was no way back. He couldn't get into the office. Like a condemned man, he ate the equivalent of a hearty breakfast and let tomorrow take care of itself.

The next morning, he retrieved the gun, put it in his coat and never left the cubicle all day, even for lunch. That night, it was deposited in the wardrobe. '*What happens if Mrs Barrow goes into the wardrobe finding the money and the gun? She would phone the police.*' Over the next few days, George went about his normal work pattern.

He was awaiting detailed arrangements from Aileen Whyte about his trip to London. George was excited at the thought of meeting her again. A sad male fantasy enveloped him. "Don't be silly.' he told himself, "you have misunderstood her."

He wondered if he could get through the security checks at Heathrow with the briefcase. He could go to London and disappear there, but he realised there was little chance of getting through security, plus he would never see Aileen again.

Aileen Whyte phoned him on Thursday and asked him to come over on the following Monday to complete the arrangements for his trip to London. Aileen suggested George take leave the next week. She said she had tried to send a message to Hamish Campbell to say someone with cash was coming over in about ten days, adding that if George was missing out on his evening meal, she would have food ready.

He was quite intrigued by this. Aileen Whyte had not asked him for any personal details, but he got the impression she knew he lived in lodgings, or at least that he was on his own. He was sure Baileys were more involved in this arrangement than just facilitating an employee as a glorified message boy. One distraction from the worry about what to do about the briefcase was thinking about Aileen.

George saw Alan Carson. He explained he felt under the weather, as Alan had noticed, and he wanted to take two weeks and one day's leave, starting with tomorrow, Friday. A bone of contention from all George's managers, since he and Irene had split, was his refusal to take his holidays. Carson took it as a compliment to his management style that George had come to him to ask to take his annual leave, albeit with just two months of the holiday leave year left and 19 days still outstanding.

That night George lay awake. He could hardly phone the police and ask if anything of interest had happened in Shaftsbury Square, but he knew someone who would know. On Friday morning, he told Mrs Barrow he was having holidays and would go away for the weekend. She was surprised but pleased. "Such a worker that Mr McNeill, he takes no holidays. I think he was so devastated by the breakup of his marriage he hides in work" she confided to her friends.

George phoned Matt Robb and asked him if he fancied lunch today. Robb was keen. From his tone George knew he was not aware of anything amiss in the Square, so either the police had not yet gone to look at the CCTV or they had done it in a way that had not alerted Robb that his 'friend' George McNeill was a person of interest. If George appeared on the screen, he would be an unknown person unless Robb was present.

Even if they did not ask him, he would blurt out, "There's an old school pal of mine."

He and Robb went to a small restaurant on Botanic Avenue. George paid in Euros because he had got too much out for his holiday, he explained. "Where are you going?" asked Robb.

"Oh, down South, just driving."

Robb sniffed, couldn't see the sense of that. A bar in a nice Spanish resort. Start the day with an Ulster Fry or a full English, or whatever, and then drink."

"And then what?" asked George.

"Same again next day for two weeks."

"What about the beach?" George asked. Robb just shrugged.

"Matt, I have time today. I would love to take you up on your invitation to see the CCTV operation."

"Brilliant, it's state-of-the art." He rode back on his claim of being the manager. As far as George could make out, he was a shift supervisor and did the rotas, etc. They went into the building, up the stairs, and into the darkened screen room.

There were about ten screens and Robb's colleague was sitting there, "Saw you guys coming," he said. George studied the screens as his eyes became accustomed to the gloom. Screen one was on but blank: Donegal Pass, Botanic Avenue, Bradbury Place, Donegal Road, Great Victoria Street, Bedford Street, Square East, Square West, Square South.

"What about Square North?" George asked, proud of his calm delivery. It was the one with the refurbished conveniences.

"That screen has been broken for three weeks. I told my boss, but they had to order parts from England."

"Ah," said George, "that must be annoying."

Robb just shrugged, "Not my fault if they won't carry parts. Mind you," and added as an afterthought, "The police were in the other day, and they were livid, as if it was my fault. I just told them to "go and do one."

George doubted if he put it to them quite like that.

"Oh, look," said George, "I have an appointment. I must fly." He promised to be in touch for that elusive drink when he got back from his break.

So that was why the police had not picked him up, though it did not explain why they had made no public appeal for help about the slayings. What would the men's relatives be saying? Would they go to the press? Tricky, 'My drug dealer son was shot in a public loo in Shaftsbury Square doing a deal. If any other drug dealer could help the police with their enquiries, the family would be delighted.'. What are the odds of neither family going public?

Apart from checking with Robb, another other thing George wanted to do was treat himself to a nice car. It was his one real weakness in the acquisitive world. He had a couple of weeks' liberty ahead and he thought he would enjoy it as best he could.

Two years before, on an earlier trip down South, he decided he should go to the centre of Ireland. Since he had already been to Donegal, Galway, Kerry, Cork and Wicklow, he drove down to Drogheda, then on to Mullingar and ended up in Athlone, where he stayed in a pleasant guest house. He went to Limerick. On the trip, he drove out on the N6 but took a turn off near Birr and decided on the scenic route. Two miles down the road, he came to a crossroads and noticed a car sales sign and a row of cars, Peugeots, Mitsubishis, Fords and half a dozen sports cars of varying vintage. He stopped, got out and pottered around. He looked at the sports cars, though all but two were over ten years old and seemed to have high mileages and encounters with objects that had failed to give way. He was conscious of a figure shuffling out of the cabin.

An older man who seemed tiny, about 5ft 3ins if that. He was dressed in a striped shirt, check trousers and a waistcoat that was too large for him.

"Are you after wanting to buy a car?" the figure asked.

"I am just looking around."

"Just as well," said the man, "Himself' is away to the city," the implication being if 'himself' was not around, no cars were sold.

George laughed, "Just as well. I am not spending my money if 'himself' is in Dublin."

The little man looked puzzled, “Dublin,” as if that was the far side of the moon rather than, the nation’s capital, “he’s in Galway, his bit of stuff’s there.”

George was sure ‘himself’ was married and wondered at the little man telling a stranger about his boss’s private ‘affairs’, in every sense of those words. However, now that he had stopped looking at the sports cars, his attention was taken by a large white Mercedes about one-year-old.

It had low mileage, pristine body work and the overall condition superb, the price was twenty thousand Euros, George could only dream of the lottery numbers.

“Nice, isn’t it?” said the little man. “The boss likes to have one top class car in stock, round here the farmers and their sons get carried away and buy sports cars or big luxury vehicles. Then they then can’t get sheep into the back seat, and they all end up coming back to Fords.”

George remembered that previous trip. He could return to that obscure out of the way car lot with cash in his pocket and treat himself.

Earlier in the year Jan became interested in a car in Drogheda and George went with him to look at it. Of course, as men do, he ‘lost his heart’ to the car and ‘needed’ to buy it. He notified the HMRC, got the vehicle approved and then taxed and of course insured. George recalled this whole rigmarole as he helped Jan with the process, but as long as there were registration documents, he was relaxed about driving North. He would have time to do the paperwork. He would not defer the pleasure of the drive home, especially as he would lose his liberty soon. George slept better than he ever did. The prospect of prison, losing his job and pension, far from terrifying him, made him quite gung-ho for some odd reason.

At the Lisburn Road Divisional Police HQ, the slayings in Shaftsbury Square were handed over to Inspector Alan Walker, one of the rising detective stars of the Police Service of Northern Ireland. Schooled in the old RUC in his early years of service, Walker, now part of a modern breed of cop focussed on solving crimes rather than combating para-military terrorism. His sidekick, John Farrell, a couple of years older, tied himself to Walker recognising that the latter's capabilities were going to propel him, and anyone associated with him, to successful careers.

Walker had two children. His wife Amy was a lab technician at Queen's University, their eldest child, Jane, inherited her parents' forensic skills and hoped to do medicine at Uni. Their son lived for playing Rugby. Farrell married later in life and his children were quite young, though there was a stepson from his wife's first marriage who wanted to join the police. Farrell's wife Sharon was a nurse at the Ulster hospital.

They reported to Billy Robertson, old school RUC, not at all dismayed at the death of either an ex-Republican drugs dealer or, a foreigner. Robertson loathed Walker. He recognised the younger man's skills kept the bosses off his back. Still, he detested Walker. His cleverness, the way more senior officers regarded Walker's opinions and would almost 'shush' Robertson in a meeting, eager to hear what his underlings take was on a serious crime. Robertson exerted himself and instructed that no details were to be made public while the police beavered away in the background.

Walker and Farrell both argued to 'get it out there' but Robertson could not be moved, nor was the rationalisation behind his decision at all clear, more a case of him exerting his authority.

"When there was a killing at the height of the 'Troubles' we didn't put everything in the public domain, but later, when we could charge someone, they would often let slip vital evidence linking them to the crime."

"That might be fine when you have a fair idea who did the killing, but not in this case like," argued Walker, but to no avail.

Fired up with all the adrenalin from the events earlier in the week, on the Saturday George drove south retracing his steps to Athlone and beyond, all the while dreaming of coming home in the big Mercedes or a 5 series BMW. As he drove down the country roads outside Athlone, he didn't have an address for the car lot. He stumbled on it before when he had come off the main road by accident. He reached a crossroads and came upon it, not imposing but standing out just a little because of its unlikely appearance on a quiet country road. A notice proclaimed, 'Honest Sean Fagan's Best Auto Deals.' That notice was not present on his earlier visit. At first, the collection of cars appeared the same as two years before. What stood out was a black Range Rover Vogue with dark tinted windows.

Two characters stumbled from the little cabin headed 'Office'. The familiar diminutive figure he encountered two years before, the other 'Honest Sean.' He looked as if he came straight from central casting as the Irish answer to Arthur Daley. He wore a continual smile, a flat cap set at a jaunty angle, and an ill-fitting blue suit.

George said nothing but nodded at the Range Rover. "Nice car."

Now 'Honest Sean' prided himself on being able to tell the difference between time wasters and real customers, but he wasn't certain about George.

George said, "Nice to see you again," to the little man whose response suggested he had no recollection of George. Sean's eyes focussed on the ten-year-old Escort George came in. "Probably a time waster".

He turned his attention to the Rover and with a flourish he recited, "Less than one-year-old, fourteen thousand miles, 4 x 4, premium sound system with CD changer, 5-speed automatic gearbox, air suspension, bi-exon head lamps, 4.4 petrol engine, and full of BMW technology, based on the seven series BMW you know, Mr er...?"

George ignored that. "And all for thirty-five thousand Euros." continued Sean.

"Yes," said George, "and about 17 miles to the gallon."

"I suppose in the city that would be about right, perhaps 20 mpg, but it's a vehicle for rough terrain."

'Like Belfast's roads' George said into himself.

Sean became bored. If George examined one of the Peugeots, a sale might have been on. Time to wind this up. He walked back into the office.

George said to the little guy, "How's his love life?"

He gawped for a minute, then winked. George enjoyed this new persona. He had so much money he didn't have to try with people.

He walked past the wee man and into the office while the little guy went over to valet a car. Sean was surprised as George took a seat without being asked.

"Here's the deal," said George, "I will give you thirty thousand Euros for the Range Rover and you can have my Escort, which must be worth about three thousand."

"Two, at the most," said Sean almost by reflex.

“Whatever,” responded George.

“Thirty thousand plus your old Escort. I don’t know, thirty-five is a fair price.”

“Have you many better offers?” asked his would be customer.

Sean said nothing. God, he hated arrogant Northerners. He did not have many Northern Irish customers, but if he had, he would have hated them all.

George moved in for the kill, “Thirty thousand in cash.”

Sean’s eyes widened, “Have you just robbed a bank?”

Then he wished he hadn’t because as likely as not the Belfast man robbed banks. That’s what they did.

“I want to buy it and I want to take it away today.”

Sean interjected, “But the registration, sorting the finances, all that.”

“I will get the cash now,” said George.

Sean said, “No offence, but how do I know the money is legitimate?”

Again, he regretted speaking out, gosh he was pushing it. If this fellow came from a Northern terrorist organisation, he could pull a gun and shoot him.

George smiled. “Wait a minute.” And he headed out to the Escort.

Sean needed time to think. Should he phone the Gardai? Was the money fake? Could it be the proceeds of a robbery, 'stop, stop, I need time to think?' He wanted a cash deal. Profits were not good at the best of times, and these were not the best of times. George returned with his case and opened it,

Sean's eyes widened. "Be careful. I don't want the 'wee shit' to see that. He would stab the pair of us for two hundred euros."

The 'wee shit' in question lathered away at a Ford Fiesta.

George was at his persuasive best, "How far away is your bank?"

"Thirty kilometres."

"Look it's now ten to one. Phone your manager, get an appointment, take ten thousand euros, you choose, bring them to the bank, say you have a customer, who wants to buy a car for cash, and the bank can tell you if the cash is genuine."

Sean sat back. He was being bounced into a decision. If the Northerner disappeared with the Range Rover and the cash was fake, his business wouldn't survive. If he could get that money, there were many possibilities.

"You trust me to go off to town with your cash?" asked Sean.

"Hell no," said George, "I am coming with you."

George raised one more stipulation, and it decided Sean.

"I need you to give me a bill of sale saying I bought the car for fifteen thousand euros."

Sean knew one other crucial thing he was not for sharing. Rover's deal with BMW was finishing and Ford intended to acquire the company. It was a long-drawn-out affair because of the various Rover brands and the US market. Sean heard a reliable whisper from a cousin who worked in the main Rover plant in the English midlands that a replacement model was under development. This Rover would depreciate, and Sean could explain to any interested party, like the tax people, which is why he let it go cheaply. He could also pretend the Escort was worth more than the three thousand he would allow against the Rover. Two men bent on instant gratification.

They set off for the bank in Fagan's well-worn Mitsubishi saloon. Like most car dealers, his own car was ancient and held together by something quite flimsy. At first, they drove in silence, then Sean Fagan chatted. George recognised that on the surface it was more than just chitchat. Like any car salesman, Fagan wanted information to earn more off his potential customer. In George's case, he wanted to assess risk to himself and his business in this unexpected enterprise he still felt "bounced" into.

"Aye, we had our own branch of the bank once, but they closed it last year. It's called progress." said Sean. "I transferred my account to Portlaoise even though it's 45 minutes up the road. They wanted me to transfer it to Galway, and I told them, the hell I will, I will boost a small-town branch rather than feed your centralising policy."

George grunted. The banking system of Ireland held no interest to him, although he shivered at the mention of 'Portlaoise'. It possessed a maximum-security prison, one just right for someone involved in drug dealing, murder, and the theft of half a million euros.

"So, what is it you do yourself?" Sean attempted.

"I am in financial services."

("What the hell does that mean bank robber, lottery winner, murderer of small local car dealers?")

George interrupted the car dealer's thoughts, "You should describe me as a farmer from the North who doesn't trust banks, and who pays cash. They will love that."

Sean grunted in return. Two can play the taciturn game, but George remained unmoved by the journey in silence. He just imagined driving that big Range Rover home.

They parked near the bank,

"Just remember a farmer from the North who likes to pay cash," he said to Sean.

"What happens if they don't play ball?" said Fagan, losing his nerve.

"No problem, "I will just shoot them, you as well."

Sean's eyes lit up in terror. ("I was right, Now the truth is out.")

He turned towards George, who grinned at him and stuck his thumbs in his jacket, pulling it outwards to show he had no gun.

"If they won't play ball, you lose a sale and I drive home in my old Escort, unless I head to Dublin and find a car dealer with more clout with his bank."

"Dublin," Sean spoke angrily, "full of car thieves, drug dealers and the car salesmen that get my profession a bad name. You are better off with me."

He exited the car, walked around the corner and into the street with the bank. George also got out of the car. 45 minutes in that old sweaty atmosphere was enough. He wound down all the windows to make the journey back pleasanter and stood leaning against the car.

As George enjoyed the afternoon sunshine, a voice behind him said,

"How are you doing today, sir?"

George turned to see a Garda in uniform standing about four feet away. He hadn't heard the policeman approach; forty-five minutes of Sean's old engine must have deafened him. George smiled.

"Ah - fine, fine, loving this sunshine."

"You are not a local person?" interjected the Garda quizzically.

Before he could respond, Sean returned, too quickly. Would Sean panic at the sight of the Garda?

"Ah, Seamus, so this is where they stationed you now. Are you on the wrong side of Inspector O'Malley again?"

"Indeed, Sean, indeed, but a man must do what the great and good ordains for him."

Small talk went on between them until the policeman continued on his beat, leaving with a cheerful, "Good afternoon to you both."

George was determined he wouldn't show Sean how much the Garda's appearance spooked him.

"What happened in the bank?" he snapped.

"It's fine, they need an hour to deal with it. The Deputy Manager is their currency expert, and he is finishing a meeting."

Just long enough to phone Dublin, identify the proceeds of a robbery and get the Serious Crime Squad, or whatever they were called in the Republic of Ireland, down here was George's pessimistic take on this development.

"Let's go to the pub," suggested Sean, and they went to a local hostelry.

"What are you having?" asked Sean.

"Just a half pint of lager," replied George.

"I will have the same."

George was relieved his chauffer back down that twisty road was limiting himself to a half pint of lager. They drank in relative silence. George offered to buy a round.

"Slainte," said Sean. "I'll have a whiskey."

George went for a soft drink, but Sean shouted to him and the barman, "Make that a double." An interesting drive back to the car lot awaited George. Sean went back to the bank while George waited by the car. Sean reappeared.

"They are happy with your money. I just deposited it in my account. I assume that is OK with you." George nodded.

They returned without incident to Sean's car sales.

Sean manoeuvred the Land Rover down from the platform and they went into the office. George carried the suitcase with him throughout their journey, although, when talking to the Garda, it remained stashed out of sight in the car. He brought it to the pub, though.

"I don't know your name," said Sean. His fourth try, but his most direct one to elicit a name from George.

George gave him his name. There was no point avoiding that any longer. He gave Fagan the details, also his address as the Barrows, implying he lived there. He counted out the balance of the money which the car dealer put in a small safe. One of those would be useful he said to himself. A suitcase in a wardrobe was not secure. He remembered conversations with old ladies he visited when he first started at Baileys who kept their money under their mattress or in a few jars. He had urged them to put it in a bank.

Sean reminded him he would need to tax the car. George phoned his insurance firm from Sean's office to learn his premium would double. They would send the documents first class, but he might not get them until Tuesday. George would then get the road tax and his certificate of ownership arranged. Paperwork sorted, George pointed the big Range Rover north and drove home content with himself. Three miles from Athlone, he filled his vehicle with fuel. Fagan was stingy with the fuel. George bought the petrol with cash, of course.

At the non-existent border, he saw a police car parked. If they pulled him over, he would have some explaining to do about the lack of a road tax disc, but the police made no move.

As a law-abiding citizen, he was never conscious of the police. Now they were around every corner; funny what an unacknowledged guilty conscience will do. He drove within himself, getting used to the size of his car, the automatic gearbox, and the power under the bonnet.

He loved his sense of liberation. The 'old George' was gone forever. He concentrated on driving the Range Rover. Then it came into his mind his life was all make believe. It would come to an unpleasant halt once the police detained him. What appeared worth the risk a short time ago was now dangerous? He shivered, but he concentrated on his driving.

He parked up in front of the Barrows' dilapidated old garage. They came out to admire his car, though neither had a clue about cars. They agreed it was "big" and "very black." He went to his room. George enjoyed his feeling of empowerment. He attributed it to the money and to the gun. At night looked at both. He held the gun, fascinated by its cold touch and its heaviness.

On the Sunday, he drove over to take Terry out as he missed his game on the Saturday and more or less insisted Melissa came too. They went to a McDonald's in a state-of-the-art Range Rover. Irene did not seem to notice, but his children were impressed by his car.

"Have you been promoted?" Terry asked.

"Sort of." said George.

"I have my provisional licence now," said Terry. "Can I learn in this?"

"Nope, but I will help to pay for your driving lessons."

"Will you?"

"Yes, I will speak to your mother when we get back."

Irene experienced guilt feelings when she met George. Her friends, her sister, her mother all advised against the marriage, "Liking him is not enough to make a marriage."

It became a more and more an unsatisfying relationship; the affairs were relief, but they didn't satisfy her either. Had she deprived the children of a dad? Before the children were born, she remembered, with too much drink in him, George had revealed grand plans in a drunken, confused, garbled torrent. She could not recall the details, but they briefly added unusual spice to their relationship.

Chapter 3

The Emissary

On the Monday George took a drive, ending up in Bangor. He got out for a walk thinking of his meeting with Aileen Whyte that evening. She had been in his thoughts a lot since their first meeting and he admitted to himself she intrigued him, more than intrigued. When he first met her, she was cool, every inch the ice maiden she had been dubbed when younger. She mellowed when she met Thomas Whyte, the rising political star, with a quote for every occasion. He would have been described as debonair in another age. This mellowing became more pronounced when her children were born. Initially, she behaved distant, professional with George, but then that moment of emotion and more unexpectedly, the kiss at the end, "her knight in shining armour." Grief can affect people differently, and George could not believe he attracted her. Perhaps best described as a port in her storm. What made him laugh to himself is the notion he was attracted to her. Can attraction happen after such a fleeting encounter? He looked forward to seeing her again but was realistic enough to think she would have regained her composure sufficiently to return to being reserved. He drove up to see Jan to get one of his special cakes and to show off the car.

Elena greeted him with the usual hug and kiss, Jan with his handshake and humorous jibes:

"Ah ha, George, I assume it is tea with a lady and at her residence. Is this the start of a romance?"

George's face reddened, and Elena looked quizzically at him. As he left the Tieleman's, he had now shown his new toy to everyone of any importance to him except his brother. Suddenly, it didn't feel so grand. Was it really worth the sacrifices?

He drove over to Aileen's house at 6.00 pm. On his first visit he left his car down the drive, visible from the house but far enough away not to be available to much scrutiny. He was a little self-conscious because of its shabby appearance on this 'posh' drive. He drove the Range Rover right up to the turning circle beside the front door. There was no sign of the policeman.

His confidence surged, as if he had consumed a substance which empowered him, well he had, E500,000. By the time he jumped down from the car, Aileen opened the door and came down to greet him, hand outstretched. No welcoming kiss, he noted.

"Mr McNeill, George," she declared ushering him in, as if surprised to see him.

She thanked him for the cake, and they went into a front room, different from the one they were in before, less formally furnished, more comfortably appointed with settees at right angles, ornaments and a less formal light fitting. She wore a white smock over navy trousers and makeup. Thinking back, she hadn't worn makeup the last time, or did he just imagine that? Certainly, she looked less pale and drawn. The big brown eyes were livelier, welcoming even.

"I want you to meet my daughters. Abigail, Rosemary, come down a minute, please."

Both girls came downstairs. Abbi 15, going on 22 and her sister 13. They were miniature Aileen's, slim, petite, dark brown hair, with quite reserved expressions.

"This is Mr McNeill, who is helping me with important business at present."

Both girls shook hands and offered the same shy, brief smile. George was ill at ease.

His experience of girls was limited to polar opposites, Melissa's disinterest, or Elena's almost hero worship, but this was different. He was aware of being scrutinised by both girls and that he would be the subject of a joint analysis once they returned upstairs.

He didn't even know how he should start a conversation with them, though as the adult it fell to him.

George wondered if he was the least mature person in the room and decided that was the case. 'Don't ask them about school, because that's what all adults do when they meet young people for the first time.' He remembered a band Melissa liked, and he asked if they were fans.

Rosemary at once, "Yes, Cal, the lead singer, is dreamy."

Abbi sniffed as if to say, "Little girls' stuff," but said, "Maybe a couple of years ago."

Aileen took control; "Back to your homework please," and they left, Abbi marching out of the room, Rosemary following with a quick look over her shoulder and a brief smile as she moved out the door.

"They are at a good school," ('as in expensive' George thought), "and the beauty is they can board there if I get elected, and if the Head Teacher can cope with sharing power with Abbi. I will be in Westminster from Monday morning until Thursday evening, I will put the kettle on so we could have our tea. The girls won't be joining us."

As he sat on his own George reckoned things had moved up a notch, Aileen Whyte would not casually have introduced him to her daughters if she intended to soon dispense with him. Also, while she would guess he read rumours she sought her late husband's seat, the fact she confirmed it directly to him drew him more into an inner circle. He wasn't clear why, but this sharp, very political woman would rarely act without a reason.

"When I was young, I wanted to go into politics. My father cautioned me Northern Ireland wasn't ready for a woman playing a prominent political role. I listened to him and learned how he worked audiences, how he handled rooms full of supporters. How to give a thumbs up here and hug there, binding people to you, the people you need to give your support foundation." She paused and went on.

"My views concerning the core policies are different now from those I held when my father enthralled me. I know how to get a standing ovation in a wee hall in Derriaghy or how to present as articulate and modern in the media. My principles have altered in terms of pragmatism, but the Party is less into embracing this Millennium. It needs nursing to get there."

George absorbed this. Politics or the elasticity of its principles did not worry him, but he recognised it could be a drug to certain people. Aileen was one of those people.

"I hope you don't mind eating in the kitchen," said Aileen as she led him through. "I asked them to withdraw the police guard, a little OTT, at the moment."

They had homemade soup, and she made a nice salad with quiche and her own potato salad. They exchanged small talk.

"Your daughters are lovely; they take after you."

Aileen ignored that, "You have a couple of children."

She clearly knew he was divorced and acknowledged it and expressed sympathy without being intrusive or patronising.

"You are so kind to do this, go to all this trouble for a stranger." adding, "They are not even paying you that much."

George noted "they," as he suspected, "they" were probably either the Party and or Baileys. It was a slip. He was not meant to know outside elements were involved in his commissioning. It was meant to be a private arrangement between a client and a Baileys employee recommended by the firm.

The firm was well connected to the Party, through Aileen's father and old man, Walter Andrews, the firm's senior partner. The latter was rarely seen these days, although over the years George met him several times. He married Augustus Baileys eldest daughter after the war and had been brought straight into the firm and worked there for fifty years.

Now in semi-retirement, Walter did not involve himself in day-to-day business. His shareholding meant he carried the most clout of all the partners. He considered himself the guardian of the firm's original values.

The chit-chat was relaxed. He mentioned his children and Jan and Elena.

Aileen asked about his relationship with Melissa and sympathised when he said they were never close; with Terry, it was different, and George suggested boys were less complex.

"Children, young people are complicated, Abbi and I were once so close, but she is quite angry at the minute, angry with her dad over the scandal, over taking his own life, angry with me for not preventing it all, I suppose, but she won't talk about it," Aileen said this wistfully, as if remembering happier times.

"I am sorry..." but before George could say more, Aileen cut in:

"Rosemary is more relaxed. She was very upset at her dad's death, initially almost inconsolable, but she gives me wee hugs all the time." A silence ensued.

"Well," said George to break the tension, "boys are less demanding. All Terry is interested in is how good my car is, and will I come and watch him play football?" As he laughed at his own little joke, Aileen responded.

"You have a nice car. It's not the same as the one you were in last time?"

That surprised George. 'Whoa, where did that come from?'

"I stood at the landing widow and watched you drive off." She explained.

George tried to put crumbs from Jan's cake back from the tablecloth to his plate.

Aileen laughed; "Don't worry, I will clean up afterwards. His Belgian baker friend and the beautiful daughter intrigued her, and she laughed at George's account of giving fatherly advice to Elena on her love life. Aileen took out three envelopes from the drawer.

"This is Campbell's last known address. Here is the three thousand pounds for him and the third envelope is your fee. It is not much for all you are doing but if I am elected........"

George interrupted, "Aileen, I would do this for nothing, just as your, er... friend."

This was only their second meeting, coupled with the phone calls. He stopped, anxious at his presumption of a friendship that he wanted, but she...., he wasn't certain.

Either Aileen didn't pick up on the silent pleading in his comment or she affected not to notice it. She simply smiled and said, "Thank you."

"One of our Party's MPs will pass by Campbell's address on Tuesday, he went past it earlier in the week and thought it looked derelict."

George felt a pang of jealousy. Did the MP have 'his eye' on this vulnerable widow and then he realised he, George, had 'his eye' on her. He was in no position to mount a criticism. What has happened to me? He did not know this woman and yet already she had a hold on him, on his emotions. Did he even have emotions?

'He' turned out to be Barry Downs MP, who was Aileen's cousin, part of the family political dynasty. Downs promised to telephone Aileen on Wednesday to confirm what he found, and Aileen suggested she ring George to advise him.

"Well, I have business nearby on Wednesday. If it suits, I could pop in."

They agreed noon would suit her commitments and his 'business meeting.'

George was keen to see her again. Aileen might think it unnecessary to meet for a matter that could be settled by phone, but in his view if any complications arose because of her cousin's phone call it might be good to talk, and he got to see her again. They left the kitchen, George stood back to let Aileen exit first, and she smiled at his gesture as she opened the door.

Now or never, could he, would he, what if she got upset or screamed with the girls upstairs?

She held the door as he went past, he put his hand down to her waist and bent towards her she went to give him a peck on the cheek, he kissed her briefly on the lips. They stood looking at each other, she held his arms knowing he wanted to embrace her, her brown eyes were moist, but she said nothing. It felt so strange being held by a man, one she hardly knew. Some instinct told him it should go no further, he turned away and then trotted down the steps.

As he walked round to the driver's side he glanced back, the front door was closed. Aileen watched from the landing window again, oh well 'in for a penny', at least he made a gesture. She could call Baileys, cancel him, get another emissary, and never see him again. He hesitated as he opened the car door, thinking how sad that would be.

Then Abbi marched from behind the double garage purposefully towards him. George saw a determined look on the young girl's face and the old George was tempted to jump into the car and drive away fast. She wished to speak to him, and it would be better manners to wait.

Abbi marched right up to him. He felt she was going to knock him over due to the pace of her arrival, but she stopped inches from him and spoke.

"Are you my mother's boyfriend?" Her eyes were flashing with anger, and she clenched her fists.

‘Dear God,’ thought George, ‘surely, we will not have a fight here in the driveway. Even if her mother was beginning to like me an encounter like that would finish it.’

George stepped back as far as the motor would let him. “No, that is only the second time I have met your mother. Your father and I did business over several years, it is - was, him I knew.”

Abbi also stepped back. Not the response she expected. “Oh,” she stated.

George regained his composure. “I am doing business with your mum, so I will no doubt see you again, Abbi.” With that he walked round, climbed into the Land Rover and started the engine, moving cautiously as Abbi hovered close to the car.

She motioned to him, and he wound down the electric window.

“Nice car,” and disappeared as quickly as she came.

Aileen stood at her favoured spot. She couldn’t remember when she first stood and watched visitors leave from this window. This included family, friends, political allies, even Thomas. She would replay the events of the previous hours analysing and re-analysing what transpired.

Aileen laughed to herself at George’s clumsy attempt at a kiss, not flattered exactly but amused, even slightly pleased. He presented differently from their first encounter, confident, even his speech was no longer slow and deliberate. George had appeared submissive, compliant, eager to please. Now, he seemed taller or walking taller, as if he was trying to take control. After a ‘second’ encounter, ‘Well we will see about that. Where did the big posh car come from? It didn’t fit the briefing from Baileys?’

'George McNeill is a nice, gentle guy, minor clerk in the firm, stable, been there for yonks, won't rock the boat, he will just do as he is told.' In fact, he appeared genuinely nice, concerned for her and keen to please. He needed the money, but not a doormat after all. Aileen was intrigued. Then, to her horror, she watched as Abbi strode purposefully towards George.

'Oh, for God's sake Abbi, just simmer down.'. Aileen murmured, knowing her eldest daughter's capacity for confrontation if something did not suit. George drove off unscathed. 'Lucky him' was Aileen's take.

On Tuesday George went to his brother's, he phoned to say he was in the neighbourhood and David said, "would you like to have a bite to eat?" and never one to turn down a free meal George agreed. He popped into Jan's for a cake. It worked well last time.

Elena stood chatting to a young guy festooned in tattoos and jewellery. She smiled at George and introduced him to 'Troy'. They shook hands and Elena said, "George is my uncle, he thinks the world of me."

George flushed and Elena laughed. Troy laughed also, well used to Elena's provocative sense of humour. George snatched a look at Elena. Where was the little girl with the serious face and the pig tails?

Elana possessed an olive complexion and dark hair, not black but a deep shiny brown eye, and long slim legs. She reminded George of a French model or actress he saw in a newspaper, but he couldn't remember. Jan came down the steps and asked if the cake was for "that special someone."

George explained he was visiting his brother's for tea, which dampened the expectations. Jan invited him to dinner the following week to celebrate Elena's acceptance for the Law Faculty at Queens University. She planned to live at home during her first year, at least.

His car got the reaction that he wanted from David. They enjoyed the meal, but there is only so long you can talk about a car, especially with his brother's aging Volvo sitting in the drive.

"So," said David, "you won the lottery?" He was aware of George's unrealistic aspirations,

"I have additional responsibilities and rewards at Baileys."

"Irene will be pleased then," said Moira, with a hint of sarcasm.

George raised his intention to acquire property, a house for himself and a couple of flats to rent out to boost his pension.

"I have seen daytime TV programmes on property." He regurgitated points he recalled from the programme, it sounded convincing, if you had money.

"Yes," said George, "acquire ex-Local Authority housing, good quality build, renovate and rent out or sell on at a profit."

"Local Authority Housing, do you mean Housing Executive?" asked David. What was available in the London Borough of Hammersmith wouldn't apply in Belfast, "Ah well I might get it in England or Scotland," George responded as he sought to extricate himself from the difficulty his grandiose scheme landed him in. Eventually, he headed down the road to the Barrows.

"I have never heard George say so much" Moira said of her brother-in-law. "I think he said more in my presence tonight in one conversation than in all our conversations in the twenty years I have known him."

“Do you think he is having a breakdown? He sure is behaving differently.” was David’s take. He shivered. If George was indeed falling apart, he and perhaps young Terry were the only actual family who would be dragged into whatever the doctors would propose.

The next day, George drove on the now familiar route to Aileen’s house. Little else had been in his mind since their last meeting. He had looked forward to it since he left on Monday. She would have accepted doing the business by phone, not as desperate to see him as he was to see her. Just before he got to his car, he tried to think of that last minute in her company, before Abbi appeared

A little kiss was not enough to jeopardise whatever relationship might develop. ‘Man up’ George said to himself. Though a lifetime spent avoiding ‘manning up’ is not the best groundwork for a situation like this. He parked and marched up to the door trying to appear ‘a devil may care man of the world who kisses lots of women. ‘They should count themselves lucky, eh, Aileen?’.

Aileen opened the door, again the formal handshake and welcomed him into her house with a slight smile. She affected a business-like demeanour. They walked into the informal reception room.

“Please take a seat. I haven’t heard from Campbell since our last meeting. Barry went past his address, and he said it was all boarded up and no sign of anyone living there so getting to Campbell might be problematic.”

“Did your husband mention any other friends in London who might know Campbell?” He tried to be sensitive, but she flashed him a look.

“No, funnily enough, he never mentioned to me, his wife, any details concerning his boyfriends.”

They sat in silence. The rebuke was the first negativity in their contact, assuming George's kiss as he left on Monday wasn't a negativity.

Finally, Aileen said. "I am sorry George, I didn't mean to snap, it's all just a strain, what with the death, the selection, the by election, the effect on the Abbi and Rosemary…"

George leaned forward and squeezed her hand. "I can resolve this bit," he whispered, and she brightened up immediately. *'Could we just pop up to your bedroom and have passionate sex as the girls are out and as a token of your gratitude?'* was what he would have liked to add....... but didn't.

Aileen spoke. "I see Abbi cornered you as you were leaving on Monday evening." So, Aileen watched.

"Yes," he agreed, "she wanted to know if we were...?"

Aileen interrupted, "What did you say?"

"I just said we only met twice, and that I knew her father better and that you and I have business to complete."

Aileen looked relieved. "She is a deep one, angry at me and at the same time protective of me. You made an impression on her, I'm just not sure what impression." Then she suddenly clasped her hand to her mouth.

"I know something that might just help." She rushed upstairs and came down with a purple business card.

"This was among what we cleared out when we gave up Thomas's London flat."

George took the card. ‘The Purple Heart Club’ emblazoned on it with a silhouette of a man dancing. It was situated in Soho with a map showing the junction between Charing Cross Road and Shaftesbury Avenue. He put it in his wallet.

“Right,” he said, “I am off to London this evening,” and he stood up. “Returning on Friday night. I will let you know what I find.” With that, he began to leave.

Aileen fussed over him as he left.

“Thank you so much George, what you are doing means so much to me, I can never be grateful enough.”

He was tempted to say well for a start we could......, then instinct told George playing it enigmatically would be best, he just said.

“I will sort this.” There was no kiss or handshake and he jumped into his car and headed for the City Airport; for his 2.00 pm flight.

The sense of sorting things was not making much in the way of music at the Lisburn Road Police station. They contacted the Community Safety CCTV unit.

“What do you make of him?” they debated in relation to Robb.

“A bit of an overblown twat and when he could have provided a useful lead, his bloody system doesn’t work because no one carries a key spare part, some safety experts.” Farrell suggested.

“Don’t forget he emailed his boss three weeks earlier,” added Walker.

“Yeah, I guess he emails them so often over trivia, they just ignore him. Still if we get nothing else,

“I need to go back and see him, put on a bit more pressure.”

“John, one thing.”

“What?”

“Always remember, there are no such things as coincidences. “

As George sat on the plane, he read an article in a flight magazine entitled ‘What makes a man in Manhattan’. Apparently, how you dress says a lot about you to other people. Many observers can tell by the cut of your suit or your tailor, the shirts, shoes you wear, even your make of watch. They all speak volumes.

Not to George, he worked to a three-year cycle; Year One, blue suit for summer, Year Two, grey suit for winter, Year three, casual jacket and trousers, shirts, then back to year one. During their marriage, Irene encouraged him to be less staid, but eventually gave up. At Baileys,

George always smartly turned out but dull. In the flight magazine, those who wished to compete with ‘Manhattan Man’ needed to go to Savile Row. George made a note to do shopping in London. A man of distinction who hopes to squire an MP and invest in property needs to dress for it. Foreign to George’s normal instincts though it might be but everything else had changed in and around him, why not the way he presented himself?

He found the hotel easily arriving just before 4.00 pm. A porter grabbed his case, he checked in and the porter accompanied him to his room not fazed by being offered a ten-euro tip. George went straight out, arriving first in Trafalgar Square, then into Piccadilly Circus. He walked up Regent Street, getting his bearings, enjoying London’s September late afternoon warmth.

George couldn't help thinking that a few weeks ago he would have been terrified at the prospect of what he was now doing, buying an expensive car, dealing with a well-known public figure, lusting after her, carrying out a mission like this. It is strange how quickly money in your pocket or the bottom of your wardrobe empowers you. He walked up to Oxford Circus, turned down near Bond Street and headed back towards Regent Street when he saw a sign 'Savile Row Tailoring'.

First, he came to a large shop. George walked in. "Bespoke Suits" proclaimed a banner hanging from the ceiling. A busy place and George saw he was the oldest person in the shop. He left quickly. In the second shop there were more assistants than customers. There was an Arab family with two assistants in attendance and, he assumed by two assistants at the changing room entrance, more customers in there. George hesitated, and an assistant made their way towards him and again he quickly exited.

He wandered across the street to smaller premises, a less well-lit window display, braced himself and marched in. The shop was 1950s in both decor and smell, there were no suits or mannequins, just rails and rails of cloth, wool mostly, cotton, and linen too. George paused as he accustomed himself to the slightly more restrained lighting.

A minute later a deep voice said, "Good evening, Sir, how may I be of assistance?"

George peered into the far corner where he observed a long counter. Behind it a small man, balding, with tufts of unruly grey hair above each ear and tiny glasses perched on the end of his nose, peered at George.

George went to speak but because of his nervousness couldn't bring out a coherent sentence, he mumbled with the only recognisable sound being "suit."

Levi Cohen served them all in his time, well-known actors, BBC news readers and politicians but no footballers or pop stars.

They belonged across the street. Levi prided himself on a personal service that gave quality and met the customers' requirements, not a sale at any price.

May of his customers were regulars, whose fathers had also been tailored by Levi. He enjoyed the intimacy of providing a service for familiar people, chats about their businesses, their families and Levi's too. "My son is doing a PhD in micro-biology. He has no interest in being a tailor," he often commented ruefully.

More random customers would drop in and Levi felt confident he could assess their needs after the briefest of conversation. It was a game he played. George, he thought, too slim for a Polish builder, demeanour too retiring for a Russian, but that guttural and hesitant use of the English language created confusion.

The man misjudged the prices of an establishment like his. Levi could direct him somewhere more within his price range. He needed to alert the customer to costs, which would enable him to dive out the door and avoid further embarrassment.

"A suit sir, for business. I could do you a single-breasted navy blue, pure new wool two piece for around five thousand pounds."

George gulped and Levi went back to the counter to continue his paperwork. He expected to hear the door closing behind this Eastern European with the limited command of English. George's gulp wasn't due to the price. He had twelve thousand euros with him, as well as the money Aileen gave him. His gulp was because of his irritation at not being able to take control of his situation.

"OK," said George.

Levi paused. Not the response he expected. He became business-like and showed George dozens of reams of blue cloth picking up differences George did not understand and could not see.

Levi decided on the blue wool he thought best, not navy, and George went along with that. He began the measuring process. It was up close and personal, too personal for a man of George's delicate sensibilities, but the little tailor was a master of his business.

"Now that we have done all the hard work measuring you, perhaps sir would like to order another suit, save you having to return to the UK just for that."

This confused George, 'return to the UK', but he agreed he needed to be smarter. It goes with the car. Once again, he blurted out, "OK."

"I think a grey would be ideal for Sir."

George nodded. Blue and grey suits were his mantra. They examined more rails of cloth. They were undecided between a light grey, a medium and an "almost" charcoal hound's tooth. They went for the medium grey.

"The grey suit is dearer than the blue but let us say nine thousand five hundred for both, would that be satisfactory?" expecting Gorge to say eight and they would settle around nine depending on George's bartering skills.

"Will Sir be happy to leave a deposit of, say, two thousand pounds?"

George explained he preferred to pay cash and would pay all of it today. Levi's estimation of his customer rose. Usually, only Russians or Arabs were wealthy enough to talk like that. Levi would have been prepared to be bartered down to nine thousand pounds for the two suits, so he said.

"I would like to give you shirts as a mark of our appreciation of your custom. Let me check your collar size, - good. So, this plain white, then a sky blue will go with both suits, as will the white and a narrow blue striped with button-down collar, and a light grey, yes, they are all fine with both suits. Now ties that match the shirts, a maroon, a navy with gold Fleur De Lys, a gold/ yellow with a motif and a royal blue and silver striped. How is that sir?"

"That is terrific. I'm afraid I only have euros."

"Of course, sir, our European neighbours are always welcome here."

He took out a calculator and arrived at a figure of ten thousand seven hundred Euros, near enough. "Delivery in Europe is, of course, free sir." George gave him the Barrows Belfast address.

"Belfast," muttered Levi, then repeated "Belfast".

"Is that OK?" asked George.

"Yes, of course." said Levi, "it will take two weeks, I will work on them over the weekend."

Levi brightened up, the shirts would set a customer back one hundred pounds each, and another two hundred for the ties. They shook hands. The entire experience lasted less than an hour.

George returned to his hotel feeling pleased with himself. He slept well and enjoyed a full breakfast. He remembered movies he and Terry went to, secret agents on special missions. At least he wouldn't have to kill to carry out his mission.

His credibility with Aileen depended on contacting Campbell. Failure would mean; "Goodbye Mr McNeill, thank you for everything. We will approach a professional."

Why did this woman attract and instil apprehension in him? The level of physical attraction surprised him most.

He wanted to make love to a woman he did not know, whose every being oozed a sense of power and purpose that even a hint of some weeks ago would have terrified him.

An enormous change happened to him over a brief period; the big event, finding the money and taking it brought the change. He became scared at what happened to him and what might befall him in the future.

He headed up to Leicester Square and tracked back towards Westminster, trying to find where Campbell lived. When he arrived, far from there being no activity, there were guys in high viz suits and white helmets all over the building. George stood and watched until an older guy with a Southern Irish brogue spoke to him.

"Can you tell me what happened to the people who lived here?" asked George. His fellow countryman proved a mine of information.

"Oh, it has lain empty for years. Developers watched the property price rise and fall. It served as a squat for a couple of years and when the developers tried to get a court order, the Westminster City Council stated they would have to submit a planning application and start work to make the building safe so that happened this week."

George nodded and went back over the bridge and up Charing Cross Road to find the Purple Heart Club. The Club was locked with no sign of life. He called into an Asian newsagent nearby and asked the proprietor when the club opened. The man just shrugged his shoulders. George got a distinct impression he did not approve of the club.

As George left the shop, a young customer followed him out. He caught George's arm,

"Thursday, Friday and Saturday, the Club opens at 3 o'clock." He volunteered, "Other days it doesn't open until 6.00 pm."

George thanked the guy, who added, "Maybe see you in there later."

On the off-chance George asked if he knew a Hamish Campbell but his new 'friend' shook his head.

He wandered around for a while amazed at the theatres, never having attended a live show. As a child, his parents assumed the noise of the pantomime would "upset the boys."

Irene took Terry and Melissa, but George 'ducked' out.

He returned to the club after 3 pm. It being dark inside, George struggled with the gloom at first. There were few people around. He asked a girl in the cloakroom if she knew Hamish, but she shook her head and a security man also said he didn't know him.

He spoke to a person organising the bar, who asked George why he wanted to know. George explained Hamish had been in a relationship with a relative, now deceased, of a family who engaged George to contact Hamish regarding an inheritance. The man looked dubious at this story but told George to wait. As he did so, his 'friend' from the newsagent appeared and began chatting.

Then another young guy appeared. The two younger men eyed each other with evident dislike.

“You wanted to contact Hamish Campbell?” said the recent arrival.

George repeated his story. The man told him to wait,

“I can’t give you Hamish’s details unless he agrees.”

He went off and George tried as politely as he could to disengage from the ‘friend’. Hamish’s pal reappeared to his relief with Hamish on a mobile phone. George spoke to Hamish and explained

“Mrs Whyte asked me to meet with you. You are expecting me I believe?”

“Have you brought my money?” Hamish demanded.

“Yes, I have it,” not wanting to broadcast, he was carrying a large sum of cash.

“OK,” the voice said, “Pete, whose phone this is, will give you directions. “

Pete became chattier. Hamish was in a relationship with a man called Hans, who lived in Northeast London, near Chingford. This meant nothing to George, much to Pete’s amazement. He wrote the address down, then wrote either ‘Overground to Chingford or Central Line Underground to Woodford,’ he added. “It’s a ten-minute walk from Woodford Station. That’s the best way. People will give you directions.”

George headed off, almost boarding on the wrong underground line, but caught on in time and got to Woodford. Armed with directions from a chatty West Indian lady, he arrived at Hamish’s address fifteen minutes after he left the station. An interesting road, on one side were huge villas, purpose-built flats from the 1930s and, on the other side of the street, were beautiful, detached houses, expensive looking with trees behind them, the edge of Epping Forest.

George climbed the stairs to the top flat and knocked. An older man in his mid-fifties opened the door. His accented voice was hard to place but he introduced himself as 'Hans'. He conducted George into the lounge. He saw a corridor to his left that led to a kitchen and one behind him, perhaps to bedrooms.

Hans motioned him to sit down. George talked German cars and how he longed to visit Berlin. Hans appeared unimpressed then Hamish appeared. At first sight, George saw a handsome man in his early twenties. He spoke with a high-pitched Scottish accent, Edinburgh rather than Glasgow, as he could understand his every word. Hamish sat in the seat Hans vacated, Campbell was older than George's initial assessment. His red eyes were puffy and although small and slim, he did not look well. Hans meanwhile disappeared into the bedroom corridor.

"Hans doesn't know about my relationship with Thomas," Hamish said in guarded tones. He went on, "He is Dutch."

Oops, that explained why Berlin and Mercedes cars weren't appreciated.

"Have you brought my money?" George handed him the envelope and Hamish counted it, then he raised his voice.

"Three thousand pounds. I have a journalist prepared to give me twenty thousand for my story, more if I can rope in a cabinet minister or a member of the Royal Family. Thomas had all these connections, you know?"

'Did that explain all the sensitivity around? It wasn't just concerning Thomas.'

"Look Hamish, be realistic," said George, "I don't know how much they will give you, but Mrs Whyte told me to be prepared to come back to London. If she gave you all the money at once, there is nothing to prevent you from going to a journalist as well."

Hamish sniffed.

"It is only of interest for a while. That mad cow drove poor Thomas to distraction, forced him to have kids. She was always on his case, he feared her."

He then whispered. "Thomas and I were in love, he promised to set me up with my own place, he promised me he would leave her," tears formed in the Scotsman's eyes.

"I remember when I first left Edinburgh, a disappointment and an embarrassment to my parents, Thomas let me down too."

For a moment, George felt sympathy. 'I suppose he is mourning too, maybe more than Aileen.'

"Right, give me your mobile number and either Mrs. Whyte or I will be in touch in two weeks."

As a parting shot, he said, "Hamish, everyone wants to be the hero in a story about themselves, in fact we are all minor players in someone else's story. It is just the way it is."

After securing Hamish's number, George took his exit. His intervention bought Aileen more time. The selection process would be over soon, the by election three weeks, at the most four, after that.

Hamish closed the door behind George.

“Everything all right, love?” said Hans. Hamish nodded and went into the bathroom and sat on the toilet, needing space on his own. The tears flowed down his cheeks and his eyes moistened. The Hepatitis B he suffered from made him increasingly unwell. Hamish remembered all the men who used and abused him as a younger person. He believed Thomas was the one for him. They made grand plans and then Thomas, too, betrayed him by killing himself.

A coward’s way out, abandoning someone he claimed to love. Thomas could not live with facing the reality of who he was, rather than who he spent so much energy trying to be. Well, he, Hamish would get something out of it.

George went back to his hotel, collected his luggage, and caught the last flight back to Belfast. The news had been on, reporting yet another stabbing of a black teenager. The sixth this year already. Violent place London.

He returned to the Barrows and phoned Aileen from his mobile, a state of the art recently acquired addition. She asked him what happened, and he said it went OK, but if she could make a dinner date on Friday evening, he would give her all the details then. She paused for a moment and then said her mother would be prepared to babysit the girls on Friday night. George said he would pick her up at 7.00 pm.

George slept well, dreaming of Jewish tailors, Scottish mourners, onrushing noisy tube trains and London accents. During the past week, he packed in more activity than in the past twenty years. If you include the incident in the Edwardian conveniences, then more than in his whole life. The thought of the killings depressed him, that had not gone away. The next day he banked his fee for his London commission. Rather he put it in his building society savings account thinking ‘now is the time to get a place of my own.’

He phoned David at work, "David I need to take a guest to a posh restaurant, have you any ideas?" David suggested a restaurant attached to a hotel halfway between Cultra and Hollywood and said George might get a cancellation there.

The voice on the phone sounded patronising." You are fortunate, due to a cancellation I can squeeze you in. We are usually booked two weeks in advance.

David then phoned Moira, saying, "He wants to go to a posh restaurant now. What are we going to do?"

Moira's reply was less than helpful. "Remember a year after we got married you said you were fed up with Belfast, fed up with worrying over your parents and George and at the right time that we should emigrate to Australia.... well now might be that time."

It proved to be a week of meals. George purchased the obligatory bottle of wine and enjoyed a meal at Jan's with Elena and two of her friends.

The girls were witty, especially when George described his trip to London. They had all been heaps of times, of course. He strung out the story of the embarrassing fitting for the suits but didn't mention the purpose of his visit or Hamish. When he left, Jan said. Elena. "Our George has changed. He went nowhere before, he drove an old jalopy, he rarely ever spoke except about the business."

"He used to chat with me, Papa," Elena replied.

"Did he mention these sorts of things or hold court, telling a story?" Jan posed the question.

"No, I suppose he didn't. I hope he is alright." They glanced at each other.

He drove to Aileen's. Abbi opened the door and ushered him inside. George felt like every seventeen-year-old boy who calls to take a girl to the High School prom and her dad conducts him into the house, ostensibly and to his daughter's impression with friendliness, with an implicit nod towards a cupboard where his loaded shotgun is kept.

"How are you today, Mr McNeill? Are you and Mum just doing business again?"

'Wait a minute, is this a fifteen-year-old's attempt at sarcasm?'

He tried to take control. "Hello young Abbi, how are you, how was school today, you know it's so important for youngsters like you to work hard so that you have a nice career when you become an adult, although that's a long way away isn't it?"

George tone was patronising, and Abbi pulled a face.

"Hello Mr McNeill," said an attractive grey-haired woman in her later sixties walking out of the formal drawing room with her hand outstretched.'

"I am Aileen's mother." She didn't give her first name, and George remembered she stayed out of the limelight of her husband's career, only ever seen on election nights accompanying him to yet another winning poll.

"It is so nice to meet you. Aileen is getting ready. She has told me how helpful you have been to her in this disagreeable business," then she glanced at Abbi. Her lips pursed and for a fleeting second George detected disapproval in her face, body language, his mind and then that middle class politeness returned.

George's thought Aileen would age like this elegant woman who decried colouring, her grey hair cut in a fashionable manner, no attempt at pretence. Flaunt your natural attributes. Abbi sat beside her grandmother, hands clasped on her knees, on a settee facing George, for all the world like a job interview.

Aileen swept in, made up to the nines, with her hair tied up behind, silhouetting that pretty face. George stood up and complemented Aileen on the dress, a tight black cocktail dress with tiny straps across her shoulders and more than a hint of cleavage.

"Thank you, George," said Aileen, and they went to the car. George opened the passenger door for Aileen and as he walked around to the driver's side, he said goodbye to Aileen's mother who turned to walk back into the house and to Abbi, who raised her finger as if to say, 'remember the shotgun in the cupboard'.

George heard Aileen laugh because she saw the gesture from her eldest daughter as he climbed into the Range Rover.

"I am afraid Abbi has taken her father's view of you, George, whereas I quite like you," Aileen teased and they drove to Cultra.

When they arrived at the restaurant, George believed the Maître D was the voice on the phone at pains to point how fortunate he was to get the cancellation. Somehow, without directly saying, he exuded, 'now if we had known it was Mrs Whyte, a reservation would have been made, come what may.'

George could have described the meeting with Campbell by phone but again he pushed for the meeting. Aileen proved a witty and charming companion full of exuberance. She looked gorgeous and eyes in the restaurant turned to her. She must have been aware that after her husband's recent death and Northern Ireland, being Northern Ireland, many people would think it unbecoming she should be out with a male friend enjoying herself. Others understood that life must go on and that all marriages are not what they seem. Either way, Aileen was quite relaxed.

They tittle-tattled about her mother, whom Aileen hinted had little time for Aileen's late husband; the girls, and then George went into detail about London. He described the "squat", the club, and the trip out to Chingford, Hamish's latest relationship, and George's assessment of Hamish. For light relief, he added mistaking Hans for a German, which Aileen found funny, but also mentioned Hamish's claim regarding the journalist.

Aileen confided the selection was in the bag. It would be formalised on Tuesday. The Party grandees were keen she would stand and, unless a real Aileen scandal emerged, anything relating to Thomas would help her in the eyes of the electorate.

"I think Campbell is a sick man, also I believe he will sell anything he can regardless of any agreement. I do not trust him one bit." said George.

"Do you think his partner is in it too?" Aileen asked.

"No, I don't think he mentioned it to Hans, well not yet."

"The by election will be called for mid-October, 5 weeks away. I would like you to go back to Campbell with another payment in two weeks, and we do one more in early October."

"He could have leverage through the reporter with a young, attractive recently elected MP.".

To his surprise, Aileen flushed but said, "Young, thank you for that, kind sir. It is not UK headlines that matter," she replied in a business-like tone. "It is only the Northern Ireland press impact which affects my selection or the Party's chance of holding the seat. We have a built-in majority. We are convinced any scandal aimed at Thomas will create a bounce in my favour."

George saw a calculated, ambitious, even ruthless edge to Aileen that could be a little disconcerting. But then a man who steals half a million in euros from criminal drug gangs cannot be too critical. As they left, George wished once again he had his own home and could take Aileen there. Instead, they headed back for the Malone Road.

Once they stopped outside, Aileen said, "I can't invite you in with my mother and the girls there," then she added, "but I would like to."

They kissed passionately. George caressed her and kissed the top of her breasts. This exhilaration with a woman was new to him and he became aroused, but Aileen brought matters under control with a common sense: "We cannot make love in a car, in my drive, anyway it's much too soon."

George mumbled his agreement, trying to hide his disappointment. She got out of the car tossing a "phone me next week," in his direction and dived up the steps and into the house.

Chapter 4

On becoming a Man of Property

During his recent travelling and week off, George developed a plan. He wanted to leave Baileys securing at least part of his pension. He assumed the edifice he built would soon be destroyed by a court case and imprisonment. Fantasies like his involving Aileen never ended in happiness. A shrewd politician like she is her would dump him before the effluence collided with the air conditioning.

For over two years he considered purchasing a house, chatted to James McKay, an estate agent who was a brother-in-law of a friend of David's. George wanted to start on the property ladder. In his more usual indecisive phase, he called with McKay every four or five months, humming and hawing and unable to decide. McKay pointed at a picture of a house for sale.

"Look, you don't have to move in. Rent it out but act before property prices rise."

On the Monday after his Friday night dinner with Aileen, he called at McKay's office without an appointment.

"James," said his receptionist on the intercom, "that Mr McNeil has come in on the off chance you are free."

James sighed. George was hard work, an indecisive character who fluttered around for a couple of years 'maybe' purchasing a flat, then 'maybe not'. A nice enough guy, but so tentative. One minute agreeing 'yes', he should put in an offer and then drawing back. If it wasn't for his brother-in-law, James would have told George to return when he became clearer exactly what he wants to do. He had space, so he told Mary to show George in.

"Right, James, I need to get moving, and I want to acquire properties to rent. Remember that little two-bedroom house on the Ormeau Road, sixty thousand pounds? I'm prepared to make an offer.

"Whoa," sighed James. "That was six months ago. It has long gone."

"Oh," said George, unable to comprehend that life did not stand still, waiting for his metamorphosis. James looked at his old-fashioned roll cardex.

"Are you interested in that area? Let us see what we have. Ah, just a couple of streets behind the Ormeau Bakery, a similar property, fifty-five thousand pounds. Mind you, it needs a bit of work done to it. The owner is a little old lady who has gone into a care home and her son is selling it. He's a bit of a wide boy, but the mother thinks the sun shines out of his arse. Strikes me when he gets the money, she will be lucky if he visits her once a year. He lives down off Donegal Pass."

James wasn't prepared for what came next.

"Can you give me his name and address and I can see him and reduce the price?"

James fixed George with an icy stare. "George that's what you pay me to do, I will put in a lower offer."

"I am not trying to do you out of your commission, James, it's just I feel persuasive."

Where was the walking monument to indecisiveness? They argued briefly but James agreed to speak to the seller, an Eric Grimshaw, and see if he would meet George.

Grimshaw was desperate to unload the property and he agreed right away, inviting George to his mother's house later that afternoon.

George then said, "Now, I have fourteen thousand pounds savings in the building society," made up with his part of the equity on the marital home, Aileen's three thousand and other savings he made since he moved into the Barrows house. "You also manage rented property for an ongoing fee, don't you?"

James agreed and brightened up even further. George headed off and James collapsed into his chair. It would all go wrong when George tried to negotiate a price, then he would come to his senses and let James handle it. He phoned his brother-in-law for solace, who phoned David McNeill. The latter was becoming more stressed by his brother's behaviour with each contact.

George drove to the address James gave him. Far from being "a wide boy", Grimshaw proved a furtive looking character with beady eyes never looking George straight in the eye in their exchanges.

He showed George around and acknowledged the house needed a modern kitchen. He never commented on the bathroom or the backyard with a crumbling out house and uneven flagstones.

George made notes and muttered calculations out loud, "Bathroom, kitchen, sort out back yard, total redecoration from top to bottom, all carpets in a skip, hmm, now let me see."

"It's like this Mr Grimshaw, can I call you Eric?" Without waiting for a reply,

"Eric, I want to get a property."

Grimshaw saw an advantage. 'This guy will give me the fifty-five thousand because he needs a property quickly.'

"I will need to put in a bathroom and kitchen, ten thousand pounds, sort the back yard, demolish the outhouse, let me, see? I tell you what I will offer you forty thousand pounds. Are we agreed?"

"No, we aren't agreed," Grimshaw was annoyed. His hopes were raised and then dashed. "Fifty thousand," he countered.

"Eric, I need to hurry. There are four other properties I want to see. My last offer is forty-five thousand, and I will give you fifteen thousand in cash this week. I appreciate you may have a other buyers interested, so if we don't agree now, I will need to withdraw my offer."

Eric hesitated. He did not have one expression of interest. To 'push' the sale he could install a bathroom and kitchen, but that meant he would only have forty-five thousand to show for it. That amounted to the same settlement George offered, but if he accepted it, he would not have to organise the bathroom and kitchen, the yard and the carpets. He dwelt on the fifteen thousand in cash. What type of person carried that amount cash? Who did they work for or represent? It was scary; Eric did not want involved with an 'organisation' or a criminal gang, but he wanted the money. He heard himself say,

"OK, I agree, forty-five thousand, but there must be fifteen thousand in cash,"

That was the easiest part. He phoned James, who agreed to have papers ready for signing on Thursday morning.

James warned the papers would cover a purchase price of thirty thousand. He could authorise the mortgage although a few phone calls would be needed. As a customer with the society for many years obtaining a property at half the asking price, he saw no problem. He undertook to speak to his solicitor friend on Tuesday. He wasn't looking forward to that. How did George strike such a good deal, then again best he shouldn't pursue the 'how?'

"Now Eric, I will bring the just over sixteen thousand euros in cash with me on Thursday. When we have finished at the estate agent and signed the papers, we can go to your bank and lodge it."

Eric needed to think through the euro's element, but the cash was the key factor for him.

"Could we not go to the bank first?" the implication being, 'You are a shark who will make me sign for thirty thousand and then not give me any cash and I can do nothing.'

George considered this.

"OK, let's go to the bank first thing on Thursday and deposit your cash."

Eric couldn't resist saying, "Are you not afraid I might then demand the forty-five thousand at the estate agent's and then just walk away with your cash and sell the house to someone else." He smiled at the humour of his outsmarting George. That is what concerned George, but he turned to the smaller man, brought his face up close to Eric's. Abbi would have been proud of that and the menacing tone he adopted.

"That would mean you and I would not be getting on so well, and we don't want that, do we?"

Eric shivered. "Just a little joke," he said limply.

George knew he would have no trouble with Eric. James' solicitor maybe, but not Eric.

In the second part of his plan, he needed to get a property for himself. He was due back in work the following Monday. He looked at houses in East and South Belfast during Thursday and Friday, but they were all over one hundred and fifty thousand pounds and George recognised they would not lend themselves to a quick cash 'bung.'

He drove to Glengormley in North Belfast and looked at a bungalow near the Tieleman's. However, the same issue arose. Nice enough property in a quiet area, it needed work, but still too expensive for a cash bonus to create affordability.

He went from North to South Belfast, first by the North Circular Road, but then entered what during the 'Troubles' would have been less peaceful territory between Andersonstown and Finaghy. He hadn't been in this part of town for years and noted a lot of redevelopments, new buildings and added roads.

He drove down a familiar-looking street. Riverdale Avenue West stretched out long and curved, its name rang a bell. All the houses were modern, late seventies, detached, with pleasant gardens and driveways but the speed bumps were horrendous. He slowed the Range Rover.

Then he remembered that in the late 1970s and 1980s the road served as a rat run for Loyalist gangs from South Belfast and Republican gangs from West Belfast waging war on each other and on people not involved in the 'Troubles'.

In 1982 an IRA active service unit carrying explosives was spooked by the unexpected appearance of an army patrol. They sped up and were decimated by the explosion from their own vehicle. The bumps were heightened to prevent explosives being safely carried over.

George recalled, not long after the houses were built in 1978, another serious event took place. The west end of the avenue was purchased by up-and-coming Catholic families, while the South end accommodated Protestant families. There were a few Protestant families at the Catholic end and vice versa. The residents in the street lived amicably enough.

They were teachers, shop owners, Local Government and Health Board employees who got the chance to buy attractive properties at bargain prices because of the avenue's proximity to two opposing flash points. As a result, both the RUC and the Army had a regular presence manning roadblocks halfway down the avenue.

Following a bomb blast in a Protestant area that killed several shoppers and a toddler, a Loyalist mob sallied forth down the Avenue, stoning the Catholic houses at the Protestant end, setting one partly alight. The residents, including Protestant neighbours, got the Catholic families to safety. Not to be outdone, a Republican mob gathered a couple of nights later and attacked the Protestant houses at 'their' end of the street.

The Army was at the bottom of the avenue where the Republican attack took place. Again, neighbours rallied around until the police and Army appeared and drove the mob back. Many considered the second attack intended to draw the security forces into an ambush and when they drove the mob off, they came under sniper fire.

Over the next few days, TV news cameras observed, as City Council employees, under the Army's watchful eye, cleared up the rubble in the street. Damage to the houses was slight: broken windows and paint daubed on doors. But the assailants failed to get all their targets correct.

One house carried the emblem 'Orange Bastard' which, as the owner said on the evening news "was an unexpected term of abuse to him, given his twin brother was Monsignor Mullally, Parish Priest of St Comgall's RC church on the Falls Road."

In recent years, the Avenue proved peaceful, the residents raised their families, prospered, got older and the 'mixed' community lived in peace. A Channel 4 documentary that featured on national television revealed that in the middle of the "mob attacks", two enterprising residents swapped houses. Both houses were identical in build. One had a better kitchen, the other a better bathroom and garden. No money changed hands. The Catholic owner went to the Catholic end and the Protestant family to the Protestant end. Both families remained in touch and friendly and were featured in a 'feel good' documentary two years after the Good Friday agreement.

Halfway down the street, George noticed a derelict house at odds with the neighbouring, well-maintained villas. Out of curiosity, he parked. As he left the car and looked towards the house, he shivered. It was one of those late October evenings, it would be dark soon, but the sun had shone all day. It was cooler now; he wore a sweater David and Moira bought him the previous Christmas but again he shivered. George did not see a For Sale sign but pushed past the broken gate and walked up a path. The garden and the driveway to the garage were covered in weeds and the garage door hung off its hinges. George tried it, but it had been wedged to stop vandals from entering. Metal covering hung over the front door and the windows. George went around the back, there were fields behind the house and boarded up door and windows.

A narrow unpaved lane lay between the fields and the garden. The back garden contrasted even more with the manicured lawns and pruned trees and hedges of the houses on either side. 'Now this has potential.'

George came back to the front garden and then to the gate, turning around to take in a full picture of the house.

He didn't see a man standing in the driveway next door.

"Hello."

George, so engrossed, gave a start.

"Sorry," said the man, "I gave you a fright."

George smiled ruefully. "Yes, well, I was just looking at the house, nice roof." he commented.

"Yes," his new 'friend,' agreed, "these all have tiles rather than slates. I don't think they wear so well if a property is neglected, the house has a history."

Raising the neglected nature of the property gave George the chance to catch up on the house's history.

The man introduced himself as Gerard O'Callaghan, one of the original owners. He moved in twenty-four years before with his wife, Grace. He would be conversant with whatever incidents were part of the history. As is normal in Northern Ireland, you don't begin a conversation relating to the 'Troubles' until you establish rapport, even trust, with a person you just met.

"The house is as good as any other in the street, but the owner moved to Dublin in 1988." He paused.

There was something important concerning the owner, but Gerard was reluctant to develop it.

“The garden could be brought under control easily enough, but it will need a new boiler and heating system.”.

George couldn’t understand why anyone would leave their house for sixteen years and not try to sell it. After more pleasantries, George asked how he would contact the owner.

Gerard fixed his gaze at him and then said meaningfully. “This is Paddy McCann’s house.”

George thought, ‘Who the hell is Paddy McCann? A news reader, footballer, a singer?’

He was a celebrity, but not one George recognised.

He remembered the days of the barricades around the City Centre, the bus searches, the nightly shootings, the street disturbances, and the horrible sound of bombs going off, but he wasn’t interested in politics. George was determined at all costs to avoid violence.

Paddy McCann worked in his father’s building firm. As a younger man in the 1970s, he was interned and served two prison sentences for being, ‘a member of an illegal organisation’ and ‘being in possession of a firearm.’ From 1978, he went off the Security Forces radar. He married Deirdre O’Turlough, whose father many believed to be a member of the IRA’s ruling Army Council. The couple had a son and a daughter.

In late 1985, an informer revealed to Special Branch that McCann masterminded a series of bombings and shootings in the city. Despite exhaustive detective work, no evidence could be uncovered but someone ‘let slip’ the suspicions about McCann to a Loyalist source.

On the night of the 19 April 1986 a Loyalist gang made their way across the fields behind the house and riddled it with automatic fire.

Deirdre McCann and her daughter, Orla, aged 6, were killed and Paddy McCann was maimed. His son Conor, aged four, escaped unhurt.

Gerard was first upon the scene, went into the house calling for Grace to get an ambulance and cradled the dying mother in his arms. McCann remained in hospital for four months, and Conor went to his grandparents. Paddy McCann returned to the house with his son six months after the attack.

"I don't think he was ever the same man again, although rumour has it, he was still .... his voice trailed off, "involved. McCann stayed here, on and off for two years. Grace got close to the wee boy. He played with our Larry, although Larry's a couple of years older. We still get a Christmas card from Conor. Paddy has a flat in Dublin and eventually Conor went to New Jersey. I believe Paddy commutes between there and Dublin. He came back twice, told me he planned to sell, that was in 1994 and then again in 2001. I phoned him to tell him the roof lost a lot of tiles. He came up, sorted the roof and the damp proof course. Deirdre's dad used to come over to tend the garden and air the house twice a year, until he became ill. He was always tense here, upset because his daughter and granddaughter died there, and he said "hated" the house, but he wanted Conor to benefit from it. "

Gerard mentioned that he, "Cut the grass until three years ago when, I did my back".

"I phoned Paddy about the garage door six months ago, but I wedged it shut and he said to leave it at that. I think the house has such a painful memory for him he wants to forget it exists."

Gerard took a deep breath. "The house is an eyesore. It attracts teenagers from behind the fields and it needs to be lived in soon, or it will never be lived in again. There is one nine doors down that has been on the market for five months with no actual offers. I could contact him on your behalf if you like, but I can't give you his number, you understand."

George nodded. "I am interested. If he wanted, I could meet him in Dublin, I often work down South. Have you been inside the house recently?"

"It is eighteen months since I have been inside the house. It was dry, musty even then." As an ex-heating engineer, Gerard believed a replacement heating system would be needed, plus a kitchen. George gave Gerard his number, shook hands saying, "I hope we will become neighbours."

He knew he should leave details of himself for onward transmission. George explained he worked in finance for Baileys and was building a small portfolio of properties, but if he bought this house, he intended to live in it. He left and went back to Barrows.

He phoned Aileen, as they hadn't seen each other since the previous Friday. "Hi Aileen, it's George. How are things with you?"

Aileen paused before she said anything. "Good," she said, "I was selected as the candidate on Tuesday might and our Chief Whip moved the writ yesterday, so the election is on 14th October. We don't want a long campaign."

"Fantastic news," George groaned inwardly, realising he forgot the selection on Tuesday and how important it was to Aileen. He should have been in touch to wish her well. Black mark. "We should meet up and celebrate," he said.

"That would be nice. I will be up to my eyes on the campaign trail, but I will phone you and you can come over for coffee."

In one fell swoop, she took control of the relatio
have to await her pleasure.

He made one more half-hearted attempt. "OK, if y
won't miss me too much, then."

Aileen laughed, "I am sure she will cope.... but George......"

"Yes," he replied.

"Thank you for phoning, you are a good friend."

He noticed a small builder's yard on the Mountpottinger road, 'Hugh McKinstry and Son'. The name rang a bell because he had seen a reference to the firm on an email circulating in Accounts that the firm was going to fail, and no loan should be advanced if they contacted Baileys.

He called in on the Saturday and spoke to McKinstry. The man was depressed. Equipment lay around beside an old van. He mentioned he auctioned most of his tools and materials. Hugh cheered up when George asked if he could do renovations and install kitchens in two houses he bought.

"You could go to direct kitchen installers and buy 'off the shelf" products. I could save you a lot of money by installing my own purpose build kitchens to fit your houses. My son is a time served joiner and my brother-in-law could install and fit bathrooms, for a lower price."

George mentioned a cash discount, McKinstry's eyes danced at the prospect of a cash deal. Hugh struggled. An excellent craftsman, but a poor businessman.

Just a few miles from the Mountpottinger Road, the police investigators were finding their own barriers in a moribund investigation. Farrell went back to Robb. He retrieved nothing from the camera, though the screen was up and running as it now had its spare part. Robb excitedly pointed at live screens of the whole of Shaftsbury Square.

"We are interested in that date in August. Can you remember anything unusual?"

"What happened, Sergeant?" asked Robb again.

"Never mind, it's classified." replied Farrell wearily.

"Just thought of something." Robb brightened up, "an old schoolmate of mine does that walk every day, he could help."

"Right, have you his name and address or phone number?"

Robb hesitated, "His name is George McNeill; he works in a finance firm near the city centre."

Farrell couldn't prevent rolling his eyes heavenwards. Farrell and Walker put their heads together:

"So, he doesn't have a phone number for this George McNeill, and he isn't certain where he works. Great.

Look, check all the George McNeill's in the phone book, including the unclassified, and the Finance firms in Bedford Street, Great Victoria Street and Bradbury Place and the Donegal Squares, all of them, North, South, East and West."

George returned to work. Only two weeks had elapsed, but so much happened recently, he welcomed the routine. When he got home one evening, Mrs Barrow sounded excited: "George, George, there is a big package that has just been delivered from London. Watch, it is heavy. Mr Barrow and I carried it in together."

Not that heavy, two suits, a few shirts. Mrs Barrow was just trying to spark a conversation because the mystery package intrigued her, the first delivered to George in three years.

"What do you think is in it and who is it from?" she asked Mr Barrow for the third time.

The next day, George handed his 'old' blue suit to Mrs Barrow for one of 'her' charities.

After ten days back at work, he spoke to Peter Donald.

"Peter, it would be a good time for me to move on and seek fresh opportunities."

"Are you sure George? You're a fixture here. We would be sorry to lose you?"

Peter unaware of the 'new' George and not being aware of comments made in Accounts about how chatty George had become. All the women concluded,' There must be a new woman in his life.' Most of the men assumed he started drinking seriously. George handed in his four weeks' notice. The other partners asked Peter Donald to check all was well with George, after all 'he might be having a breakdown.'

"Can't get over it," Peter reported back. "He's in terrific form. He has just acquired a house, maybe a second. He sees a future in property development."

Old Mr Andrews came in to see George. He was not the least concerned about his welfare,

"I trust, George, you will complete the tasks Aileen Whyte needs done?"

George assured him that would remain a priority.

"Good," said the old man, "I think we will register you as a consultant with Baileys. You never know what other jobs might come up where we need someone with your expertise to undertake for us."

The old man's instinct was to bind George to the firm in case they needed him for more work on the Aileen Whyte matter, or any other business.

"Leave that with me."

There was a friendly farewell in the office with gifts presented. George was wearing an expensive looking blue suit, light blue shirt and maroon tie.

"Very smart," said Patsy, trying to provoke Mandy. "He looks quite attractive; the power we women have over men."

"Harrumph," went Mandy, even more furious at George for having a nice suit and a relationship.

George was determined his departure from Baileys would be by the book. He was accorded Board Room for his presentation, an inner sanctum not often seen by any employees except those who knew him for years. Later he went to a meal with select colleagues. Three of the Partners attended and paid for the meal, much to the delight of Alan Carson, Gus, and Dan. A larger group met at a city centre pub, although the Partners had gone home by then. George bought everyone a drink. At the end of the evening, a group of younger colleagues headed to a club while the older ones and 'marrieds' guessed it was time to go home.

George drank too much, and, without being aware of it, followed others to the club where he ended up chatting with people he only knew to see. People paired off or headed home and George found only he and Mandy were left from the original Baileys group and both were the worse for wear.

Mandy said at one point, "I hated you for ...... me thinking you were a Partner." George couldn't follow the logic of this, but had enough booze in him to nod, as if it made sense.

At 3.00 am, they left the club to get a taxi and Mandy said she intended staying with a friend, 'Claire', out the Cregagh Road. They got a taxi there and George got out and accompanied her into the friend's house. They found a key under a stone at the front door.

"Shush, "Mandy kept saying as they went up the stairs with a finger over her mouth, although she was the only one making a sound. They undressed each other, fell into the bed and George managed to make love to her, before falling asleep on Mandy's ample bosom.

A less satisfied Mandy dropped off as well.

She woke at six and gazed in horror at George asleep beside her, thanking her lucky stars she would not see him at work again. She went into her friend's bedroom, waking her.

"Mandy, oh God, what time is it.... did you have to waken me?" asked Claire.

"I have come home with a guy from the office I don't want to see." she whispered.

“You are not leaving him here with me? Is he married or something?”

“No, look, he is harmless, I just don’t want to see him. You will get rid of him easily enough.”

Claire closed her eyes as if in pain, “How can you do this?”

“Don’t worry, it will be fine, “said Mandy. “I will phone you tomorrow. He is a pushover,” and she giggled and again Claire closed her eyes as if in pain, but before she could say another thing, Mandy disappeared, and she heard the front door close.

Claire lay in bed for another hour and a half, hardly daring to close her eyes and cursing Mandy to the high heavens. She got up after 7.30 am and tiptoed into the bathroom for a shower. All was silent from the spare bedroom, apart from the rhythmic sound of snoring. As she went downstairs, she wondered if the unexpected and unwanted guest might be attractive. Now that would be ironic. Then she remembered Mandy brought him and shook her head. He would just be another man with a fetish for big breasts.

George woke closer to 9 o’clock, feeling rough. He wasn’t sure what happened the previous night. He came here, wherever here was, with Mandy. There was no sign of her. He gathered his clothes; his smart suit lay crumpled, but no sign either of them were sick over it. Had he and Mandy....no surely not. He went to the bathroom, washed, dressed and, step by step, made his way down the stairs, partly because he felt decidedly hung over and he wanted to escape before Mandy appeared. As he reached the bottom step, he espied the snib Yale lock on the front door that would allow him to exit without being noticed.

“Good morning,” a voice said from behind him.

George looked around. A petite woman in her housecoat leant against the kitchen door her arms folded. She was late twenties or early thirties, with short blond hair and a pretty face. George turned and put his forefinger to his lips as if to say, 'be quiet.'

"Don't worry," she laughed, "Mandy's gone."

George straightened up,

"Come on into the kitchen," she said, "and have some breakfast, I'm Claire."

"I'm George and sorry, but I am a little rough this morning."

Claire commented. "Look, you are lucky to get out alive after a night with Mandy," And pleased with her own humour, she put the kettle on.

They chatted and George kept down coffee and toast. Claire and Mandy went all the way back to school.

"She keeps getting involved with the wrong men, either feckless ones, drunks or marrieds. It's the same wherever she goes."

Claire was divorced and in no hurry to enter another relationship. George nodded.

"I went to London in my early twenties and met and married my ex-husband. I was a classroom assistant in a local Primary School."

She undertook training and loved both the job and working with young children. George suspected she would have liked a child of her own.

“I went to London on business two weeks ago, my first time, mostly in the centre

“If you live in London, you do not go to the tourist bits around the centre of the city. So, what have you on for the rest of today?” asked Claire,” Not a lot I hope because you do look quite rough around the edges if you don’t mind me saying so?”

George just nodded in agreement; under no illusion that the ‘scars’ of last night’s activities were draped over him in every sense. He brightened up talking about Terry and Melissa, how hard he found it to make a relationship with his daughter, but he would continue to ‘stick in’ there.

At 10.30 am George felt he could brave Mrs Barrow,

“Thanks for the coffee and the bed for the night,” as he got up to leave.

“You can pay me back by taking me out to dinner sometime,” Claire could hardly believe herself saying. “We must do that,” agreed George, “as long as you don’t bring Mandy. Give me your number.”

She wrote it down on a scrap of paper and saw him to the door. They said goodbye and Claire advised him to “get that nice suit cleaned.”

He headed off down the street towards the Cregagh Road, enjoying the fresh air and happy for the half-hour walk that would bring him to the Barrows.

Claire closed her door thinking, ‘what have I done after all I have sworn?’ and how much she would say to Mandy......... or rather how little she would say to Mandy. She liked what little she experienced of George and smiled to herself, hoping he might take up the hint of taking her out to dinner, but if he didn't, so what. She enjoyed the chat. It was normal and nice, no agendas. She met many of Mandy's conquests over the years, going back to when they first started dating boys. None of the guys Claire went out with were ever keen to pursue double dates because Mandy's beaus were a bit off-putting.

Mandy's men fell into four groups. There were the married men, older than Mandy who just wanted a one-night stand, Claire never met them but got a blow-by-blow account of how they were infatuated with her, but "probably wouldn't leave their wives for her." Then there were the 'jack the lad' salesmen and delivery drivers with the same motivation but wanted more than one-night stands. There were guys Mandy got a crush on and pursued until they succumbed and then went into hiding, changed their phone numbers, or 'acquired' a girlfriend or partner, or 'went back to a former partner and were full of apologies. Then there were nicer guys whom Claire liked, who were dumped after a few dates.

Claire also remembered all the fun when she first went to London, shared with a group of girls. Some of her pals, including Mandy, would visit. Then her daddy died, soon after she met "him," before they married, it was all meals, holidays, and nights out. Afterwards he became more controlling, unpleasant if work became stressful and she decided to leave. That was a catalyst for more unpleasantness mixed with pleading to 'give it one more chance 'and then the relief of just going home, being free, and creating a fresh existence in her own home.

That weekend, George wasn't in any fit state to take in Terry's football game. He endured Mrs. Barrows' inquisitorial, almost hostile looks. He left his suit into a speciality dry cleaner in the city centre. The assistant there purred over the quality of the cloth, the cut and its newness. To his relief nothing had been spilled on it.

Claire was nice. He might phone her and ask her out for dinner. She suggested it.

He liked her pretty face, her upturned little nose, the husky voice with a local accent but modulated by her time in London. However, he wanted to concentrate on his relationship, such as it was, with Aileen.

He took Terry and Melissa out to Donaghadee for lunch. He booked a table in a young person friendly restaurant in the town. Melissa played with the mobile phone he bought her while he and Terry analysed the games played in the English Premiership on Saturday.

Aileen, her daughters, and a friend with her two daughters came in. Aileen spotted George, came over, kissed him on the cheek and demanded to be introduced to his children, not gushing but taking charge.

"Oh George, is this Terry and Melissa?"

Melissa became star struck as she immediately recognised Aileen. Terry did not know her. He inherited his father's eye for current events and celebrities but was quite taken with Abbi. Abbi was going to walk off to their table. She ignored George but stood and chatted to a tongue-tied Terry. 'Not his fault. His father is a total arse.'

Aileen introduced her friend, Caroline, and Rosemary was friendly towards George. It occurred to Aileen that Rosemary might be making a point to her sister. Rosemary also chatted to Melissa for a short time and then the Whyte party made their way to their own table.

As the girls chatted and fiddled with their phones, Caroline whispered to Aileen.

"So, is that the new man in your life?"

Aileen said, a little too firmly. "Caroline, don't be ridiculous, he is just a friend who has helped me."

"I bet," said Caroline, "but the way he gazed at you, I wish my husband, or indeed any man looked at me like that, in fact strike 'my husband 'from the record and just leave in any other man." They both laughed.

Chapter 5

A Home of His Own

George and Hugh McKinstry collaborated in refurbishing the house. Hugh's cousin was a paper hanger and although George would have settled for emulsion everywhere, Hugh persuaded him to wallpaper the lounges, stairs, landing, and the hall.

He met Aileen briefly at her campaign headquarters. During their brief conversation, they were interrupted seven times by different people, "Aileen this" and "Aileen that." George possessed zero interest in politics before he met Aileen, and his brief experience in the frenetic campaign office only confirmed the wisdom of this. She gave him an envelope with the three thousand pounds in cash for Hamish's next payment and added that in future Baileys would pay George through his consultancy role. Just for a minute, he was treated like the 'hired help'.

More satisfaction came from a call on his mobile. "George McNeill?" a voice snarled.

"Yes," said George.

"This is McCann," the guttural voice announced.

George hesitated for a moment, Paddy McCann.

They agreed George would go to Dublin. They would meet in a pub on the city's north side. He tried to do background research on McCann but could find little in the way of newspaper cuttings, although he discovered one or two photographs at Republican funerals in the 1970s. Then no other mentions until a big splash around the slaying of his wife and daughter in April 1986, with a photo insert based on a funeral in the top corner of the article. He could find nothing around the time of the Good Friday Agreement. George remained curious, who exactly was Paddy McCann? He had never encountered someone with that level of involvement in the 'Troubles'

They met in a snug in the Rising of the Moon pub. McCann proved a wee Belfast man with a broad accent who didn't shake hands or smile. At least George did not adopt a "pally" attitude, it would not go down well. Your natural intelligence can make you wary of certain approaches. When McCann arrived, he brought a fresh element to George's experiences.

"There is a possibility I am under surveillance by the Garda Special Branch. I take precautions to avoid being followed."

He recently returned from New Jersey, he mentioned, and would not, under any circumstances, enter Northern Ireland.

George nodded but went straight to the point. He explained he 'happened' upon the house by accident.

McCann interjected, "Aye, you wouldn't be up that way much, would you?"

George ignored this; The post Peace Agreement community relations mantra did not attract Paddy.

"Gerard, next door is really helpful.

"He's a decent person, Gerry," agreed Paddy. He paused.

McCann became misty eyed. God, a Belfast hard man like him.

Then having your wife and daughter murdered in front of your eyes would affect anyone, even one who sent other people to an early grave. George waited. He did not want to intrude or offer patronising sympathy for events that did not involve him. What "these sorts of people" did to each other in the bad days had nothing to do with him either then or now.

After a suitable time for this reflection, George made his pitch,

"The houses on Riverdale Avenue are selling for £125,000. Your house needs a fair amount of work done.

A boiler and heating system would need to be installed and a damp proofing course a swell. Then there would be repairing the garage door and decorating. Also, the front and back gardens need work. "

He added. "Another house further down the street has lain empty, with no realistic offers in five months. George summarised the picture well and offered Eighty-two thousand euros, cash.

McCann's response caught him on the hop. "OK, fine by me. You said cash, in euros."

George nodded, and they shook hands. The euros presented no problem to Paddy. The difference in the currencies meant nothing to George. He possessed a magic money tree in his wardrobe. Paddy explained his solicitor in Dublin would sort out the paperwork. George would need one in the North to tie up the odds and ends.

'I hope McKay doesn't create over this. All I am doing is giving him work and money.'

The men agreed. George would return to Dublin with the cash once the paperwork was completed. Again, a fair amount of trust was needed, but George sensed Paddy McCann wanted rid of that house.

McCann knew anyone trying to defraud him ... well, it just wouldn't be a clever idea.

McCann lived a solitary existence in Dublin. His visits to New Jersey with his son and grandchildren were the highlights of his life. He went at Christmas and New Year and for a month in the summer. He worked on construction sites. After his son moved to the US, against his better judgement, he involved himself again in Republican activities, though nothing illegal. He attended Sinn Fein meetings, canvassed for their candidates in local and national elections. He avoided being propelled into senior roles. His former colleagues accepted after the tragic death of his wife and daughter, he should be left alone to raise his son. The Garda kept him on their list of 'people of interest.'

His closest friend in Dublin, an associate from the mid-1970s, was Joe Higgins. Joe served time in the Irish Republic for possession of weapons and an operation at Crossmaglen on the Irish border. Higgins owned a small electrical contracting firm and offered Paddy job opportunities when the latter moved to Dublin. His eldest son, Joe jnr, worked with his dad at first in an apprenticeship role. Of Higgins' two other sons: Rory was a student and the youngest, Artie, was still at school.

People Paddy knew were dead or drifting out of the movement. When the Peace Agreement and ceasefire took hold, others became disillusioned and moved to smaller, more extreme groups. Paddy's reputation was diminishing, but he didn't recognise he wasn't the force he used to be. At an Ard Fheis in 1997 that he spoke at, he fell out with Northern comrades from a later generation. The dispute concerned support for the Northern Leadership inching towards a historic agreement. Despite Paddy's reservations, he stayed loyal to the 'top' men. He did not handle the dispute well and adopted a menacing attitude towards those with whom he disagreed who were pursuing a harder line.

Paddy left the Ard Fheis after the dispute and went to meet Joe and his eldest son at a local hostelry when three of his protagonists attacked him. It took place near the pub and both Higgins poured out and a fist battle ensued until the Garda arrived. Witnesses testified that Paddy was set upon, and the other men ran off. This affray sealed even further an enduring friendship.

Having returned from Dublin, George flew off again to London. He made his way to Woodford again. He climbed the stairs to the top flat. Hamish opened the door in a temper and launched into a tirade, "That bloody woman's incessant demands killed Thomas. I have been in touch with a journalist from a national newspaper and we are negotiating a price for my story."

Why would you say that to a man with an envelope full of cash?

"OK, I will return to Belfast with this cash. Do you think they will let me keep it for my trouble?" George pondered aloud.

Hamish's eyes lit up in panic and he tried to grab the envelope. George was not a physical person, but he pulled the envelope back in time, think Abbi.

"Look you little prick, "*We, 'who the hell is this 'we,'* "are sick to the back teeth of your threats. If I give you this money and you go near a national newspaper, the next guy they send over will add you to an extension to the M 25. Do you understand?"

Hamish nodded meekly; he knew from a phone call before George arrived that this opportunity with the newspaper was gone. George handed him the envelope.

Earlier in the day, at an editorial meeting in Wapping, an eager young journalist was told.

"First, the guy is dead. Second, his widow, with her young daughters, is perceived as akin to a saint in Northern Ireland. Third, we are not wanting to start another war with the LGBT movement and fourth, every story has its moment, and this one passed the day after he died. The fact the Sundays ran it killed it once and for all, that's life mate." The journalist phoned Hamish with the bad news.

After George left, Hans arrived home. He recognised George as they passed on the pavement, although George either did not see him or not chosen to acknowledge him.

He found an inconsolable Hamish in a rage with three thousand pounds lying on the table. Seeing Hamish's rage, he wondered if this volatile Scot and he were suited?

George phoned Aileen on Saturday. She sounded exhausted with only three campaigning days remaining before the by election. This being Northern Ireland, there would be no campaigning the next day, Sunday.

"I will contact you next week. At least tomorrow you can get a rest."

On Sunday morning, a Dublin newspaper with considerable sales North of the Border featured a picture of George and Aileen coming out of the restaurant near Hollywood. George walked slightly ahead of Aileen, holding her hand. Aileen trailed behind him, with a clutch bag in one hand and the other holding George's. Hardly the most scandalous picture in the world. Many innocent males might have held the hand of a female friend experiencing a sorrowful time. The headline proclaimed: "TRAGIC WIDOW FINDS NEW LOVE."

Neatly timed for election week with no actual story, just a rehash of the one on Thomas' death. Aileen phoned him and appraised him of the newspaper picture.

Aileen began, "We," (*them again they get everywhere was George's take*), "will put out a statement. You and I should speak tomorrow," she commanded. "When the press approach you say nothing, is that clear, nothing."

George came as close to being annoyed at her tone as he could be. Silence.

"George, if you care for me at all, please do as I ask."

'As I ask, that's better. I wonder what you will ask when they publish the photos of me, two dead drug dealers and half a million stolen euros.' Thought George.

Peter Donald went "Oops," and Irene was beside herself not knowing whether to laugh or cry. Poor Mrs Barrow was unaware of the 'scandal' until she went to the bingo on Monday, but her pals were full of it. They hadn't connected George to her. Uncharacteristically, she decided not to enlighten them.

A statement appeared in the Monday papers: 'Aileen Whyte wishes to state that she is not in a relationship with any person, has not been in a relationship with any person and with her daughters continues to mourn the tragic loss of her husband, the girls' father. Following the tradition set by her father, she is pursuing a path of public service.

The Mr McNeill in the Sunday newspaper photograph is a family friend helping in her election and they were having an informal meal to discuss final campaign tactics.'

The press searched for George without success. 'He doesn't seem to exist,' one editor mused, as every McNeill in the book claimed no knowledge of George. That included his brother David, in an absolute state over the article and photo, Moira loved it.

Three days later, Aileen won her seat with a comfortable majority. George tried to catch her on the phone but got no joy. He texted her his congratulations with a few xxs included.

She texted back to apologise, said life was 'blistering' at present but would settle down and she would phone him. One small x. accompanied the text.

Mandy met with Claire for coffee on the Tuesday.

"I need advice Claire; I want to go to the papers and reveal that George and I slept together in your house. We even had sex....... not that memorable sex."

"Really, Mandy, do I need to be told that? Anyway, this is not your story. Did you see the press release? They are just friends; you are not involved in any way? Even though you might wish it, you will not become a celebrity because of this. I am quite sorry for him; he appeared all right to me."

"Oh, wait a moment. You don't even know him, Claire, or hang on, did something happen after I left? You didn't, did you... the papers would pay a fortune for that story? Sex stud has orgy and takes prospective MP out for a meal."

"Mandy, please don't judge me by your own warped standards. Only you would want to 'star' in an orgy to get your name and photo in the papers. We shared toast and coffee. I talked to him. All you have ever done is flash at him, then glower at him and then have sex with him, a typical Mandy in depth relationship."

"Now, now Claire, don't get shirty."

The women paused, collected their breaths, then burst out laughing. Claire confessed she gave George her number, but he hadn't been in touch.

"I wouldn't have minded going out to dinner with him," she murmured, almost but not quite to herself.

The next weeks into late October were a whirl of signing papers relating to the house, pleading with McKinstry to leave the Ormeau property and go to Riverdale Avenue and work on it. West Belfast was not McKinstry's normal stamping ground, a bit too close to Andersonstown for his liking. George pleaded and pleaded and then offered a thousand-euro bonus if McKinstry, his son- and brother-in-law, did up his house.

"Why didn't you say that before?" He went to Riverdale, surveyed the house,

"We can remove the shutters, fix the garage door, do the damp proof course, and decorate for..." They set a price.

Gerard's son cut the grass front and back and while the gardens remained overgrown with bushes needing pruning, and shrubs and trees also requiring attention, it looked less like an abandoned property. Gerard told him of his connections, who could install the heating system, including radiators and a boiler. McKinstry recommended a custom fit kitchen and bathroom for the Riverdale property.

George bought furniture, paying cash in euros.

He added a couple of double beds, two wardrobes, one with a long mirror, a three-piece suite, a comfortable armchair, and a dining room suite, as well as kitchen utensils and a TV and a few soft furnishings. In addition, he bought furniture and white appliances for the house he intended to rent out; they were not as expensive as the ones in Riverdale, all paid in euros.

Perhaps half of Northern Ireland went from Sterling to the Euro zone without it being announced. He knew he spent almost two hundred thousand euros of the kitty.

An interesting conversation would arise if the owners of the money turned up, or the police. David and Moira were impressed with the house. Moira made various suggestions, including softer furnishings, George said he might rent out the house.

A few days earlier, John Farrell burst into Walker's office and beckoned him down to the small room where the crime scene images of the Shaftsbury Square murders were displayed. The room possessed a desk, two chairs and, on a wall, two photographs taken at Belfast City Mortuary. There were cards above each photo reading 'Fedor Pakas b 1981 died August 2004' and 'Patrick Quinn b 1982 died August 2004,' plus photos of the Square and the refurbished toilets. Other police officers bantered Alan and John over their 'progress' on the case, or lack of it. Police work is often painstaking, but to Superintendent Robertson this case was a waste of time and he pulled them off the investigation to deal with more immediate priorities. In fairness, there had been little progress since August, so that wasn't unreasonable. An excited Farrell began,

"I followed your suggestion, asked around and," he raised his voice in triumph, "I have got our Mr McNeill. He is like a ghost, he doesn't have an address, he isn't in the phone book or on the voters' register, but I have found him. I went to a firm called Baileys and spoke to the receptionist. She said a George McNeill left their company six weeks ago, having worked there for twenty years, caught people by surprise. Now is that a coincidence?"

Walker ignored the provocation. It was Farrell's day, a day of old-fashioned police legwork.

"Did she have his address? "

"Well, I didn't say I was from the police, but-" said Farrell, drawing himself up, "through her I got a photograph of him."

"WHAT?"

"She mentioned he appeared in the front of one of the Sundays and I know a guy who works in the picture section in their Belfast Office, and he got me this." So, saying Farrell brought out with a flourish a large glossy photograph of McNeill and Aileen Whyte, the recently elected MP.

"All we need is his where he lives."

"Fuck me," Walker's responded, "now it's getting interesting. Billy Robertson will do his nut at her involvement. Won't go down well in the lodges either."

Walker looked askance at the photo, not because of McNeill, but he knew Aileen Whyte's involvement would complicate matters, especially with 'upstairs.' They added the photograph to the wall with the words 'George McNeill' above it. Farrell summed it up commenting,

"We can hardly approach her and ask who he is, not knowing what that will bring to light or the storm it will create around our heads."

"Too right," said his boss, "the guy is merely a potential witness. We only want to ask him if he was there the day those guys were killed and if he remembers anything. We can then cross him off our list. I don't think we mention this to that bastard Robertson yet. We have nothing to go on of any substance.

It is odd he left his employer then after all those years too, and that he is so difficult to find. Whatever you say, I don't believe in coincidences, but let's see if anything else comes up. At least we know where he worked. We can find a discrete way into that for his address. Check to see if he is on any of our files. Ask that mate of yours at Special Branch, he often has odd bits of intelligence and--"

"What?"

"John, there are no such thing as coincidences in our game."

Two days later, the daughter of a consultant surgeon at the Royal Victoria Hospital was the victim of a brutal murder on her way home from Queens University.

Walker and Farrell were brought straight in on the case on a twelve-hour shift basis. 'Shaftsbury Square' went on the back burner again.

A disabled neighbour across the street humorously gave him a "telling off "for the state of his garden. A keen gardener, because of a stroke though he struggled to do much gardening himself. he said,

"I use a guy to do his heavy work. I can introduce you if you like."

George nodded.

"I just give him instructions. The guy's name is Martin Breen, he is always looking for more work. He is willing, a hard grafter, though not in any way imaginative. I would give him advice and plan the garden for you as long as you wouldn't mind. Before my stroke, I tried to help Gerry, but he said the owner was a bit funny. In the ten years I have lived here, I have never seen him."

George jumped at the offer. A few nights later, having finished his latest stint across the road, Martin Breen called at his door, a slight wiry, dark-haired figure. One of those people who never looked you in the eye but were always smiling as if at some private joke. They settled on a rate. George said it would be in cash and in euros, euros because he travelled with his work in the EU. Breen agreed. With an input from the neighbour across the street, Breen began work preparing the garden for winter and spring. The only disquieting thing when George mentioned it to Gerard O'Callaghan, the latter seemed less than enamoured.

George hadn't seen Aileen since that brief encounter in the Election campaign office. Would she phone him? She would be busy at Westminster. She had to be sworn in, find an office, attend many political group meetings. As an Opposition MP, albeit in a small party, she undertook a shadow brief, in her case the Home Office. The girls would soon have to be settled into Boarding School.

Also, when she came back in Belfast, each Thursday evening there were surgeries, local party branch meetings, liaising with MLAs (Members of the Assembly). Deep down, he was testing her to see if she had a genuine interest in him or was it all merely a convenience during the Hamish incident?

Aileen prepared to close her office in London for the Christmas recess. She was pleased with Josh, the assistant she recruited; a young, bright guy who graduated several years ago from Cambridge. He went on an extended backpacking holiday to India and Australia and came home in late Autumn, too late to get employment. He landed on his feet when Aileen's advert for a Parliamentary research assistant came out in early November. He lacked Parliamentary contacts around Westminster to help her with detailed business.

Once more, she struck lucky with Ann Clayton, a secretary to one of the Conservative Party's longest serving MPs for many years. When he stood down, she agreed to work for his successor. A sensible arrangement, but unlike his predecessor, this MP was a micro-manager and insisted on everything going through him. They clashed frequently, and she resigned. The MP, conscious her unexplained departure, could have a negative impact since he was trying to make his mark in the Party needed to act. He spoke to one of the Whips who suggested to Ann he would arrange for her to go to the next Tory MP elected.

Aileen's election sped up the opportunity. The Whip did some networking with Aileen's party leader. Where might she get a secretary seven weeks before Christmas? She arranged a meeting with Ann, and they took to each other. Ann insisted on starting right away, which suited Aileen. She made a point of saying nothing regarding her previous employer, although Aileen received some background information from the Whip.

Ann also knew Thomas, but never mentioned this to Aileen. Her attitude to Josh hovered between a caring aunt and a bossy but kind school matron, which, as a former public-school boarder, he recognised.

When the boarding school element in Josh was mentioned, a shiver ran up her spine. The girls wanted to wait until the term after Christmas began before they boarded, and Aileen still carried guilt over her daughters leaving home and moving four, maybe five miles away. Perhaps these days, the girls were more relaxed with their grandmother. Aileen radiated far too much drama, no doubt because of her election campaign, but maybe anyway. Her mother agreed to stay over at least three nights a week, though not without creating a disapproving/martyred atmosphere.

Aileen chose not to accept the disruption as that big an issue. After all her parents spent most of their married life in the house. Being Aileen, she made this point to her mother.

"The thing is, Aileen, all politicians think everything should revolve around their needs, the Party's needs and the constituency's needs. I put up with forty years of that dance; I don't want another generation of it."

Aileen acknowledged this. In retaliation for staying with "her grandchildren," her mother then tried to raise the relationship with George, following the newspaper speculation. A step too far for Aileen, and she told her mother so.

At Westminster she got support from Sir Toby Hazlehurst, a former Tory Grandee and junior Home Office minister who appointed himself her guardian. They met when she went for an initial briefing over her 'shadowing role'. He behaved in a solicitous manner towards her and helping solve several practical problems as she found her way around the Westminster maze. Being seen walking into the Palace of Westminster with a long-standing MP and a government minister enabled the police and House of Commons staff recognising her more quickly than usual. Also, she was elected in a Bye Election, and this helped too, not like the hordes of new MPs after a General Election.

A Home Office junior minister in the previous Tory Government which Hazlehurst loved never having expected, in twenty years in the Commons, to achieve Ministerial Office. His appointment was a compromise between an able EU 'Remainer' and an out-and-out EU 'leaver'. Toby fitted the bill as an MP with some quasi-liberal pretensions. After his party lost the 1998 election, Toby being at a loose end and pursued other interests. This included several interns and young advisors, some of whom made discreet complaints, regarding his 'wandering hands' and his inappropriate comments. Hazlehurst had to be spoken' to by a senior member of the party.

The perfect storm for a candidate seeking reselection happened when someone leaked to his local constituency that Toby was ‘disciplined’ for inappropriate behaviour. An ambitious local party member began to demand the constituency party and its MP adopt a no compromise ‘get out of the EU’ approach. Toby failed to recognise the seriousness of the issue. He attempted to calm branch members by playing the elder statesman. Other old enmities surfaced, including an affair with a previous constituency chairman’s wife that still rankled. Local papers dropped hints he would be deselected; they were being briefed by someone inside the branch.

In the Commons, he remained popular with some, as his invitations to his grouse shooting estate in the Scottish Highlands were much sought after. Toby became angry at the bickering in the local party and in a fit of pique he jumped ship and became a Labour MP. He claimed at heart he wanted to remain in the EU. Toby knew that by a slender majority, most of his constituents in his Home Counties seat were fans of Remain, but his local party were opposed. If he split the vote and let in a Lib Dem, that would chastise his enemies. As a well-established MP, he carried a personal vote, but this always proves smaller than a sitting MP thinks. Toby might be re-elected with cross-party voting.

The local Labour Party swallowed years of hostility and were persuaded to adopt him as their candidate to win the seat. This enraged Toby’s opponents, which delighted him. He was quite prepared to lose his place in the Commons just to see their faces when he canvassed, or on the next election night.

A portion of Toby’s family considerable funds were tied up in local businesses and lots of working people were employed in his businesses and were likely to support him, especially if he stood for a Party, they were more likely to vote for. He was elected. A coterie of Labour intellectuals was appalled at the total lack of principle recognising it for a shoddy deal.

The Chief Whip, "Well Prime Minister a small reshuffle at this point in your premiership is a good idea."

"Yes, but not the major offices of state, just enough to give the media something to play with and disconcert the opposition."

"Why not offer Toby Hazlehurst his old job as Minister of State at the Home Office. Think how that will play out with the opposition."

The PM chuckled, "Yes I like that." and Hazlehurst returned to the Home Office in his previous role. This led to emotive Ministerial Question Times, with Sir Toby espousing the opposite position from the ones he took relatively recently in the same role for his former Party.

Many Hansard quotes were thrown at him to embarrass him, but the angrier his ex-Tory colleagues got, the more he revelled in it. It was A sketch writers' heaven and Sir Toby often featured in the papers, and not always for the right reasons, but he loved the drama. His Tory chums refused to ostracise him in the bars. The prospect of the August grouse shoot invitation still influenced them. One ex-colleague with whom he maintained a cordial relationship going back to their days at Oxford remonstrated with him; "Toby, tone it down a bit."

"But Humphrey, I am too rich to care." he replied.

He had known Thomas and was quite taken with the young widow in her first days, as she took her oath and made an early, brief, but emotional, maiden speech, including a fulsome tribute to her late husband.

'That was quite arousing,' Toby told himself, he didn't say it to anyone else. Her only negative experience of him happened when they parted in a corridor near the Chamber, Hazlehurst patted her bottom, so fleeting Aileen wondered if she imagined it or if it had been accidental.

She did, however, have an odd experience walking into the Chamber two days before the Christmas recess when a left-wing female Labour MP, Stella McGovern, fell into step with her. After a gentle chat about how Aileen settling in, did she have all her support organised and how hard each Sunday night was saying goodbye to the kids.

"I have seen you a few times with Toby Hazlehurst.":

"Oh, he has been kind towards me.".

As they reached the chamber, Stella took her wrist, "Be careful of him. He has an appalling reputation with women. It's easy to assume, if you are a mature woman, you can handle men like him. He is persistent and, if he senses he has an opportunity, quite unpleasant." With that, she trotted up the steps on the Opposition benches.

Aileen took it as an excellent piece of intelligence. She mentioned the conversation to the discrete Ann, assuming she would say little. Ann's reply surprised her.

"Keep him at arm's length and never be caught on your own with him," an uncharacteristic, almost indiscreet response.

In a quiet bar in Westminster, with a few of his longstanding chums from the 'Club,' Hazlehurst held forth. "Almost snared that Irish filly," he claimed. "Fifty guineas, I bang her senseless before the Easter recess."

At night, curled up in her small but comfortable flat, Aileen usually slept well. On this night, having drunk too many coffees as she tried to get through a mountain of paperwork between 7.00 pm and midnight, she lay awake unable to sleep and George came into her thoughts.

She wasn't prepared to admit to herself that George attracted her. She liked him. They did not know each other well, but there was a lot of contact during a stressful period in her life.

The MP regretted they almost lost touch because of the Election and post-election Westminster debacle. She remembered him kissing her the first time and then, after the ill-fated dinner; she felt his passion and hers too, but she controlled that situation. Should she leave it? Did she miss a man in her life? There hadn't been one for a long time.

Yet George was dependable, so quiet, such a comfort and he boosted her by his presence, almost an ally that she could trust, trust being a big thing to her after Thomas.

Thomas's priority, she reasoned, like most men, was Thomas, and she knew that from soon after they were married. George was different, not demanding, but focussed on her. She missed him.

The election was frenetic, and she concentrated on that leaving little time for anything else, but George, in an odd way, became important to her.

'Gracious me, I can't be falling in love, too old for that nonsense. I will phone him over the holidays. 'Her last day in London involved some frenetic shopping for Christmas presents.

She gave Ann and Josh theirs, but she wanted something special for the girls and, of course, for her mother. On an impulse, she bought George quite an expensive watch. Aileen wasn't sure how he managed after he retired from Baileys and the watch might be a bit of a boost.

She heard a consultancy role might be found for him. She owed him not just for what he did, but the way he did it, discreet without pre-judging or intruding into her deeper self.

Aileen flew back to Belfast with some other Northern Ireland MPs and then made her way home. Since the weekly trek to Westminster began, Aileen found it a strange feeling when she came home. She loved this house. Apart from three years when she and Thomas were first married, it was the only place she lived in. Soon it would be too big for her. Abbi would go to university. Maybe not in Ireland. Rosemary would follow in Ireland though, at least.

The house in Riverdale became habitable ten days before Christmas, and George sat Mr and Mrs Barrow down and explained that he bought a house.

"Oh, where?" Mrs Barrow exclaimed.

As he described it and thanked them for all their kindness somehow, he 'forgot' to answer her question. He moved his belongings out. He needed to find a source of regular income. James reckoned that the house on the Ormeau Road he owned would yield £350 pm, less the fee to James for letting/managing the property. As it was too close to Christmas to advertise, McKinstry was diverted to work on Riverdale

Chapter 6

It all gets social, and George has guests.

Three days before Christmas, George sat in his home, enjoying his own space. Better plans needed to be in place if his house of cards caved in, or rather, when his house of cards caved in. Although relieved the Barrows, nice enough people, were not on top of him all the time, Martin Breen, the gardener, slipped into their role. He popped around to see if there were any odd jobs he could do. He needed the garage cleared and the garden done. In winter, there is less to do in the garden. Breen was almost clinging to him. He sometimes drove to Riverdale in his old van, other times he walked. He never mentioned having a family. On evenings he worked all day but had no van, George offered to drive him home. Breen would have none of it. Happy enough on George's turf, but he did not want George on his.

Once, after doing sterling work clearing the build-up of rubbish, George gave him a can of beer. One can become three and then whiskey was drunk. It created too intimate a link with Breen. He became more familiar, called 'George,' George. The latter became anxious that Breen, with associates, might rob him. Perhaps his own guilt raised these feelings, he guessed Breen believed he kept cash on the premises. When Breen consumed the drink, he mentioned he served prison sentences during the 'Troubles.'

"Nothing against Protestants, Mr McNeill." (George was still Mr McNeill in those early days,) "But them and the Brits did a lot of violence and damage round where I live. I lost friends."

He then became morose and said no more. A look in his eye suggested his incarceration was not anything trivial. George did not interrogate him further, but Gerry O'Callaghan made a typical cryptic comment,

"I am not a big fan of that guy, Breen." He added nothing further. George was thinking through this comment when his mobile rang. It was Aileen. His heart jumped, and he became quite excited at hearing from her and her initiating the contact.

"Are you going away over Christmas, New Year?" This raised an unexpected dilemma, Christmas with Abbi ...'

He hedged his bets. "Well, I go to my brother's on Christmas Day and the Tieleman's on Boxing Day. They have a big family event with relatives coming over from Belgium."

The invitation Aileen made was different. "There is a charity dinner and auction at Belfast City Hall on New Year's night. Would you like to come?"

George hesitated. After the newspaper photo was, she suggesting he come as her partner. The 'scandal' would not worry him for a moment, especially if it resulted in him sleeping with Aileen.

"You will need to bring a partner and it will be a black tie. Please say you can come; I would love it if you were there supporting me during my speech. If you come here on Christmas Eve, I can give you the invitation. Please say you will."

"Yes, Aileen, I'd love to come. "He could always be "ill" on the night if he couldn't sort something out. Which George would appear the new George or the one who would like to hide in a corner and speak only if spoken to? Had a spell been put on him, would it wear off at midnight on New Year's Eve?

If he was going to the Charity Auction at the City Hall on the 1st of January, he would ask Elena to go.

"Sounds as if you'll be busy."

George explained one of Jan's brother's and his wife would stay at Riverdale, "and we haven't even seen it." Jan complained to Elena.

George would pick up Jan's brother and his wife on Christmas Eve and bring them to his house, depositing them back at Tieleman's on Christmas morning before he arrived at David's. A few years ago, when Jan's relatives' children were younger, he and Elena travelled to Belgium. But for the past few years, the relatives enjoyed coming to Ireland.

"The young people prefer to go out on their own," one of Jan's sisters-in-law complained, "We never see them.

Elena did not like the change. She missed seeing her cousins, but she also loved the house being full at Christmas.

Aileen listened. This family was important to George. She spoke of her and the girls' Christmas plans. He dwelt on how soft spoken she could be on occasions. Gone was the "West Wing" shoot from the hip. Aileen, decisions made at once, commands issued without pause or hesitation. He remembered it only too well from his experience at her election campaign office.

George bought presents for Melissa, Moira, his brother, nephew, and Elena. Terry wanted money, and the Tielemans didn't exchange presents but had a secret Santa at their Boxing Day family party, George got Jan's brother Pieter.

George always brought Elena a present. In the past, he struggled with gift buying. Terry and Melissa now helped with ideas or at least reacted to his, "Oh God, Dad, not that for a sixteen-year-old girl."

As he brought ironing upstairs, he found a scrap of paper which he tried to interpret earlier. He found it in his suit when it returned from the cleaners after his 'leaving' night.' The effect of the speciality cleaning, plus passage of time and house move, resulted in it fading and being indecipherable. It was a telephone number; perhaps Mandy's, and he amused himself trying to find the numbers. He concluded that the numbers ended in either four, six or five, eight. As he wrote out the two combinations of numbers, he remembered Mandy's pal giving him the scrap of paper. He owed her a meal for the breakfast and the bed for the night. What was her name? He recalled a petite woman with a pretty face and short blond hair. They had a fun chat, were relaxed, and shared more intimate information about previous partners than strangers do. On an impulse he tried the number ending in four six, 'this call cannot be connected,' said a voice.

The next morning, he phoned Baileys which was due to shut at lunchtime for the holidays and spoke to Mandy. An odd conversation, Mandy had no man for Christmas. She would have to rely on the office Christmas party again, but no matter how desperate, George's phone call offered no temptation. After a perfunctory enquiry concerning her health, he asked for her friend's number. Of course, he hadn't her name, but he reasoned Mandy would say it when he mentioned 'her friend', 'Oh, do you mean X?'

That is what happened. Mandy said, "Oh, Claire Cooper?"

George responded, "Yes Claire," Mandy gave him the number, remembering her and Claire's conversation.

As soon as she put the phone down, Mandy phoned Claire. "Guess who was on the phone looking for your number?"

Claire didn't get it in one or two, but on three, "George, what does he want?"

"I do not know, but it's Christmas, so go for it. You don't know what you'll get from it."

"Well, Mandy talking about people getting things, if you are having one-night stands' drinking too much, be careful or you might end up with an STD or worse."

"Oh Claire, come on, 'one-night stands' me? It was only the one, and with 'Your' George."

"He is not 'my' George and I remember the postman from Newtownards and the...."

"All right, all right, but you have to phone me tonight. I demand to know every word he says and every word you say. No holding back, mind"

Claire grunted noncommittally and said, "Bye."

George expected Mandy would warn Claire. It would be better for Claire to be prepared, so he waited for twenty minutes before he phoned her. Her tone, when they spoke, confirmed that Mandy prepared her for the call.

"How are things with you?" There was a little chit chat between them, then, "I promised to take you out for a meal. Have you any free time over the holidays?"

"I am tied up with family things over Christmas."

"Are you free on Boxing Day in the evening? Could you accompany me to my friends, the Tielemans', party? "Jan often told him to being someone. Claire tried to buy time by mentioning her arrangements, but said to herself, 'Boxing Day when I return from Liz's can be downer,' so she agreed, careful not to sound too eager.

"I could leave early. The family wouldn't mind, but you need to pick me up at my sisters in Rosetta."

George's turn to draw a deep breath, old George, meeting the family of a girl he met once. She gave him directions.

"That is terrific, see you at 7.00 pm. The Tielemans' meal is at 8.00 pm. When Claire and George hung up, both were fighting the same feelings.

Is this a mistake?' Neither knew the other. A pleasant conversation over breakfast doesn't lay the foundation for anything but 'hey ho' it's a party, other people will be there, refuge can be found in a crowd. A first date has to start somewhere, it can end there as smoothly. Claire remembered him talking about his children and his ex-wife whilst she shared about her marriage. An honest exchange, she liked that.

On 24 December, George made his way to Aileen's house. Abbi opened the door.

"Abbi, lovely to see you, you are looking good, out on the town tonight with the guys and gals?" Rosemary stood inside the hall and tried, with difficulty, to suppress a giggle.

'Out on the town, with a mother like mine? Shows how little you know her.' but Abbi said nothing, putting on her brightest, fakest smile.

“Mr McNeill, always a pleasure to meet you. What a surprise. My Grandmother told me you finished your business with my Mum.” (*‘So why don’t you fuck off, you lecherous bastard’*).

“Mum,” she shouted.

George must be able to handle this joust with someone not yet sixteen. His voice was soft. “Abbi, I am always eager to see if I can help your mother with your and Rosemary’s upbringing.”

Abbi digested this with horror, to George’s delight, but then shouted, “Mr McNeill thinks I should go to Jennifer Caldwell’s party.”

Aileen came from the kitchen. “Abbi, we have dealt with that, and Mr McNeill doesn’t know Jennifer or what mums have told me about her parties.”

She shooed the girls upstairs. “MUM,” was Abbi’s despairing cry as she left.

Aileen brought George into the kitchen, where coffee percolated.

As she did, George ventured, “You know, I am a dab hand at dealing with young women who are not conforming to their parents’ expectations. I could always speak to Abbi for you.”

She gaped but then remembered his encounter with Elena and laughed.” I think you got off lightly with Elena. You wouldn’t with Abbi.”

Aileen motioned George to a chair and gestured towards Fortnum and Mason biscuits and handed over the Charity Dinner and Auction invitation.

"You might bring Elena; at her age and stage she would enjoy it or Melissa."

Aileen was keen to meet the beautiful, young Irish/Belgian girl she heard so much.

"I guess Elena would enjoy it, she is just that bit more mature. Anyway, how are you doing?"

She described various events a newly elected MP did, staff recruiting, the famous political personalities she met. "A virtual trip through the past two years' Question Time, "she concluded.

George did not want to embarrass himself by admitting he didn't recognise most of the names. At least he had heard of Question Time, even seen it after a Thursday night Europa League games.

She glanced at her watch. "My hairdresser is due any minute."

It wouldn't be Aileen that she didn't go to the hairdressers. The hairdresser comes to Aileen.

"I am hoping she will fit in a brief cut with the girls. Rosemary's is too long, and Abbi is being difficult, "Aileen continued.

'Abbi being difficult surely not,' again an unspoken thought.

If Abbi and George's unspoken thoughts ever met, it would be akin to World War Three.

"Abbi wants the top of her hair purple, and one side shaved. We agreed I will get a colouring for the top that will wash out, but no shaved side bits. We have a big family do later in Christmas week. If I have one more aunt saying Abbi is like me as a teenager, I will swing for them."

It might be the aunts had a point, but he wouldn't achieve his desires by sharing this.

"Are you likely to be in London in the New Year?"

"Oh yes, I am due over on business, "though this only occurred after Aileen's question. Meeting her on neutral territory would lessen the barriers. She mentioned Sir Toby and how she needed to put him in his place. He had invited her to dinner, and they agreed on a date towards the end of January.

"I don't wish to take advantage of our friendship, but if I bring you along, he will know...... I wasn't on my own."

I am past hired help status now protector, which is an improvement. If you kiss an errand boy, up the ante to your bodyguard, or had Aileen not seen that movie?

"I don't want to fall out with him. He is useful at present. I prefer to put him in his place, gently, so no swords at dawn." she laughed. "Am I taking advantage of your good nature?"

"Feel free,"

George got up to leave faced with his usual dilemma, but before he did anything, Aileen asked him to wait, ran upstairs and brought down a small, gift-wrapped box.

George spluttered, "I haven't...."

Aileen interrupted, "You have done so much for me; it is my way of saying thanks."

Still, any hired help, the cleaner and the gardener might get similar gifts. His momentum carried him to the door, Aileen was stepping into the room, handing him the present, and they came together, almost colliding. George put his hands on her shoulders and kissed her. Aileen kissed him back, placing her hand on his arm as a gentle restraint. The moment was broken by the doorbell and Abbi running down the stairs shouting.

"It's Carol, Mum."

Carol proved to be five feet tall, with oodles of ringlets of red hair, and smiled at George. She carried a large vanity case with the tools of her trade in it.

The girls came down into the hallway as he walked out.

"Have a nice Christmas," he shouted. Rosemary waved and replied, 'same to you'. He turned towards Abbi running his hand over the side of his head and winked. Rosemary got it in one and burst out laughing. It then dawned on Abbi what he was referring to: her shaved side hair ambitions.

Aileen didn't notice and shouted after him. "Remember, don't bid for anything at the auction, it will cost you a fortune."

George hurried to the car before Abbi remembered where her grandfather's shotgun was.

He called at the Tielemans' picking up Jan's brother and his wife to bring them to his house and mentioned he was bringing a friend to the evening party on Boxing Day, if that was, OK?

"Of course, of course." said Jan. Elena was intrigued to hear George was bringing a female guest called Claire to the event, intrigued, and put out. As a little girl, she told everyone, including George, she intended marrying him when she grew up. As she became more mature, their relationship changed, but she retained an almost proprietorial interest in him. She wasn't pleased others would take the time from him that was due to her. She did not invite any of her admirers, assuming she would spend time with George. They were always teammates for the games, and Elena sat beside him at the dinner table. When she was younger, it caused great amusement to her extended family in recent years, but they became accustomed to it.

On Christmas Day, George drove his house guests to Mass. He met Grace and Gerard outside the church. The latter raised his eyebrows but, as ever, made no comment. George hadn't intended to enter the church but out of curiosity, he accompanied his friends into the church. He was not a man of faith; he wasn't raised in one. George had never been to a Catholic service; he found the church peaceful and the carols enjoyable. He ended up shaking hands and exchanging season's greetings with a few neighbours who were having to reset assumptions, wrongly, as it happened. For a place beset by religious energy, it is never the 'done' thing in Northern Ireland to discuss someone's religion directly. Assumptions might be based on schools attended, Christian and surnames, parts of the city someone is brought up, but the direct question is never put, "Are you a.....?"

George opened his presents from Terry and Melissa, from his brother and came to Aileen's gift. It was a watch; he was struck by how heavy it was. It was better than his old one, so he put it on. They went to Tieleman's for a snack lunch, given the amount of alcohol consumed on Christmas Eve the copious amounts that would be drunk that evening, the afternoon proved a respite. Christmas presents were exchanged, his watch was admired. Most recognised the European brand, but no one mentioned the price, George wasn't aware of how expensive a Breitling is.

"Have you been treating yourself?" Jan asked.

“No, it was a present. More a ‘thank you’ than a Christmas present, “he added, as much as to reassure himself he shouldn’t have bought Aileen a gift although he suspected he should have.

He missed an opportunity, trying to change the subject, he ended up in the same issue.

“What have you bought your young lady for Christmas?” one of Jan’s sisters asked George. The look on his face answered her question. She couldn’t suppress an “Oh!”

Elena took charge and grabbed his arm. “Now Aunty Aline, they don’t know each other well. You heard him say they have only met once. Don’t hassle poor George, she is just a friend.”

George headed off for his first Christmas Dinner at his brother’s. Christmas Day could prove tense at David and Moira’s, but the latter warned her husband

“Do not, under any circumstances, raise, posh car, new house or Aileen Whyte. It is none of our business.” she insisted.

They enjoyed the meal and exchanged presents. George fetched Terry and Melissa for their customary hour with their dad on Christmas Day. Again, presents were shared. George made his excuse to leave on the way to return his children to Irene, saying, “tomorrow will be a long affair.”. When they arrived at Irene’s house, she wanted to chat, but he needed to go to Jan’s for Pieter and Bebbie. Boxing Day would be a long event.

George drove Pieter and Bebbie to Tielemans’ at 2.00 pm, on Boxing Day, and caught up on their family business. As was their custom, they didn’t interrogate George, but enquired how Terry and Melissa were faring. They were intrigued to be meeting his companion for the evening’s dinner. No one mentioned it, but the whole family, after all these years he attended alone, would be fascinated. Elena felt something changed, the only person taking it in their stride was Jan, who let it all pass over his head.

How would Claire manage in this firmament? Usually, he took a taxi home on Boxing Day because of the drinking, but he had to drive his guests to his house and leave Claire home. He didn't mind abstaining, although he hoped it would not result in his being less sociable and confident.

Claire was in a total panic. Why did she accept the invitation to attend a party with a man she didn't know and a group of strangers, foreigners? She could have stayed safe and comfortable at her sister's.

Her sister and her brother-in-law, Kevin, teased her." Claire, time you came out of your shell, take a risk, meet new people, have unique experiences."

Claire wasn't sure. Well, she was. It was too late, she had only herself to blame. No, wait a minute. She had Mandy to blame. They were both at their respective mothers' houses, so after a few glasses of wine over dinner, she phoned Mandy

"You got me into this," Claire hissed down her phone so her mother and the family wouldn't hear.

"Happy Christmas Claire. The first time you have phoned me to wish me Happy Christmas in all the years, including school, we have known each other. I am fine, thank you. Are you having an enjoyable festive season?"

"Don't give me that. You heard me."

“I didn’t give George your number remember.” Pause. “You did, so you can’t blame me. Anyway, I didn’t know he was a serial sex killer. You’ll go out with a bang, girl.”

Despite herself, Claire couldn’t help laughing. “What am I going to wear?”

“Ask Liz but something short, you have nice legs, low cut because you have nice ....”

Claire cut her off. “Yeah, yeah, I am not you. I don’t advertise my wares.”

Mandy’s turn to interrupt. “What about that bikini in Ibiza......?”

Claire cut in. “Over ten years ago, madam. I hadn’t even met ‘thingy’ from the deepest pit in Hell, then.”

“Oh, did you get even a card from your former beloved? “

“No, they will think a pen is too sharp an implement in whatever secure facility he is incarcerated.”

Mandy again, “Now come on Claire, get a bit of Christmas spirit, that’s hard on him even for you.”

“I suppose so, Jim (Thingy) wasn’t that awful, vain, selfish, bad tempered, insensitive, dishonest, and unfit to be the life partner of a decent human being. “

“Tomorrow will be fine. George exasperated me, not sure why, but Patsy is the most balanced person I have worked with ever. She has known him for years. She says he is a nice guy, who is quiet, but life is passing him by, and he is trying to break out of his shell. He won’t be exciting, but tomorrow could be fun, up to a point. Don't expect fireworks if you take him home though."

"That won't be happening," said Claire grimly.

"I say that too, every time," responded Mandy wistfully.

They chatted on as Mandy described a night involving two French sailors, which left Claire howling with laughter.

"Neither of them?" she added.

It was Mandy's turn to sound grim. "No neither, just my luck." On that cheerful note, they ended their call with Mandy demanding a full report of tomorrow's events.

Claire responded. "You will be told as much as I deem acceptable. Enjoy the holiday girl and leave the rest of the French Navy to its own devices."

George left at 6.30 pm to pick up Claire. Liz invited him in, and he was a few minutes early. He was friendly towards her because, apart from her hair being darker, she was the image of her younger sister. He was conscious the house was quite full, but he was ushered into a small dining room off the hall, which was empty, cleared for his arrival, he surmised.

People, all female, were half in and half out of the living room and the kitchen, ostensibly chatting to relatives, but he guessed, trying to get a glimpse of him.

Earlier, Claire raised the Aileen Whyte newspaper story. None of those present moved in the Aileen Whyte circles, but they saw her on TV, remembered her father and her husband's tragic death and the newspaper pictures. Unaware of all this, George only had to deal with

Liz. She was relaxed and pleasant. A little girl aged five or six ran in and entwined herself in her mother.

This is Karen," said Liz. George asked the youngster what Santa Claus brought her. It eased the tension as the child chatted describing her presents.

Claire entered the room, she looked stunning, a tight yellow cocktail dress, cut low at the front. She peered at him. "Just put my lenses in," she announced. She couldn't remember what George looked like, either.

He wore casual clothes; she remembered his expensive blue suit more than she remembered him and somehow assumed he would wear it tonight. George gave her a peck on the cheek, breaking the spell of him standing ogling her.

"You two have a lovely evening," adding, as only a sister would, "She is terrified of meeting your friends, so take care of my baby sister."

Claire gave her sister a dirty look, but George took her hand,

"She will knock them all dead,"

'You too. I'll be bound,' Liz guessed as she ushered them out the door.

Claire spoke incessantly as they drove across the city, sounding apprehensive. George picked up on that and chatted back in a reassuring manner. Claire berated herself. A date with him would be fine, but taking on his friends, foreigners, too. How daft was that?

"How was your Christmas? See lots of family and friends?"

“The group at my sister’s is almost the same as the one at my mother’s yesterday, bar a couple of aunts and uncles who go to their own children on Boxing Day and with the addition of my brother-in-law Kevin’s, parents. We have talked ourselves out.”. Claire remarked.

“My sister’s father-in-law’s golf trials and tribulations are all that’s fresh and doesn’t interest even him, I suspect. But I always begin, ‘Eddie, how is your game?’ Big mistake?”

Claire brought a bottle of wine and an expensive face cream for Elena. Jan grabbed Claire as soon as they arrived, more or less ignored George and with his arm around hers brought Claire around each of his relatives, telling an amusing and not always flattering story about each. Far from Claire being intimidated, it was the relatives who looked panicky wondering what gory old family secret was to be unleashed.

George himself stood beside Elena, who, almost despite herself, said,

“That is a lovely dress. She has a figure to die for, George, and she is stunning too.”

George invited Claire on a whim. When she entered the room at her sister’s house, he was gob smacked. During the drive and going into the Jan’s house; he put that to one side. Seeing her being conducted around the room by Jan he fixed his gaze on her, Claire looked gorgeous.

“She is very pretty.” Said Elena, George nodded.

The evening proved enjoyable. The meal was its usual success with Jan and one of his sisters, who was a chef, excelling. Then one of Jan’s sisters grabbed Claire and danced with her. Jen danced with

Elena, and they swopped partners. George did not feel left out just relieved not to be dancing. They played charades and other party games, which got funnier as the night progressed and the alcohol kicked in. The only slight tension occurred when someone mentioned the expensive watch George wore. Claire had seen the expensive watch earlier and took from the conversation it was a present. The family worked hard to change the subject. Why are they so tense over George's watch?

Claire paced herself with the booze. Elena found two half full glasses of wine behind photographs on the sideboard the next morning.

Elena and Claire did a kitchen clean up as the older folk showed signs of tiredness and too much booze. "How are you enjoying the University? Have you specific plans for the future?"

Elena confessed she dreaded telling her father she wouldn't enter the business, but after the initial argument it calmed down. She also described to Claire experiences with George when she was young,

"I had such a crush on him," they both laughed, "when I was 6."

"Dad and I have a close relationship with George, but he regrets he and Melissa don't.

George says she is like her mother," and then Elena held up her two forefingers in a sign of a cross, "He always does that when he mentions Melissa and Terry's mother."

It was late and time to load Jan's relatives into the car and drive them to his house. Jan suggested he leave Claire and come back for her, but his brother-in-law was asleep on his feet and his wife, supported by Claire, stated, "We should go." They left and drove across West Belfast towards the south of the city. Despite being a

Belfast girl, Claire had never been to West Belfast. She visited Benidorm, Crete, Ibiza, Paris, but West Belfast would have been a step too much. This journey would have been impossible for them a few years ago. She liked his house despite its soulless air; functional but furnished in a sparse manner. Emulsion without wallpaper, functional lamp shades on the ceiling lights but no side lamps, chairs and tables but no ornaments. Nowhere did it suggest it was a home. It resembled a hotel suite, a comfortable one, but only that. It was apparent a woman did not live there, no soft furnishings and the spartan appearance confirmed this.

"To be honest George, not knowing you and going to meet all these strangers........ I dreaded this evening," Claire confessed.

George nodded but didn't share his own apprehension.

"They were such lovely people, so kind, so generous, especially Jan and by the end of the evening Elena even forgave me for coming with you."

They both laughed.

George, once the Tieleman's were dispatched to bed, asked Claire if she would like to stay the night. She hesitated for a minute, George was chancing his arm, but she answered 'No,' thinking, 'not on a first date pal.' She accepted a coffee which George needed to revive his spirits and his energy. After the coffee they set across South Belfast to the East, it being late on the 26 December, there was little traffic to worry them.

Claire guided George to her house, he wasn't in any condition on his last visit to remember. She remarked at the size of George's vehicle in her street of small houses and compact cars. They parked ten doors from her house and George walked her to her door.

Claire drank sparingly that evening, it was natural, on a chilly night, for him to put his arm around her and for her to snuggle in against the winter chill. As she opened the door, she hesitated, and they began kissing, more and more passionately.

They almost fell into the house; George pushed the door closed with his foot. They took off their coats and stumbled up the stairs and collapsed on Claire's bed. George unzipped the dress and helped ease her out of it. Claire froze.

She gazed at him, weighing up if it would be a step too far but she responded to his more and more passionate kisses. He took off his sweater and trousers and unclipped her bra. She slid down her pants and then his. He remembered to remove his socks. They kissed with increasing passion. George caressed her shoulder and arm, slid his hand to her buttocks and caressed those.

Claire held him tighter, caressed his cheek, moved her hands inside his shirt and stroked him, feeling him becoming more and more aroused. and they made love. It exhilarated George, brought a passion he never experienced. This female partner was more satisfied than his previous one in this house, though not, in this bedroom.

George woke at 6.30 am, pleased with himself. The last thing he remembered was the sight of a naked Claire skipping to the bathroom to remove her lenses. She cuddled back in, and they both plunged into a deep sleep. He kissed her shoulder as he watched her sleeping. Her makeup was a bit smudged; so tired she only had time to remove her lenses.

Claire stirred. She opened one eye, then the other, and smiled at him.

She covered herself with the duvet, saying.

“You need to run Pieter and Bebbie to Jan’s to say goodbye and leave for the airport, their flight is at 1.00 pm.”

He would be able to get home, have a shower, shave, and drive over to Jan’s. The other Tielemans would have already left except Jan’s older sister, she already planned to stay on for a few more days. Elena and her aunt spent a lot of time with each other over the years, the closest person to a Mother Elena had since her mother’s death. At 12, she could fly unaccompanied to visit her aunt. Jan found the separation sad, almost like losing his wife all over again, even if only for a few days. He couldn’t go with her if the bakery was busy, it wasn’t workable.

Last night, Claire appeared special. This morning, he wasn’t so sure. For different reasons, neither was Claire.

George dressed, “I have something I want to ask you, I’ll phone tomorrow evening,” he gave her a quick kiss and rushed downstairs.

Claire lay on, trying to assemble everything that had happened the night before in her mind. The evening went in an unintended direction at the end. Did she accept it as an experience, an enjoyable experience, and refuse further invitations? That did not appeal. He mightn’t phone her. Did he just enjoy the sex, the relationship might last for a while until that attraction ended? Also, what did he mean he wanted to ask her something, this was mysterious, exciting, scary, worrying? There were three messages from Mandy last night, one this morning already.

Her phone rang.

“Mandy, stop harassing me. I have only woken up,” she barked into the mobile.

"Er, it's Liz, dear," a voice said, "just phoning to see how last night was. I knew you were worried. I take it you Mandy has been phoning nonstop, she doesn't grow up, twenty-nine going on sixteen."

They both chuckled. Then Liz suggested, "I take it he is still not there?"

"Of course not." Claire replied with a clear conscience.

"The Belgians were nice and made me so welcome. George was fine, quiet, but he seems like that most of the time. He has these high, chatty moments and then he subsides."

"Will you be seeing him again?"

"He said he would phone me. I hope he does— I think."

"Right, see you on Saturday at Mum's. She has been worrying too."

"Oh God, you said nothing to Mum, did you?"

"Come on Claire, she was there last night. They all knew you had a date. He looked nice. I liked him and Karen, liked him."

"OK see you Sat., Sis."

Mandy rang next. "Right, every minute, tell me is he still with you, —is he?"

"Certainly not."

"Oh, you released him early?"

“Would you believe it if I claimed he didn’t stay all night? I didn’t make him breakfast, he is not here now, look I will prove it. GEORGE, GEORGE ARE YOU HERE?” She bellowed. “See, not a sound.”

At least the breakfast bit was true, and he left at 6.30 am so he didn’t remain all night.

“Hmn, you wouldn’t lie to your Auntie Mandy, would you? “And before Claire could respond. “Yes, you would. Gosh you can be so secretive.”

No one could accuse Mandy of being too subtle, but Claire filled her inquisitive pal with carefully chosen highlights.

“The others will be disappointed at the lack of tasty bits.”

“What, are you going to phone the girls with details of my all too innocent date?”

“Yes. Naturally Lillian and Mo have already been on to me.”

Silence, then Claire responded, “Tell me Mandy when he was here with you, did he sleep on his back too, bye?”

She hung up as Mandy screamed, “I KNEW IT, I KNEW IT!”

Claire wanted a nice, long soak in a hot tub. I will make sure my I switch off my mobile phone. That will teach Mandy. As she ran the bath, George’s comment, ‘I have something to ask you,’ came back. Why didn’t he do it there and then? Maybe he is a spontaneous person, has fallen in love with me and is going to propose?’ God, I hope not. That’s daft, but why wait until tomorrow evening?

George did his taxi duties and headed for Donegal. He planned to buy one more property, an inexpensive run down one for which he could pay cash and hire local builders to refurbish.

He spent a significant portion of the original half million and he wanted to keep 250,000 euros as a bargaining chip either with the Authorities or with 'them,' whoever 'them' are. His second foray to Donegal and no more successful than the first. He tried the beautiful Atlantic coast as far North as he could go.

George needed a bolt hole to store the money and the Glock handgun in case his house was searched, somewhere no one connected to him could be associated with, but all the cottages were too expensive, six figures bought as second homes by people from Belfast or expat Scottish residents or Dubliners. The driving provided useful to plan ahead. He already decided he would ask Claire to attend the charity dinner and auction rather than Elena. He remembered the Boxing night passion, a rerun of that appealed. Well, at least until his relationship with Aileen moved to the next stage or crashed in flames. Claire was not likely to be serious over him, they only just met. Yes, they made love, it was so nice, but the occasion influenced it, nothing to get carried away over.

Her marriage experience sounded worse than his and she did not want a partner. She wanted an enjoyable night out, he wouldn't be hurting her feelings, a friendship with benefits. Then the briefcase came into his mind, and the men in Shaftsbury Square and what he did, George grew morose.

He phoned her as promised. Claire played it cool. Neither mentioned their night together. George told her of his dinner and auction invitation, though he did not specify who invited him.

"Claire, it would be fun at New Year. Would you be my partner?"

Another ‘date’ with the two of us and half the hoi poloi of Belfast, more people even than the Tielemans’ party. It sounded like a fun thing to do over the Festive break. An impossible man, unpredictable, too many assumptions but yet she liked him, his warmth and consideration ....

“Yes, thank you.” Then,” I don’t have a thing to wear.” In George’s view there were women’s clothes shops everywhere, how was that a problem?

“I’ll pick you up on Saturday. We are due to be seated in the banqueting hall by 7.15 pm as the ‘platform’ party would enter at 7.30 pm sharp. I must remember to get a dinner suit and bow tie before Saturday. Bye.”

As he hung up from that last comment, it dawned on Claire it was a formal ‘do’ and she would need a long dress, which she didn’t possess. Today is Wednesday. What does a girl do if she doesn’t want to spend a fortune on a dress she may never wear again? She rings her big sister.

“Liz, help. George is taking me to this dinner at the City Hall on Saturday night and I need a formal dress.”

Liz described a dress, “but remember I bought it after I had Karen, anyway I can take it in, but do you have the right shoes? You are a size smaller than me?”

“OK, I can invest in a pair of semi-formal shoes. They won’t be seen under the dress, and I can get more use out of them.”

“That is practical, typical of you. Anyway, come over Friday morning and we can try it.”

It wasn't a happy holiday season for Sammy Drennan, a twenty-one-year-old part-time handyman who was charged with the murder of an eighteen-year-old student. Walker and Farrell were relentless and identified him as a likely suspect as he worked at her parents' house. He became besotted with her and been rejected. He lay in wait for her, claiming he only intended to appeal to her one last time. The police were hard on him, and he made a tearful confession. Walker said to his partner:

"We have lost half the holiday over this. We will take a break and in the New Year return to the Shaftsbury Square case. Let us give it a bit of time, whatever Robertson says, and crack it."

In the end, Claire stayed the night at her sister's. They secluded themselves in the kitchen to do the running repairs to Liz's dress. As they chatted, Liz asked, "Well, is George the one?".

"Stop it Liz, I don't know him properly. We had a lovely evening at his friend's party, it was fun, such nice people."

"Yes, and now he is taking you somewhere quite public as his partner. Anyway, did you sleep with him? "

"No, of course not." Claire replied sharply.

"Oh, so you slept with him... on your first date," mused her sister. "Now that could be a mistake, a rule you have, you keep."

Claire considered this, could it have been a mistake? The season, the alcohol, her long abstinence from any relationships, all conspired against her.

Liz again, "What are his best points?"

"He is not bad looking, tallish, warm eyes. Does that make sense? He is quiet, well mannered, gentle, doesn't impose things that other people should do, not controlling, not like 'thing.' I feel relaxed around him."

"What are his bad points?"

"He is quiet, doesn't start conversations, stared at me a lot, takes ages to decide even over minor matters. I am not sure he trusts women; he may have secrets or gives that impression."

"Oh right, he has no conversation, no sense of humour, is indecisive, may hate women, and could be a serial sex killer. Sounds like fun company."

"Don't be silly. You know that isn't what I meant. He is quiet, but attentive, well-mannered and ... nice."

Chapter 7

The Charity Dinner and the Auction

George had to pick Claire up at Liz's, take his car to Claire's, leave it there and get a taxi. 'Hopefully this will be a rerun of the Boxing Night experience.' Aileen did not cross his mind for. A further trip to Donegal yielded possibilities of a cheap bolt hole, but for various reasons, they were ruled out.

He picked up Claire. She made an entrance wearing a long, dark blue, strapless dress, a delicate gold chain belt, with her blond hair framing her pretty face. She looked lovely. Liz gazed on approvingly at her running repairs, invisible to all but the most trained eye. They left the Range Rover, were picked up in a taxi and dropped off outside the City Hall. A typical early January night, dry, clear and freezing. The moon lit the night sky and an early frost formed. Claire took a cape; the colour was not in keeping with her dress, but it was warm. George hadn't brought a coat and shivered. They deposited Claire's cape in the cloakroom and headed to the banquet hall, queuing to look at the table plan.

A platform party was seated at a dais. There were 40 tables with twelve guests at each table, plus the top table. George noted he and Claire were in the front row, table three entitled 'Baileys.' 'I should have known'. Four of Baileys partners and their wives were at the table, with the Chief Constable, Sir Geoffrey Newton and his wife plus George and Claire.

'What am I doing here?' Claire thought. 'I have no desire to join the great and good of Belfast. We could have gone for a quiet meal and got to know one another.'

All the partners' wives knew George and Irene in their younger days with varying views on them ranging from "He seems so quiet, and she is pushy" to "I feel sorry for her. You just want to give him a shake."

Their husbands' careers moved onwards and upwards, George ended up left behind and he and Irene separated. They were sympathetic towards him. Life was not kind to George, neither in his career or his personal life. Recent events brought a whole new dynamic to George's situation. Despite his poor career progression, he was linked in the media with Aileen Whyte, MP. What would any fashionable woman give to be seen in her circles? Then tonight, accompanied by an attractive young woman, ten years his junior, he appeared different. Did he have something they all missed?

George and Claire were seated next to the Chief Constable recently appointed from England and his wife Susan. Peter Donald and his wife Mary were on their other side. They all rose as the platform party was piped on to the dais.

Old man Andrews was seated next to Aileen. George suppressed a fear she would be accompanied by a new beau, perhaps a Tory Westminster MP. He gazed at Aileen in her long white dress and her hair curled up Grecian style. The pangs of lust he often felt when he saw her rose. Claire didn't notice.

The Lord Mayor's Master of Ceremonies boomed out the order for the evening. The speeches would be first to allow guests to enjoy their meal. There would be a five-course meal, a comfort break and then a popular local comedian would conduct the auction in aid of a children's hospice and the city's homeless.

At that point George recognised Aileen must have paid for his ticket, two hundred pounds per couple. This irritated hm. Aileen knew where George was seated. She stole a look at table three, curious to see Elena. A woman she didn't know was seated beside George. She would have been late forties and opposite the Chief Constable while a younger attractive blond was seated opposite George. Aileen calculated she was in her late twenties, thirty at most. That wasn't Elena.

Introductions were completed at table three, the guests found Sir Geoffrey entertaining. He possessed a fund of political and UK wide police stories. A born raconteur he dominated the evening. Susan, also English, said little until one of the partners' wives asked her, pointedly, "And you Susan, did you work in England?"

"Before I retired last year, I was Chief Superintendent in charge of the West Midlands Serious Crime Squad and raised two kids. Life was busy," Susan conceded. Her husband said nothing but rolled his eyes. He remembered the "busyness" as more frenetic than that but kept stum. Claire was not sure if she should address Susan as Lady Newton, but the latter made a point of introducing herself as 'Susan.'

The speech was very Aileen. Earnest and forthright concerning the Hospice and its work, the needs of the homeless, "Not just at Christmas," she reminded everyone, and talked of peoples' aspirations for Northern Ireland in this season of goodwill. She told a quick couple of light stories from her Westminster experience; all well received. George wanted to stand up and applaud, but of course a standing ovation was unlikely to be the 'done' thing.

The Lord Mayor told more risqué stories but received a communication from his wife: a kick on the shin.

"Something tells me I need to wind up and let you enjoy the meal," and with thanks to various organisers he sat down and then engaged in an intense conversation with his wife.

At the 'comfort break,' Aileen excused herself to the Andrews.

"I need to circulate," and headed straight down to table three.

She shook hands with the partners and wives, most of whom she knew, Sir Geoffrey, Susan, and made a point of kissing George on both cheeks before demanding to be introduced to Claire.

"You know the press has him as my next husband," she told Claire and most laughed. Claire wasn't sure what to make of the exchange. After general chat, Aileen spoke to George, "I see you liked the watch," and smiled.

Claire didn't know Aileen. She defended them to Mandy when the press story broke, but tonight she was put in her place. Aileen swept off to visit other tables, especially where she saw party supporters or donors. A brief silence ensued while they recovered from 'Storm Aileen'.

Sir Geoffrey broke the silence. "Quite a tour de force, our latest MP."

Claire tried to adopt an impassive face but got a quick smile of understanding, or was it sympathy, from Susan? The latter would have vied with Aileen as the sharpest cookie in the room.

All this passed over George's head, but to irritate Aileen, he made several attempts at bidding during the auction. He caught her grimacing at him as if to say

'I told you not to do that.' He finally bought a picture of Fair Head on the Antrim coast by a local artist for seven hundred and fifty pounds.

He handed the staff a thousand euros, saying, "it's all for a good cause." A member of staff whispered, "He's old for me, but who wouldn't choose to be with a guy with his money? "

Claire couldn't help saying, "Your bid - that's too much money."

"I need it for the living room in the house," George stated in a grand manner.

He didn't sound like the George to whom she was attracted, and what on earth was going on between him and that bitch?

Peter Donald went up, as the other partners had, to pay respect to Walter Andrews. Andrews had been focused on the proceedings at table three throughout the break.

As Peter went to return, Andrews grabbed his arm.

"Remember that minor problem in Glasgow? I think we should send George there."

Peter replied, "Not really his bag."

Andrews inclined his head toward Aileen, on her way back to their table and Peter looked and noted, "Oh, I see, yes…. perhaps..." Andrews could not miss an opportunity to stick the knife in Cyril.

"I am still not happy about this Glasgow acquisition. We were close to being exposed to those investments in dot com enterprises. Now it's the property market. If major problems arise there, the building societies and the banks will be exposed and it will rebound on our investments."

Peter nodded, but if building societies and banks had problems, Baileys would be beneficiaries. It was crucial to be in the right place at the right time, but he did nothing. Definitely not the moment to discuss internal strife.

Walter was childless. His priority was to maintain Baileys to the standards Augustus Bailey set. His shareholding would be left to Aileen the daughter of his other old friend, Edmund. She had the proper values and the Thomas Whyte death, coupled with her re-emergence in her own right, strengthened his view Aileen was 'the right stuff' to keep the legacy. He preferred to keep less desirable influences at bay.

Oblivious of plans for his future, George and Claire left. They said their farewells, recovered the cape and found a line of taxis. Aileen kept being drawn back to George and Claire. A nice-looking girl, young, but George never mentioned her, why? She wasn't his ex-wife nor a relative. George introduced her as 'his friend'. She told herself, 'Aileen, George has a nice girlfriend, he is on his own, be pleased for him,' but she was irritated with him. Was it because he bid in the auction against her 'instructions' or he had not mentioned Claire, or was she jealous, ... surely not jealous?

George did not pick up on how quiet Claire was later in the evening. The taxi took them to her house, and they chatted. Claire mentioned she enjoyed Geoffrey and Susan's company; Peter Donald and his wife were "lovely." As a younger person or someone who did not know anyone else, it could have been boring.

Claire expected him to mention Aileen. He didn't. The taxi drew up at her house and they went inside. Claire offered George a coffee. He waited for a sign they would spend the night together; she waited for him to mention Aileen. They sipped the coffee in silence.

Claire began. "You didn't tell me Aileen Whyte bought you that expensive watch for Christmas."

Aileen's contribution to the evening at their table dawned on George at last.

“A gift for help I gave her, a little OTT, but nice.”

“You could have told me. What is the relationship between you two? She kissed you.”

“Oh, it’s what people do these days at this time of year,” dismissed George.

“She knew all the others; she didn’t kiss anybody else. Well, what is it? Are you in a relationship with her? Are you sleeping with her?”

“No, no.”

“Do you want to be?” Silence, any response, but “no, of course not” says a lot.

“You should go home, now.”

“Claire, I like you; I want us to get to know each other.”

“I will phone you a taxi.”

George went into a huff, a most unlike George mood.

“I will drive myself.”

“No George, please don’t. You have had too much to drink.”

George stormed out of the house, up the street to his car, and drove home. He did not do anything wrong. He had only two dates with Claire, he created no commitments.

He hadn’t bought her a Christmas present. OK they slept together once, but they were both adults, why was she trying to control his life? He brought her to a major function and to a party, which must mean something. Claire confronted him regarding his feelings for Aileen. He was not prepared for this there was no long-term future for him and Aileen.

He remembered when in his marriage he forgot Irene's birthday or that time when he was buying Irene's Christmas present from Melissa when the wee girl was only seven. They had gone into Bodyshop and bought all these bath oils and moisturisers that were bright Christmas colours of blue, green, red and yellow. Melissa claimed they were beautiful and was so proud of herself as she handed them to her mother on Christmas Day. George thought he did well, but when the kids went to bed, Irene turned to him.

"Since when have I had oily skin? You could at least have checked; she will want me to use them. I can't even palm them off on someone else."

His insensitivity shone through in the end, his frustration over wanting to sleep with her and guilt over his desire for Aileen led to his huff

As Liz suggested when Claire confided in her, "Men never recognise sensitivity from six inches. Women can see it at thirty thousand feet." Claire was upset as she settled for the night, flipping between being well rid of him to thinking she overreacted. She had no claim on him. How many layers were there and what were they hiding? Later, she dreamt she was in a palace running from room to room. She reached a ballroom where George and dark-haired women were dancing. Then the police appeared.

Walker phoned Farrell. "Did you get the Belfast Telegraph tonight?" he asked.

“I never take it during the holidays because all their best guys are on leave. It’s thin, but they did a feature on Cliftonville, so I bought it earlier. Haven’t opened it yet.”

“Never mind the football, go to the society and social page.”

Farrell opened the paper. The page in question contained photographs of Christmas and New Year social events.

“Don’t play silly buggers. What am I meant to be looking at...? HOLY SHIT!”

“Exactly.” A photograph of the Chief Constable, George McNeill and a pretty young blonde woman stood out.

“I wonder, did the Chief take his address?” replied Farrell playfully.

“Smart Ass.”

“Can I take it, boss, we won’t be putting this photograph up in our operations room?”

“I wouldn’t think so, but I have to tell Robertson. He will hate me even more.”

“Don’t worry about that,” responded Farrell soothingly. “I doubt if he could hate you any more than he does.”

George returned to Donegal on the 4th of January. He saw a little cottage quite near the Atlantic Ocean. It needed work, but the owner would only do things by the book. He drove inland, took a wrong turning heading for Derry, and passed an old farm road with an improvised For Sale sign. George drove up the single-track road and arrived at a farmhouse with hens running around outside and a sty with a sow and piglets in it.

An older woman and four dogs came out after he stopped the car.

"I saw your For Sale sign."

She beckoned him. "Sure, himself is in the bottom field with those few cows he has."

She led him to the side of the house, where he saw a derelict single storey building standing 50 yards from the farmhouse with a small 'lean to' at the rear. She opened the door, "Hasn't been lived in for three years, since Michael left," she added.

Then 'himself' arrived, one Matt Molloy. He had a further three dogs, was full of blarney. "What a brilliant house it would make, lick of paint here, lick of paint there, the odd replacement window."

It had 5 rooms: a kitchen, a living room, a main bedroom, and a single bedroom. The bathroom was small and in poor condition, so that meant 6 new windows and two doors.

In addition, floors would have to be repaired, plaster board put up on stone walls, a heating system installed, repairs to the roof, new kitchen, bathroom, and toilet.

"Lick of paint here, lick of paint there," repeated George, "more like thirty thousand Euros. So how much for the old cottage?"

"How about eighteen thousand euros?"

"Fifteen, cash,"

"Done. To be sure," spat in hand, handshake.

The following week, he met a solicitor in Donegal town. Matt's sons were present, they had long wanted him to give up the remainder of the once thriving farm. They gained from the sale of land, but their 'Da' couldn't let go of having farm animals and keeping the old family home. It needed money spent on it and he and his wife's pension and the little he made from dealing in a few cattle, pigs and free-range eggs was not enough. The solicitor and Matt had contacts that would help with refurbishing the old cottage. George was to spend twenty thousand Euros over the next months, but work was slow.

If he was convicted and sentenced, he would ask Jan to look after the wee cottage. When he was released, he could spend the rest of his life there, free of all these situations he got himself into. 'Will I live to retire?'

He figured the cottage was less likely to be burgled than Riverdale. Matt, Mrs Matt, she had an unpronounceable Gaelic name with quite a few 'hs', plus their seven dogs would be around. At some point, he would leave the briefcase there, but not the Glock pistol. He would like to have learned how to shoot it, but the only bullets were the ones in the magazine, less the two that killed the men in Shaftsbury Square. Could he point the gun at anyone, let alone shoot them?

His life turned busier. He was summoned into Baileys to discuss the consultancy and Aileen phoned him in a chatty mood and asked him to visit so they could plan the dinner with Sir Toby. Aileen returned from a Party meeting with the hierarchy. He held her and kissed her; "I never thanked you for the watch." She knew he wanted more but answered:

"My mother is bringing the girls soon," which was true but also had the intended effect of cooling George's ardour. As he took off his coat, she saw a new overcoat in case there might be other formal winter events. She liked what she saw. Despite the rebuff, he was as amiable as ever and she considered taking their relationship to the next stage. The London dinner was set for the second Tuesday in January, after the Recess. Parliament would be in full swing again. She would text Hazlehurst at 5.00 pm on the evening of the dinner and say a close friend unexpectedly arrived and could he join them?

If Sir Toby wasn't happy, then at least he knew the existence of a 'He'. She would find another way of parading George but keeping her own political group, especially her cousin, out of it.

In the police station, Walker and Farrell met after their New Year's break.

Farrell led, "I spoke to a woman in HR in Baileys. She was quite professional. I told her McNeill may have witnessed a crime and we need to speak to him. She gave me his address. It's up past Finaghy way. I am confident she wouldn't tell anyone, but all she knows anyway is that he is a potential witness."

Walker nodded. "That's all we know about him as well. We will go up there tonight."

George passed into reception at Baileys and asked for Peter Donald. Mandy's look told him she knew of the tension with Claire. He should front up the position with Aileen. Just then, Peter Donald's secretary came down and brought him up to the Partner's office.

Peter made straight to the point. "George, more than a year ago we were pushed," pause, "we were persuaded to expand Baileys activities. We acquired small firms doing similar work to us in Glasgow, Bristol and soon Liverpool. We have an interest in acquiring others, in Sheffield perhaps and London."

George had heard rumours; the local financial press got wind of the expansion. A most unlike Baileys thing to do. It prided itself as being a safe, purely Belfast operation dealing with regular local customers. This strategic business plan was part of an energy in the firm to diversify and expand. Old Man Andrews would hate it, but it was the way of the future. Baileys risked being taken over by a global corporation wanting to move into the Northern Ireland market, post the Good Friday Agreement. It generated a great deal of money in the Belfast economy from the United States and UK Governments. The old Irish adage applied, 'Get your retaliation in first.'

Peter was explicit, "The Partners need to ensure we have Baileys' standards in place before we re-brand these various companies. We need someone whom we trust. Who knows Baileys inside out, to go to each. Once there ferret around, find what makes the place tick, do a report saying what is the same, what is different, what should be changed and what should stay because that fits the... culture locally. A proper brief will be drawn up and a reporting arrangement for you. We can advise local management you carry major clout here. They will hate you, but that goes with the territory. We will pay you, as a consultant, five hundred pounds a day for at least four days per week, starting in Glasgow because it is the worst performing, moving to Bristol when you have finished with Glasgow. This is subject to us being satisfied with your work. We will pay your travelling expenses, provide you with accommodation and transport and any other expenses you would incur. How does that sound?"

"That is very acceptable, Peter."

It came to eight thousand pounds a month, when he had been earning three. He no longer needed the Euros. God, if only he could return them and do a deal promising to repay the balance, but to whom?

He did not realise he was being taken 'offside'. The partners were not at all certain he possessed the skills to do the job. It was a compromise. They could get rid of him if whatever issues that only

Peter and of course Walter Andrews were aware of were resolved, or if he proved useless at the task.

Peter could have added that the partners are totally divided over this expansionist strategy led by Cyril. Andrews tried to bring the majority on his side. So far, he only had one definite and one 'maybe' to withdraw from the 'across the water' plans. The main thing at the moment was to take George out of Belfast and keep him busy.

George agreed to start the following week. The formal agreement and brief would take longer to draw up and go through various processes. George was to provide brief reports each week to Peter. "First impressions can be important to record before you become too dug in."

"I will have a proper brief and contract drawn up, but we wish to move quickly on this. We have been friends a long time, George. A handshake is all that is required and don't forget to notify the tax man, or you will be hit with a stoater of a tax bill."

Hands were shaken and, on the way, out, George couldn't resist saying to Mandy,

"Baileys will see much more of me," not specifying how or why, but left her to enjoy spreading the gossip.

Peter reported to Andrews, "He is up for it."

"Do you think he can do it without messing up?"

"Yes, he is a safe pair of hands. Whatever he uncovers, we may need someone else to sort out; but remember how capably he dealt with the Thomas Whyte incident and the subsequent London element?"

"I suppose so, but it needs a specific skill set to accomplish what we have asked him to do, and I am not sure he has enough of those," the old man agreed doubtfully.

George presented himself at McIntyre and Matheson Accountants, a spectacular office in St Vincent St in Glasgow City Centre. 'Far too flashy for Baileys,' and the rent must be huge. Why, apart from prestige, would they have such an office? In fairness, they had been there for twenty years. He must check the ownership of the building. He couldn't believe they owned it; must rent their two floors.

He was shown around the office. A meeting with the 6 accountants was arranged, then another one with more senior staff. At George's suggestion, a further meeting was added with the administrative, reception staff and other employees, the guy who did HR and a woman responsible for IT.

The Scottish firm had a different client base, centred around individuals and several big Corporates whereas Baileys favoured a mixture of individuals and small local businesses. The original Partners McIntyre and Matheson were long gone. It had been acquired by a bank but then dumped during the Tech downturn in 2000. An under-funded management buyout led to Baileys' buy out. The managers involved in the original buyout had withdrawn from the firm and appointed Sandy Burney as Managing Director.

George's briefing from Peter detailed the background that exhorted him to learn the nuts and bolts of the firm and identify what was working and what wasn't, and above all, what potential was there to change to a Baileys' formula. The briefing was high on rhetoric and low on professional targets. George was realistic enough to appreciate that Peter and his colleagues needed a more sophisticated plan using a manager with more experience. Instead, George was parachuted in regardless of cost and the impact on the Glasgow firm. The overall principle was sound, but it was implausible that George would be the person to carry it off. He expressed his doubts to Peter who adopted a biblical model.

"Consider yourself as John the Baptist," said Peter, "the one who comes after you will bring change."

George did not want to jeopardize the lucrative job, so he raised no more doubts, though he recalled John the Baptist's ultimate fate was not attractive.

Standing in front of the group of six junior accountants and an older man. Making a speech terrified him. He was so ill prepared that it was only when Sandy Burney introduced him, he understood he had to start the ball rolling. Burney dropped him straight in it.

"I told you we were acquired by an Irish firm and that they would eventually explain their plans. This is George McNeill, who is going to spend time with us to learning how our operation works."

George would have to speak. He planned to say, 'I am George McNeill from Baileys in Belfast and I wanted to say that I will spend the next six months with you to learn about your firm.'

However, Burney used the only part of the speech he had ready. George stood uncomfortably in silence for a minute. This had the effect of the group suddenly focussing more intently on him, wondering what he would say, which unnerved George more. He wished he could turn and walk out of the room, but he recovered his composure.

"I look forward to meeting each of you," George was determined to string the contract out as long as possible.

"In the meantime, perhaps each of you could say how long you have worked with the firm and what general area of contracts and accounts you have."

Most people love talking about themselves. Some were briefer than others. The group spoke for fifteen minutes.

George then thanked them, "I am afraid I cannot give you any details of Baileys plans for you because they will await my report and recommendations and then Baileys, through either myself or someone else, will outline our intentions. I expect you hoped for more certainty, but I preferred to be honest with you. We are at the beginning of something, and I hope we can all be involved in it together."

He continued on almost word for word, repeating Aileen Whyte's speech at the Belfast City Hall charity dinner, expressing what she hoped to achieve as an MP and how the New Year might unfold. By any standards, it was reasonable, by George's miraculous. As the accountants left, they shook his hand and smiled. All but one, Freya. Later, he reflected on this positive experience. They detested Sandy Burney and their warmth towards him was based on the old maxim 'my enemy's enemy is my friend.' It was common knowledge Sandy Burney would be a casualty of the coming changes. Sandy thought, *'they have sent this jumped-up minor clerk. Shows how little they think of us, or me.'*

The encounter with the five senior staff was different. They were fairly monosyllabic in describing their roles. There was a tension that was not present with the junior group. George gave his 'Aileen' speech. At least he didn't freeze in front of them. The strongest personality, a tall, angular woman called Laura McKenzie, acted as the spokesperson for the group. As they were introducing themselves, Burney hissed in George's ear,

"She's a lesbian."

George passed through life unscathed by any of Belfast's usual prejudices over religion, colour, class, or sexuality. He would not find prejudice now, despite Burney's problem. He suspected it was as much because of Laura's strident tones and authoritative delivery as her sexuality. She asked the right questions, in a clear and pointed way, and deduced George might be out of his depth, but avoided commenting. The group showed in their body language less hostility to Burney. More comfortable with him, George guessed, because Laura, as their unofficial leader, had him under control. Laura did her homework.

The previous week, she contacted a friend in Belfast and asked her to make enquires.

The response, "George McNeill, according to my information Laura, was a plodding junior accountant. A quiet, decent guy, a loner. With Baileys for over twenty years. He left a few months ago unexpectedly. Getting the Glasgow role surprised the person I asked."

The meeting with the other staff was pleasanter. A re-run of the event with the more junior accountants.

George flew down from Glasgow to London City Airport. He took the underground to Aileen's flat. He would suggest they enter a relationship but limit it to him visiting her in London, thus keeping the Northern Ireland constraints out of the mix. Even George recognised that sounded like a commercial contract he was seeking to embark on. The sort of proposal Aileen was capable of suggesting to him because she was less certain of her feelings, and she always needed to be in control.

The uncertainty was an issue. It was too much, especially combined with the worry over the outcome of the Shaftsbury Square incident. That brought him down to earth. What lay ahead of him would be totally unacceptable to Aileen. The more they became involved, the worse it would be. His plan flipped.

By the time he arrived at the flat, his mood lightened. He would play the evening as Aileen chose, though he hadn't booked a hotel. He hoped she had a comfy couch. Her flat was in a large, terraced house with a magnificent entrance hall. There were six self-contained flats and Aileen's was on the first floor.

He rang the entrance button and when she told him to, "Come on up," he took the stairs two at a time, his rethinking energised him. He had his Glasgow bag and his Saville Row grey suit. She opened the door, and they kissed. He did not want to stop, but she pulled away and surveyed him.

"My, you look smart. Do you want a shower?"

"That would be a super idea. Are you going to join me?"

"Bad boy, I am already changed."

George laughed thinking, 'I should have arrived earlier, before she had time to change.' He salivated at the prospect of what might have happened. He had a shower; he had also brought a clean shirt.

They had a coffee and then headed to Westminster, George in his expensive suit, light blue shirt and maroon tie and Aileen also in a smart grey suit, with a pink blouse, high heels, hair piled on top. They looked every inch a Westminster power couple. During the walk, Aileen confessed she did not wish to fall out with Sir Toby.

"He opens doors that might take me several years to get through."

They were joining Sir Toby in a quiet restaurant within the Palace itself; later, more MPs would come to dine, but at 7.00 pm there were only a few interns and advisors eating, consumed by their own plots and schemes and uninterested in the three older people.

George could not understand why Sir Toby Hazlehurst was considered such a Lothario, but money and power have an aphrodisiac effect and the Minister possessed both. His own relationships with females only took off when he had half a million Euros in his back pocket, although, to be fair, neither of the females knew that. Do you exude an aura when you are rich? Toby was graciousness itself and didn't seem at all put out by Aileen's 'move.'

They chatted about political issues and people and, conscious that George was left out, the Minister brought up Northern Ireland. His grandmother came from outside Enniskillen and his father always planned they would spend a holiday there exploring old roots. He remembered her well, her stories recalling a grand country mansion, horseback riding and fishing parties from the home counties, including a brother of the King.

He also recalled her indecipherable accent, "Whereas you both, especially Aileen," he added gallantly or flirtingly, "have such lovely soft accents."

George thought he could help Aileen sustain her relationship with Toby. If George could prove useful to him, then it would seem.... he wasn't so much brought along to warn Toby off. He considered the Northern Ireland link, Toby's grandmother. He offered to track down some of the Fermanagh roots.

"You say her maiden name was Ferguson, Henrietta Ferguson, born in 1882 near a village called Derrygonnelly, County Fermanagh. The local parish church will have records if they were not destroyed."

He was not to realise that this inconsequential offer introduced a sinister element into the picture emerging elsewhere around George

McNeill. Then he and Aileen walked back arm-in-arm to her flat. They entered, George settled for a coffee, while Aileen drank a glass of wine.

She took off her jacket and kicked her high heels into the corner of the room. She looked so desirable. If George was honest, lust, at least, was rampant in those close quarters. He sat opposite her in the small sitting room while she sat with her legs curled under her on the settee opposite him.

"George, you have a 'new friend', and you will do research for a Home Office Minister."

George pooh-poohed all this, becoming embarrassed by the teasing,

"I was being friendly; it is you he wants to get into bed." Aileen's turn to blush.

Then she returned to the attack, "So who is this Catherine you brought to the dinner? You never mentioned her before."

For the first time in all his Aileen encounters, George had the upper hand. It would be a mistake to play down Claire. Aileen was well aware her name was not Catherine, and she knew George knew that. Did that slight reflect jealousy or possessiveness? He enjoyed this feeling. He was not going to blurt out, *'She is a friend of a former colleague that I had terrific sex with and invited out twice.'* Even as this came into his head an unexpected feeling, a sense of disloyalty to Claire, arose.

"Ah, Claire is a lovely girl. I met her recently. She's a friend of an acquaintance. I am on my own much of the time and she is good company."

Aileen received this non-information impassively, but her mind whirled.

'He has made it clear he wants me; I am closer to feeling the same way and now I have a rival. Or is this all a mistake? How would he fit into my political career, my life with the girls, my mother, the Party, my small but select group of loyal friends? They would be fine. All the rest, except Rosemary, would be opposed.'

George felt confused. He resigned himself that this visit was to do the correct thing and keep Aileen out of his future problems. Now, in the intimacy of her flat, he thought he was letting Claire down. He went to the bathroom and naturally ended up on the couch beside Aileen. He was closer to her than he had ever been. She smelled of an expensive perfume. She gazed at his honest face, his fair hair, long lashes, and they began caressing each other. They kissed more and more passionately, then moved into Aileen's bedroom.

The bed three quarters rather than a double, was comfortable and they undressed. Aileen appeared beautiful in the dim light of the one small lamp. Could he be on the verge of achieving what he dreamt of every night since they met? Would he be able, or would he let her down?

Feelings were rising with him, so was everything else and they made passionate love, lay back exhausted for a while, then lay caressing each other, drifting off into a light sleep and woke and made love again.

An alarm sounded at 6.00 am. George was due in Glasgow. Aileen was not due in the House until 11.00 am. He kissed her lightly and went for a shower. Was sex always like this and was he just unlucky that he and Irene had such an unfulfilling relationship? But immediately Claire entered into his mind again and guilt flowed once more.

When I am with Claire, I think of Aileen and when I am with Aileen, I think of Claire. This is too complicated. Aileen stayed silent. He wore the shirt he had worn at dinner; well seen, he doesn't live with a woman.

Aileen began, "George, last night..."

"Aileen, it was lovely; it meant such a lot..."

"I know, I enjoyed it too, but life, my life is complicated. We have to move slowly."

"Actually," he responded, "my life is complicated too."

"In what way?"

"Let's talk this over when we have more space. I need to get to the airport."

His flight did not worry him. It was how much he dared tell Aileen about the Shaftsbury Square event, and as for Claire, don't go there. If he told Aileen of either one, there would be no way back. They kissed more tenderly than passionately and agreed that George would phone on Saturday night when they were in Belfast. George picked up a taxi to the airport.

Aileen lay in bed for a while. George proved a skilled lover who found sensitive points to unleash in her a raw passion. Being with a man who craved her for herself was also a factor. Her sensitivities were exacerbated by the recent dramas in her life. These included Thomas's death, her selection, election, coming to Parliament. It touched a core deep within her, something she had always been destined for, always craved. It could be a combination of all these. She fought against this complication; the lovemaking, better than any she experienced before, more generous, more sharing, but not the priority in her life. It never would be.

Aileen wanted George close, but not too close. She couldn't explain her feelings, to herself. She lay back. She would just have to wait and see how it unfolded.

George received an office next door to Burney, who could thus monitor him. The HR guy, the previous occupant, was put out at sharing with IT given, he claimed, the sensitive nature of his business. During George's second week in Glasgow, the HR bloke called into his previous office and bemoaned his displacement. "No offence," he added as an afterthought.

"None taken," said George as the guy rummaged among his filing cabinets.

"I am having those moved at the end of the week into your office." George advised him.

"My shared office," came the pointed reply.

George had got to the fed-up stage. "Whatever," he sighed wearily.

He was unaware of Laura's informant, leaving a breathless message on her answerphone.

"I have had an update on this George McNeill. He is having an affair with an Aileen Whyte. You must have heard of her; her husband was the MP who killed himself last summer, and she was parachuted into his seat. She is regarded as the rising star of Northern Ireland politics, a future First Minister. McNeill is in the celebrity pages here with various other glamorous women. He seems a bit of a personality, and that was not what I first heard. The girl who told me says she cannot believe the transformation, but it is genuine enough. A final point, he may not be what he seems, step carefully around him. "

Laura absorbed this information. Her initial dismissive attitude to George needed reconsidered. He was so meek around the office, a wolf in sheep's clothing if ever there was. She would need to tread carefully, only too conscious of her own competence and aware the changes he may bring could affect her career.

George settled into a pattern in Glasgow, flying there on either a Monday or Tuesday, home on a Thursday or Friday. The same people were on the plane each week, he supposed regulars like him. Same people but different faces. A couple of casually dressed young women sitting at opposite ends of the cabin with their heads down, students having a weekend at home and feeling homesick. They would brighten as the plane touched down thinking of whatever students think of, parties, a waiting partner, studies. A cluster of men in their thirties and forties uniformly distinguished by already having their jackets off, their crisp white shirts putting even the cabin crew to shame, pounding away on laptops. Another group of more casually dressed guys, contract workers going to Glasgow or returning to it. Finally, George the odd fish, lost in his thoughts but engrossed in some negative private drama.

He was provided with a tenement two-bedroom flat behind the Mitchell Library. The library lights on those cold January nights showed off the building in a gothic scene appropriate for the time of year.

They illuminated his living room and main bedroom. Someone had the sense to put heavy curtains in the bedroom. If it wasn't for the eternal stairs up to the flat, it would have been perfect. Because of the stairs, George became fitter than he had been in years, but then five floors of stairs: too many stairs. It was warm, convenient, comfortably, if sparsely furnished. He busied himself in the evenings, trying to learn how to cook, with limited success at first. The flat was cleaned by a person he never saw. The TV news that evening described the horrific shooting of a man in his own car and another shot in a supermarket carpark. The deaths were described as drug related. George shivered. Violence especially related to drugs seemed at every corner he turned.

He spent time working out his feelings for Aileen but was surprised how frequently Claire came into his mind. He owed her an apology and an explanation. The old George intervened, and he put off the call.

George returned from Glasgow on the Friday evening. He looked to see if Aileen was at the airport, but there was no sign. He picked up his car, drove to Riverdale and settled into his home, relieved there were no more travels until Tuesday. The house was beginning to grow on him. It could be his home for life, whatever lay ahead. Of course, the courts could make him dispose of it to pay off the proceeds of the drug money he used. Who owned the money, who would the prosecution maintain it should be returned to, now that would be an interesting debate? Despite the passage of time George became obsessed by his actions in Shaftesbury Square.

'I mean the gun; I am not interested in guns. Never fired one, never saw one before that afternoon. Why did I pick it up? Why do I every so often take it out, feel its cold heavy steel as if it were a kind of Tolkien ring? The briefcase he acknowledged he lifted because he guessed it had money in it. Someone who had never done a dishonest thing and he had so quickly stolen a large sum. Why, why?' A bad decision, best to try to forget it.

As he unpacked, Gerry popped in.:

"I am glad you are home; two guys called to visit you. I spoke to them, but they didn't want to leave a message and that Breen guy has been around most days, just at the door not doing anything in the garden."

'Who were the 'two guys?' He felt a shiver. He hadn't told Martin Breen he would be away. The 'gardener' would be capable of breaking into the house to look for cash. He thanked Gerry and took the pizza he bought on the way home into the lounge, opened a beer, and watched TV for a while. Anything to prevent him from having to face up to the issues floating around in his life. He needed to think through the night with Aileen. He would speak to her tomorrow after he saw Terry and Melissa. George also needed to call Claire; he was more apprehensive about that.

There was a message from Jan, "Haven't seen you since the party. I know you are away at the moment but come up for tea on Sunday. Elena will be here."

His voice sounded so normal. Oh, to be Jan and only have work and a daughter to be concerned for. That was me before I took that wretched briefcase. George bowed his head. He felt tears coming to his eyes. 'What had he done?' It all seemed such fun at first, getting the Range Rover, buying the house, meeting Aileen and then Claire. Also, being at the Charity Dinner, bidding in the auction, going to Glasgow and London, dining with a government minister, like a major player, and finally the Baileys contract. It could not end well.

He fell asleep with the TV on and was wakened by the sound of a bell ringing. George glanced at the TV, but it wasn't coming from there. It was his front doorbell. He staggered to the door. The combined effect of the sleep and being cooped up on a plane caused him to be unsteady. He opened the door.

Chapter 8

A Time of Many Visits to Riverdale

"Good evening, Mr McNeill, my name is Walker, and I am a Detective Inspector with the Police Service of Northern Ireland. This is my colleague, Sergeant Farrell. May we come in?" And without waiting for a response, he entered the hall.

George gazed in wide-eyed astonishment at the two men before reacting.

"Of course, of course, come on in," although by then both police officers strode past him.

As Farrell said afterwards, he looked at us as if we had said, 'Good evening, Earthling. We have just landed from Mars. Take us to your leader.'

George prepared, even rehearsed, this moment, but it flew out the window because he was dozing and caught unprepared. The police are funny like that, not keen on warnings at all. His response was so obviously genuine that the policemen's take was he had nothing to hide. A more sophisticated response could have raised suspicions.

They would identify him through Matt. If there was a picture of him with the briefcase, that would be more worrying. There would be no record of him entering the refurbished conveniences due to the dodgy screen. His lying had worked up a notch, especially to himself, but he hadn't an answer for the briefcase. If he claimed to have picked up the briefcase in a nearby office, they could check. Suggesting, he met a guy he didn't know on the street who gave him an unsolicited briefcase with half a million Euros which he didn't mention to anybody, would not float either. Apart from the briefcase, George was ready.

He sat through police interrogations at Baileys when fraud had been uncovered. It would start off with a general pattern of questioning when they possessed several facts but couldn't connect them. Further interrogation would be more demanding, but if he could bat them away now, he might avoid further suspicion. One specific question would bring everything tumbling down, the one relating to the briefcase. He seriously considered reconnecting with Matt Robb to ferret out if there was a sight of him before and after with the briefcase, but Robb might make this query known. The fact he returned and raised the 3rd of August might raise suspicion.

Let us see what the PSNI's finest put on the table, anything he wasn't expecting? Walker began.

"Thank you for inviting us in. We called a few times this week but couldn't catch you."

"Ah, well, since the beginning of the year. I have been based in Glasgow throughout the week."

They must not be aware of his consultancy work, all they got from Baileys was his address

Farrell made a note, then added. "Is it OK if we make notes, sir?" George nodded.

Walker, "We want to see if you could help us with any information relating to a serious crime in Shaftsbury Square on the 3rd of August last year?" (Question expected).

“A serious crime in Shaftsbury Square, I don’t think I read that in the papers, anyway what sort of serious crime?”

“Two men died violently, and we believe a large sum of cash was taken.” (Expected)

“One man was a Lithuanian national involved in Dublin’s illegal drug trade the other a Belfast man, also involved in importing and distributing illegal drugs.”

“Oh, I see, I am not aware of reading or hearing that?”

Walker (cursing inwardly at Robertson’s interference), “A tactical decision.” (*to himself, ‘and a right stupid one’*), “We hoped to flush out the killer or killers.”

George inwardly, *‘Oops, someone made a mistake. I wonder why?’*

“I see, no, I saw nothing resembling that any day. I do that walk daily; you know? “

Farrell, “You didn’t notice any cars being driven at high speed in the Square or adult males running up Botanic Avenue, down Donegal Pass, or towards the Donegal Road?”

(Sort of expected) “No, I don’t think cars have been driven at speed in Shaftsbury Square since 1963.” *‘Don’t be a smart ass, it won’t help.’*

Farrell glowered.

George continued, “I walked up Bedford Street and down Great Victoria Street probably every weekday in August, I don’t remember any day particularly,” pause “but” Walker and Farrell both instinctively stiffened, “I popped into the CCTV base in the square recently, an old school chum of mine, Matt Robb manages it. He would be worth speaking too.”

George’s tone was enthusiastic, but he sensed the disappointment in the police officers’ body language as they subsided. He brought nothing new to the table.

Farrell tried a different tack, “That is a nice Range Rover sir, have you owned it long?” he looked at his notes, ‘registered August 2004.’

“Funnily enough, I got it down South, for a song, an old model.”

(George had belatedly done his homework on the Range Rover and was now aware of the BMW and Ford issues and the latest model. This followed an argument with Jan, who claimed he could not have got the car at the price he claimed unless there was something wrong with it.)

The inspector chimed in, “This house is nice, have you been here long?”

(Expected). George prepared a long-convoluted story that wasn’t convincing concerning a win on the horses with a tip from a man he didn’t know. He needed a better explanation, the consultancy came along, problem solved.

“I left my permanent post with Baileys (implying ‘I held a position you are just a fucking plod’). I received a generous severance, plus money I saved from the sale of my marital home, other savings, and Baileys rehired me as a consultant. They have me based in Glasgow, following work I did in London. I will be back in London, off to Bristol and Sheffield. A lot of time away from home, but lucrative.”

He smiled knowingly at the two cops as if to say, 'I am on the up. Do you know my friend Aileen Whyte MP, or another pal of mine, the Junior Minister at the Home Office, Sir Toby Hazlehurst?'

Walker, "A serious business. The Belfast dealers imported drugs from Liverpool. The Lithuanians had come to the North to buy them. It is one or both groups will try to sort this out, although, fortunately, we have the drugs."

The implication was clear: speak to us or else to more unsavoury characters. At that, the cops rose, shook hands, and left. They weren't aware of the briefcase and were unlikely to pursue it through witnesses. Thankfully, they didn't know that he paid cash for Riverdale.

At the station the next day, Walker telephoned Chief Superintendent David O'Connell, Head of the Dublin Metropolitan Policing Area, with responsibility for general policing and units dealing with serious crime, including homicide and drugs. They met at an Interpol conference and later at other police conferences when they were both rising stars in their respective forces and stayed in touch liaising over one or two cross border crimes.

"David O'Connell is an excellent cop, but he doesn't act by the book. In fact, he revels in chucking out the book.

He expected to be promoted to Assistant Commissioner, like our Assistant Chief Constables, several years ago but his cavalier attitude meant they didn't risk it and he resents that like mad. One of his colleagues told me his only child, a boy, died of leukaemia and David changed. He never discusses it and once let slip his wife and he hardly discussed it since their son died, not a healthy grieving process."

"Tell me David, have you guys become aware of a Lithuanian drugs gang in Dublin?"

O'Connell proved a mine of information; Lithuanian drug dealers had come to Ireland recently.

"They are trying to establish themselves and have put the local gangs' noses severely out of joint. The master mind is Andrius Pakas, now assumed to be in Central Europe somewhere, probably in either Bulgaria or Romania. His brother, Arturas, his son Vito and nephew Fedor, have been living in Dublin for over a year. Arturas lived in Liverpool for several years and has serious crime contacts there. He is fluent in English, albeit with a slight accent. We think Andrius may have targeted establishing the family in the UK or Ireland a long time ago. Your colleagues advised us a few months ago that Fedor Pakas, Andrius's son, was killed in Belfast. Interpol is explicit. Andrius Pakas is both a dangerous and a violent person, his brother, Arturas, less so, but he can be exceedingly ruthless if confronted or his status or plans threatened."

The two police officers agreed to stay in contact and O'Connell stated he would come to Belfast shortly with any further information concerning the Lithuanians.

As agreed, George phoned Aileen on Saturday. Perhaps he read too much into her tone. She sounded friendly, warm even, but omitted any reference to their night in the London flat, though he tried to raise it. Family and constituency matters would occupy her weekend, and she promised to phone him from London during the week.

"It's almost calm at Westminster compared to home. I wonder do all MPs feel that."

He spent most of Saturday afternoon with Terry and Melissa. Terry wanted to come to Glasgow. "Any chance of a ticket to an 'Old Firm' game, Dad?"

George agreed to pursue this. Melissa liked the idea of shopping in Glasgow. George believed he and Melissa were getting on better. Was there a reason for her rethinking her relationship with her father? She was less dismissive of him and more interested in seeing him than before. George suggested when the school holidays came and when Terry started college, he would bring them all over in the car. When he left them back, Irene interrogated him.

"I gather you are a consultant with Baileys. What does that involve?" *('Are you paid more?')* She added, "Are you seeing Aileen Whyte? "

George remained non-committal; all her friends were agog with the Sunday newspaper revelation. The minute a public denial appeared; they guessed there must be something in it. Irene then revealed she had entered a relationship with a divorced teacher, and they intended to set up home. He had met Terry and Melissa.

"The kids mentioned nothing to me."

"They were under strict instructions; I, and I alone, was to tell you."

George nodded. "I hope your relationship works out, Irene. I suppose I will meet the chap sometime."

Sunday was quieter, time to man up and call Claire. He owed Claire an explanation, but it would not be in her interest to develop their relationship. It would be a tough conversation. It was over two weeks since they parted. A long time for a huff. Of course, he could excuse himself, ' Well apart from now being based in Glasgow in a new job, going to London and meeting with a Home Office Minister, sleeping with the MP Claire doesn't like and being interviewed by the police over a double killing and a half million Euro heist, life was uneventful.'

George could put off phoning Claire no longer. He wanted to speak to her. He wanted it to be like before the Aileen row. Two people who liked each other were friends. Hopefully, friends with benefits. He didn't want other complicating factors he couldn't control intervening. He dialled, for a second, hoping she wasn't in, but inside he was pleased at the sound of her voice.

"Hello."

"Hi Claire, it's George." Silence.

"Hello George," very formal.

"I am phoning to apologise," he began. Neither was clear what he was apologising for, being attracted to a woman who created fantasies for half the male population in Northern Ireland and a woman more than half the female population considered a role model.

"It's just...," he continued lamely.

"George," Claire sounded warmer, less hostile, "What does Aileen Whyte mean to you. What is your relationship with her? You say you have never slept with her."

'Oops, maybe not the time for an update.'

"I will not play second fiddle to anyone. You must sort out your relationship with her and your feelings. If you do that and if I am still not involved with someone, we can talk."

'Involved with someone'. What was she trying to tell him?'

"Claire, are you involved with someone?" A hint of desperation in George's voice. He hadn't expected that.

Claire was determined to enjoy this moment. "I have been out with a guy, Colin. We met through work. He is a peripatetic adviser employed by the Education Authority. I have known him for a while, and he asked me out."

He asked her out many times, but with the issues that arose after the Charity Dinner, she finally agreed. Colin Murdoch and Claire had an enjoyable meal. He had kissed her on her doorstep and hoped to be invited in. Claire decided not to increase George's agony beyond, "He is a nice person, he has no attachments," she added pointedly.

His earlier huff had not sat well. The money and the connections did not impress Claire as much as he hoped. He regained his composure,

"I didn't handle it properly after the dinner. I should have sat down and explained it better and now I have work in Glasgow four days a week. I have wanted to phone every day since that night. I want us to be more than friends," his voice sounded softer.

"George, that cannot happen, you cannot be with me, and have your mind on another woman dropping me to run off to do her bidding. You were in London recently. Did you see her?"

'How did she know that' he spoke inwardly but avoided her question?

"Look, could we meet for lunch or a coffee? Are you free later next Saturday afternoon? Terry's game has a noon kick off, so I am free after that."

"Well ... OK," replied Claire, a bit torn.

They agreed on a city centre venue,

"Goodbye George."

"See you on Saturday, Claire."

Whatever the future held for her Claire, she was mindful of her sister's words.

"If you think he is special, you might have to fight for him."

"Yes, I suppose I will be prepared to do that."

She noted he did not say whether he met Aileen Whyte when he was in London, if he did what happened between them?

George was pleased to have re-established contact and to have a meeting in place but was jealous at the thought another man on the scene, it caught him by surprise.

Claire talked to both Mandy and Liz; she described their row over Aileen Whyte after the Charity dinner. Mandy, who was initially hostile to George, was now a fan. He lived a more exciting life than she imagined he did. The sort she would like to live with plenty of money and being seen in all the right places and with celebrities.

"Go for it girl," her advice to Claire, "Give it what you want to give, there will be interesting experiences, opportunities too, I'll be bound. He is in and out of Baileys working with the partners, although recently I overheard Peter Donald being irritated because George journeyed to London when Peter Donald thought he was in Glasgow. I have no idea why it was such an issue."

Her sister was more measured. "Claire, many men I know are attracted to Aileen Whyte. She is cool, well groomed, confident and, as Mandy says, she moves in all the right places. I have met George twice and I don't want you to take this the wrong way, but he is out of his league there. Few men will be happy in that woman's shadow, and any man will always be in her shadow. If that is the person George is, then he is not the person for you."

"Liz, when I moved to England, I was a nineteen-year-old, full of dreams and wanting to get away from Belfast after a number of shitty jobs and a couple of unpleasant encounters with men. I got carried away with Jim. He had an answer for everything, lots of money it was a ball- for a while. I married him and thought that was the way life would be. He changed after we got married. Not at once. Exciting plans were replaced by controlling. His 'devil may care' meant we lived in a tip, or we would have if I hadn't worked so hard to keep it all together."

"A lot like his dad. "said Liz. "Our daddy did not care for him at all."

"Yes, his dad treated Belfast as a colonial outpost. He was doing it a favour by coming over for the wedding. "

"Your experience was worse than mine. Kevin is an easier person to live with and once Karen was born, she ended up with a slave for life. He loved bathing the baby, reading the bedtime stories, even nappy changing. Well, he did not love that, but he did his fair share."

"My whole life with Jim went downhill, the selfishness, the drinking, coming in at all hours, lipstick on his collar. Whereas if I was on a girl's night out, he insisted on meeting me and driving me home, 'I can give your friends a lift, it is safer'. But I knew he wanted to keep an eye on me. If he did not trust me, why did he want to stay with me? Once I was certain we needed to split, it became easier or clearer. Sure, there were the temper tantrums, the tears, the threats. I could see my way. I kept my cool, manoeuvred him out, hinted after a break we might get back together, but I was certain I wanted away. Coming back to Belfast was the last piece of the jigsaw."

“You did that with a lot of maturity. You grew up at a rate of knots.”

“Once I got the job in the nursery, I was happy to be back. I do not care if I live with another man. Yet, it is so odd that I am so attracted to George. You asked me once what were his good points, and I was unconvincing. Sometimes you cannot explain what is deep inside you.”

“If he is important to you, don’t retire from the field, and let Aileen Whyte have a clear run. Be in there, but only on your terms. It could mean he gets to choose, but in the end, the final decision is down to you.”

Claire would keep her options open; she wouldn’t let George get too close, but she would keep as much control of their relationship as she could.

Mindful of his promise to Sir Toby, the following Sunday in late January, George drove west. A person in the Linenhall library advised him to go to Innismacsaint Church and to ask if anyone in the congregation did local Parish history. The area was scenically beautiful.

A few miles outside Derrygonnelly lay the Lough Naver viewpoint, which overlooks lower Lough Erne and had views of the Donegal coast to the west and the Sperrin Mountains in County Tyrone to the north and east. He came across the church and the graveyard with a number of Fergusons interred there. He called at the manse and spoke to a helpful minister.

“A member of my congregation, Mary Fraser, has written a history of the church. It hasn’t been published, but we have printed copies and many members of the congregation gave donations for copies.”

He phoned Mary Fraser, who was quite excited that a stranger from Belfast was interested in the church's history. The Minister opened the church and Mary got old Parish Records that were dusty having been stored for years in a basement. She prattled on, recounting historic events long before Henrietta's birth and George stayed patient, listened to the events, including tragic ones, over the years.

"Yes, here she is Henrietta Ferguson, born 19 April 1882, married Sir David Hazlehurst. They had two sons and a daughter. One son, William Hazlehurst MP, (Toby's father), responded to a request for a donation back in 1958 to help improve the condition of the graveyard, make safe gravestones and donated five hundred pounds. It is recorded as a generous response. He intends to come over to visit the church."

Mary gave George a copy of her potted history and added facts from her detailed notes. George made sure he donated in sterling; he was relieved not having to lie anymore why he paid only in euros.

He resolved to put all he had gleaned in a report. George's report writing was improving. He compiled the potted history, the additional details from Mary, intending to pass it all to Sir Toby. Of course, it meant he would have an excuse to visit Aileen.

Peter had been tetchy the last time he went, so he told him he would only work three days this week: Wednesday, Thursday, and Friday, because of personal business. He would go to London later on Monday, contact Aileen and then head up to Glasgow on the Wednesday.

He phoned Toby. "Hazlehurst," the voice barked.

George explained he visited County Fermanagh and had information for Sir Toby.

'Goodness gracious, the fellow went to a lot of trouble. I assumed he suggested he would do that in the vague way a politician promises to do things.'

"I am coming over on Tuesday and I will stay until Wednesday morning."

At first Toby told George to post the information but then, 'the chap might want a personal thank you, least I could do after all his trouble.'

"George, I have a brief 9.30 meeting at the Home Office on Tuesday morning then I have to be in the House for 10.45, I am sorry to cram it in but if you could come to the Home Office at 10.00 am we could grab a quick coffee?"

"Perfect." agreed George.

George flew over on the 7.00 am flight. He left a message on Aileen's phone to say he would be there from Tuesday until Wednesday morning and could they meet for dinner Tuesday evening. He thought she might have tried to put him off if they had spoken.

George entered the Home Office, passing through security, to reception.

"I have an appointment with the Minister of State at 10.00."

"Which one?" asked the woman behind the desk.

"Sir Toby Hazlehurst."

She lifted the phone. "The Minister's private secretary will be down shortly. Please take a seat behind you."

Edward Thornton was irritated; the Minister only just mentioned this appointment.

He intended to use the time before the Minister went to the House to brief him on events later in the week.

He was pleasant enough to George even though his accent was difficult to decipher, not a Buckinghamshire constituent for sure. As he conducted George towards the door to the Minister's private office, he offered to look after the A4 size brown envelope, but George clung on to it. They drank coffee and George described the old church, Mary Fraser, and the Ferguson graves and Sir Toby's father's donation to the church graveyard, Toby was not aware of this. He was quite moved at hearing about a decent his father did many years before and something positive too because the old man had a negative reputation.

After twenty minutes as he rose to leave, Toby shook hands and thanked him again. As George left, Edward noted he no longer carried the A4 envelope, and he glimpsed it on the Minister's desk. Later that day, as he walked to one of the coffee shops, a man from Special Branch he was on nodding terms with stopped him.

"Tell me Edward, who was that guy from Belfast the Minister met first thing?"

"Ah Belfast, that explains the accent. I did not receive any prior information about him. He brought a report which he gave the Minister."

The Special Branch man absorbed this, then said.

"Oh, I hate it when the Minister responsible for security matters has meetings he doesn't mention. I hope he is not trying to do a back door deal with one of the Republican splinter groups. They are acting up again, lost, nowhere to go since the Good Friday Agreement."

Edward nodded. He had no interest in Irish politics, but the encounter was not casual.

“Sir Toby mentioned he met the chap at dinner, last week I think, Aileen Whyte, the newest MP from Belfast, was there too.”

‘Curious and curiouser’ ruminated the Special Branch guy. Aileen Whyte would not be involved with any dissicent Republican group.

When he left the Home Office, George did not notice the man following him. He received a text from Aileen suggesting that she had to be at Parliament late, but they could get a ‘take away.’ She suggested George come to the flat for 9.00 pm. George texted her to ask if there was a quality Chinese restaurant, he could bring food in. Aileen texted back an hour later with a suggestion. He wandered randomly around the city centre.

The Special Branch Officer reported in, “He is on to me. He is trying to pretend he is an innocent tourist and is going to public places. He visited the Tate and then got the tube and ‘did’ Madame Tussauds. “

A second officer took over for the next shift. George ate a late lunch at an Italian restaurant off Oxford Street.

He called into see his old friend Levi and ordered a black business suit and two shirts and two matching ties. He paid with his credit card and explained he had a different address to send the suit. He would take the shirts. The Special Branch officer in charge of this operation was puzzled, but though it was unlikely George would contact dissident Republicans in London. He continued their surveillance for the rest of the day, but he felt George was aware of their presence. He could be trained and be using these activities as a smokescreen.

Aileen texted him, saying she hadn't had time for lunch, hadn't eaten since breakfast and was ravenous and looking forward to him bringing the takeaway. He wished she said she was looking forward to seeing him.

As the evening grew darker, he discovered a cosy pub near Westminster fifteen minutes from Aileen's flat. He walked to the Chinese restaurant. It wasn't a takeaway, but a proper restaurant. They did 'take away' for special customers and when George said Aileen Whyte MP, they obliged.

He got to the flat with his precious cargo and his carrier bag of shirts, underwear, and socks, all noted by the Special Branch officer. Aileen gave him a big smile as she welcomed him. He was anxious she would ask if he had a hotel for the night. He hoped she assumed he would stay with her. His experiences in Glasgow proved a lively issue. Aileen made various suggestions, including that he should tell the partners he could turn the business around. Also, he should find someone in the firm familiar with the local clientele and support their instincts on direction and pace. Aileen discussed her work and how Toby backed off but was still pleasant and even remembered to ask after George.

He took the reference to Toby and the reminder of their last time together to join her on the couch. They caressed each other and kissed more and more passionately, holding hands, moved to her bedroom, and made love. Aileen fell asleep first. He lay there wondering if their relationship had moved on, or Aileen only wanted comfort and release. Aileen was quiet as they ate breakfast. George had yet to book a ticket to Glasgow. He would go to the airport and find a flight with a spare seat. He hoped she had time to spend with him.

"George last night was enjoyable. I love having you here. It makes this flat seem less impersonal somehow, and I like your company. But

I don't think I am ready for a relationship; I am not even sure I want one again."

She looked wistful, her eyes brimming with regret for lost dreams and hopes. It was important not to pressurise her, he squeezed her arm, "I better get my flight to Glasgow."

February offers the promise of spring, cold but brighter nights, frosty mornings. George drove to Donegal. Progress was slow on the little cottage, but at least the bathroom and the bigger bedroom were finished. The kitchen and the living room remained a mess. The floors, windows, and heating system were still to be replaced.

"Those boys have been working their butts off," ventured Matt Molloy. George looked at him. He pottered around the property and Molloy left him to it. He walked around to the 'lean to' at the back of the cottage, it was full of rubbish, but George found an old chest of drawers with bits of nails, screws and other odds and ends, he moved it and with an old shovel he found and dug a hole. George put the briefcase in polythene into the hole, then moved the old chest back.

Riverdale felt 'cleaner' without the briefcase full of euros. It wouldn't have been his house in the first place without the euros he already spent. Funny how you can rationalise things if it suits you, he mused.

David O'Connell contacted Walker to arrange a date to come to Belfast to share information, but added he heard from 'sources' that the Lithuanians were also planning a visit to Belfast to locate their money.

Walker and Farrell stirred the pot with George, as they found some of his explanations unconvincing. They visited him again on a Friday night to advise him to be careful because the providers of the money were coming to Belfast to locate it.

George shrugged his shoulders, adopting the attitude, 'What has that got to do with me?' Inside he was a little anxious, but he could see no way of the drug gang identifying him or where he lived.

Davy Foster, a Sergeant in the PSNI Special Branch, called into the station. An old mate of John Farrell's, he tracked him down to the Shaftsbury Square incident room. Farrell was deep in conversation with his boss, who had come across Foster before.

In a throwaway comment he asked the Special Branch man,

"Have you guys been doing anything on continental drug gangs?"

Foster answered, "Not recently," looked up at the charts and the pictures and let out a yell, "Crikey, George McNeill."

The picture of McNeill and Aileen Whyte had been up and down on that wall a few times, the PSNI detectives were all ears.

Davy Foster explained, "We had a query from Special Branch officers based at the Home Office. Ministers like to pretend all the police anti-terrorist and security services work together and share information. Do they fuck. McNeill has had several, shall we say, unauthorised meetings, with the Minister of State responsible for security. He met him last week and handed over a report. We don't know the nature of its contents, but we are worried the Minister might do a back door deal with IRA dissidents to draw them into the Peace Process without going through channels. Special Branch followed McNeill and we understand he spent a few nights at Aileen Whyte's flat."

He continued. "They know so little facts; they don't know how McNeill, or the Minister fit in, in fact they don't know what they fit into. At least one of my colleagues believes McNeill could be an undercover MI5 agent, embedded with dissidents. The Home Office

Special Branch folk contacted us to see how close McNeill is to current Dissident IRA men or previous IRA guys."

Walker and Farrell were dumfounded by this latest twist and advised Robertson, who began to panic. They added 'possible MI5 undercover agent' to the list below George McNeill's picture.

A week later, after a tiring time in Glasgow, George was in collapse mode when he got home. Is every Friday night going to be like this?

The last time I got home, the cops came. All I wanted was a power nap. I am tired tonight too. He wavered between having a quick sleep in his chair or an early night.

He heard a quiet knock on the front door, and he walked down and opened it. At first, as he saw an older man and a younger one. Was it the police officers who visited recently?

Chapter 9

Chickens Come Home to Roost.

As he focussed, he realised the older man, dressed in an expensive suit, was older than the inspector and the younger one, in casual sporting gear, was younger than Sergeant Farrell.

"George McNeill?" asked the older guy in an accented voice and without waiting for a reply, pushed past George, and walked along the hall into the lounge. The younger man pushed George in front of him, holding his shoulders, smiling all the time. A further shock awaited George as he entered his lounge: a third man stood at the door between the kitchen and the lounge. He was dressed in a dark suit and with his hands clasped in front of his stomach for all the world like a nightclub bouncer. He ignored George and stared intently into the middle distance.

The older man introduced himself, "I am Arturas Pakas and the guy holding you is my son Vito. He wants to introduce himself properly."

Vito smiled winningly and let go of George. He then put his left arm around George's left shoulder and drove his right fist violently into the pit of George's stomach.

Arturas continued, "I know you are trying to breathe, but you can't. Do not try, it is important you stop trying, momentarily your legs can no longer support you. Don't worry, Vito will hold you. In a few seconds, you will be able to breathe through your nose, then your brain will return feelings to your legs. Unfortunately, that will be accompanied by a great deal of pain," and it was.

Everything Arturas described happened exactly as he said, apart from Vito getting fed up with supporting George and letting him collapse onto the settee. A look of irritation crossed Arturas's face at that, but Vito just shrugged, sat beside George, and patted his knee reassuringly. All this time the third man stood immobile. Without being sure why, George sensed that of all the men, he was the most dangerous.

George did not smoke. He watched in silent horror as the older man tipped a dish of pot-pourri onto the table and used the dish as an ashtray. The cigarette's sweet pungent smell bizarrely reminded him of the pipe tobacco his father smoked. The dish and the pot-pourri were a gift from his sister-in-law. 'I can only imagine what a house a man lives in alone smells like,' she cheerfully informed George.

Reality beckoned as Arturas took centre stage again. "It strikes me, my friend…"

Why on earth anything that happened in the last few minutes allowed the use of the word 'friend' was beyond George.

"We need to identify shared issues. My nephew's death has caused great angst in my family, especially to my brother Andrius. No, no," he declared as George tried to use words such as 'I wasn't involved in that.' "I realise you did not kill him, otherwise it would be my Bulgarian friend," with a nod to the 'gent' in the dark suit at the kitchen door, "who would interview you now."

Arturas closed his eyes to emphasise how awful that prospect would be. George did not doubt him for a minute. George still couldn't speak or breathe properly, though, as the pain got worse, so his breathing improved. The pain lessened and he began to think.

Despite the violence of the incident, he had been expecting an encounter with the Lithuanians, especially after Walker and Farrell's visit. Surely, he had a plan...... except he didn't.

"Let me tell you how this works. I want our half million euros. Now your nice car and your new house suggests to me you have spent say a hundred thousand," (more like two hundred George thought, closing his eyes), "that is your problem, but we are going to return in one week and you will HAVE our money. I've been in your house three times this week. We didn't find the money, so I take it you have hidden it. You have a very nosy neighbour; it wasn't easy searching the house. This God forsaken country has already claimed my nephew Fedor's life. My brother and I are angry. Someone has to pay." was Arturas's next comment.

There was a possibility up George's sleeve to deal with the Armageddon situation that he could face. He would contact the police. It would be Alan Walker. He would lose his liberty, his position with Baileys, his registration with Chartered Accountants Ireland, in effect his licence to practice. There would be the shame for Terry, Melissa, and his brother. Aileen would, of course, put out a statement. 'Mr McNeill was briefly involved helping in a very minor way in sorting out my late husband's affairs. I unaware of any wrongdoing he was involved in and met him only briefly.'

Jan would be more kindly disposed to him. He also thought Claire, on the basis women are drawn to wounded pups, might not feel too hostile towards him. By the time he was released, she would be long gone. He would lose his house, but the Donegal cottage would be his bolt hole. Jan would keep an eye on it, even use it as a breakout space for him and Elena.

"Mr McNeill, you think you can simply run to the authorities, turn yourself in, give them our money or what is left of it, and take your punishment. Really, do you think we would be that gullible? We considered creating much pain for you and you would beg to tell us where our money is. That would have been simpler, but if the money is well concealed, maybe only you could get it. Something could go wrong. We might kill you by accident during the interrogation and never find it."

George's instinct, 'kill you by accident' as opposed to the killing you will do once you have got the money. It was vital to keep Pakus and the cash separate for as long as possible until he came up with a plan. What plan? He had no Scooby of an idea.

"You have one week to get our cash. Mind you, that is a long time to think how you could frustrate us, so we have built-in safeguards. You are out of your depth. As a criminal, you are a total failure. This is important, listen up. If you cannot be here in one week with our money, we will kill Terry. Dimitar," with a nod to the Bulgarian, "will do inexcusable things to Melissa. She is fifteen, isn't she? I am afraid he has this thing about very young girls. Awful, isn't it? Don't worry, he doesn't speak much English. I find his behaviour quite repugnant, but he can be very useful. Finally, my son Vito is quite taken with Elena Tieleman. She is a real looker that one. He almost hopes you do a runner so that he can have Elena."

George felt sick. The pain of the earlier assault would be nothing as he absorbed the picture Pakas painted of what would happen to the people he loved most.

Arturas patted him on the arm, "7.00 pm next Friday, then."

George said nothing but looked at Arturas and hated him as he hated nobody else. Whatever his brother was like he couldn't be as malevolent as this person

As George looked around Vito rose to his feet and as he passed a cabinet with photographs of Terry and Melissa and Elena on top, he paused, lifted Elena's, looked at it and then turned and winked at George and made a point of licking his lips. Of Dimitar, there was no sign. He disappeared as noiselessly as he arrived.

Father and son left, and George buried his head in his hands and sat, unable to contemplate a way out of this horrible experience. He had always guessed it would end badly but not this badly. 3 to 5 years in prison, estrangement from people he only got to know recently, was not as bad a prospect as this.

This was more serious. He was outmanoeuvred. George's big mistake, among several big mistakes, was assuming he would think the same and feel the same at the end of the entire business. He had not factored in the feelings and relationships that accompanied the 'new' George. The thoroughness of the Lithuanians also caught him on the hop. They entered his house twice, searching for the money. They investigated his closest relationships and correctly identified his most vulnerable spot. He walked around the house every soften sitting down, he was in a state. He spent the night in his chair. At one stage, sobbing to himself. As a distraction and because he couldn't sleep, he put on a DVD of his favourite movie, The Magnificent Seven. It must have been before dawn. Where were Coburn and Vaughan, Bronson, and McQueen when a good guy needed them? Then the despair hit him. He wasn't a good guy. He deserved all of this.

With the film running in the background, he fell asleep but was wakened by a knock on the front door. He staggered half asleep to the door and opened it.

A voice grunted, "Hello."

George responded, "Steve McQueen -Vin?"

"What?" said the voice and brushed past him into the hall, in the manner of Alan Walker and Arturas Pakas.

It wasn't Steve McQueen. It was Martin Breen.

"You look like you had a rough night. Anyway, I just called to tell you I was up at the house several times through the week and on different occasions, I am certain there were people inside. Obviously, I didn't call the Peelers."

'No,' thought George,' regardless of the crime, you wouldn't go near the police.'

"What is that smell?" sniffed Martin. "Have you been on the wacky baccy?"

He looked at the remains of the cigarette in the dish beside the spilled pot-pouri. George made coffees. An idea was forming in his mind. Even if he could get all the cash, Pakas would want retribution for his nephew's death. It would be a family honour killing. Somebody needed to suffer, and George had a fair idea who that was.

Martin prattled on inevitably about money and the danger of keeping it in your own house and how you need friends who can handle themselves. He was more explicitly saying he knew George often kept sizeable sums of cash in the house. The idea of "needing friends" gave George a further element to his plan.

"Martin, you are right, of course. I have to do business with cash. There were people in the house, part of a European group my associates and I have... em, had a difference with?"

Breen's eyes widened in astonishment. 'I knew it, I knew it.'

"My people, well Donald is the hard case," (whoever heard of a hard man called Donald, for Christ's sake, George do better) "and Andrews the master mind, they will expect me to sort it. Do you have any contacts who would eliminate three dangerous foreign guys?"

'Are you confiding in Breen, seeking his help, plumbing the depths the voice went on? Are you setting up a killing, George? You have sunk very low?' repeated the voice in his head.

Another more pragmatic tone interrupted, *'It's them or you, it's keeping Terry, Melissa and Elena safe.'*

Breen responded at once. George could not believe what he was saying:

"I can arrange that with a friend. How much are your people offering?"

George suggested, "Ten thousand euros."

Breen bartered, "Twenty thousand for each of us, after all, you want three men killed."

George felt sick again. Then he considered the girls and Terry.

"You will need the bodies disposed of. I have done a bit of that." added Martin.

'I bet you have,' George thought. They agreed on fifteen thousand euros each.

Martin's pal, one Liam McVeigh, had been on 'operations' with him in the past.

When Martin discussed the garden, George felt he was genuinely knowledgeable. Even Gerard next door was impressed with the preparatory work Martin did for the winter and also his physical input into the digging and cutting. This was totally different. How did they go from a normal topic to planning a gangland slaying? He had doubts about Breen's capability.

Even if he could do this, George knew he would be at future risk from Martin once he paid him. He hoped reference to his imaginary gang would make Breen cautious. Breen required him to recount twice, in detail, the Lithuanians visit.

"So, the guy in the dark suit stood there. You didn't see or hear him come in, but the back door was locked. The younger guy sat there. The boss sat where? Right, once more."

Breen then, without invitation, left the lounge and went upstairs. He came back down and moved to the back door.

"Good lock. When are they coming back? Next Friday at 7.00 pm, OK? Me and Liam will be here. We will bring a van. You will need a large amount of polythene sheeting. I want you to spread it in that corner, under the TV and into the middle of the floor. Cover the settee, the TV and the chairs. Also, buy paint and paint the wall behind the TV. Say it was a diversion to take your mind off things if they ask. Don't make a point of raising it. Be natural. Leave the paint tin and the used brushes in a plastic tray there." He pointed beside the TV.

"The plan is, four minutes after they come into the house, me and Liam will take them out."

George closed his eyes momentarily, as if in pain.

Breen spoke, as reassuringly as possible.

"Look, I appreciate this is not your bag. I realise you are scared, but there is no other way. Be clear the bad blood between your people and them means they are intending to kill you either way."

George knew that. Appalled, relieved, exhilarated, scared, scared, and he so wanted to be somewhere else when this happened, but there would be no hiding place for him. Going from total despair to hope, but hope with a violent interlude, 'Why oh why had he......'

He got the paint and polythene sheeting as requested. Martin phoned his mobile and confirmed Liam McVeigh was 'up for it' and could get hold of guns. He emphasised that they would be paid in cash. George confirmed 'they' would deliver the money to him on the Friday. He didn't want Breen thinking it was in the house.

Breen and his mate Liam McVeigh called on the Saturday morning. McVeigh was a guy of few words. He paced out the kitchen, living room and stairs. George marvelled at his 'professionalism'. At least he wasn't underestimating the drug gang. He gave Martin and Liam a thousand euros each in cash.

Breen nodded, "I have debts to pay off, what will you do, Liam?"

McVeigh shrugged, "I'll do this. I have no commitments or links in Ireland except my sister, but when this is finished, I am off."

He struck even George as an odd fish. A loner, less sociable than George used to be. *He hadn't met the right two women*, George joked inwardly.

George returned to Donegal on Sunday to raid his stash for Martin and Liam's money. Late February by now, cold but dry, so the trip proved easy. He avoided the old farmer and his wife, who were out. On the Sunday night, an hour after he returned from Donegal, Breen appeared.

"It's off"

'Great,' thought George, 'it might be off for you, Martin, but it isn't off for me when these guys from Dublin arrive,' but he kept his cool.

“Why? By the way, have you brought my two thousand Euros so that I can get somebody else? (Where am I going to locate gunmen? Yul Brynner had less trouble recruiting the Seven).

“Liam could only get one gun. These are not the sort of guys you tackle with one gun, hope and a prayer.”

George paused, “Look, Martin,” in his most persuasive and reassuring tones, “my people,” (them again, the imaginary McNeill gang) “will get you a gun. I need to make a few phone calls. Come here late on Thursday and I will have a gun.”

“No,” replied Martin, “they might watch you to see if you have grassed to the peelers.”

‘Oh yes, grass to the peelers, how unsporting of me to turn to the police because a psychopathic international drug cartel wants to murder me and perhaps my kids. How totally unreasonable of me.’

Martin said, “Can you get it after you come back from Glasgow or, better still, on your way down from the airport?”

George nodded. It was if Breen had prepared this to deal with a setback. Martin continued

“When you come down from the airport on Thursday evening drive via the Falls Road. Stop at the corner of the Springfield and Falls, hospital side. I will wait there and give me the gun. For goodness’ sake, disguise the package a bit. Far too many exchange guns on that corner. We don’t want them asking questions.”

‘*I wonder whom ‘them’ are*,’ reflected George, but he said nothing and agreed. He stowed the Glock 19 in his car. He could place bubble wrap and brown paper around it. I mean is that what you do when you are passing a gun to an ex-terrorist who is going to kill foreign nationals on your behalf in your home. His final thought, *'this cannot end well for me.'*

George flew to Glasgow on the Monday. For a short time, he could banish all thoughts of Pakus and his associates coming the following Friday night. He threw himself half-heartedly into the assessment in Glasgow. People asked him if he felt OK because he was quieter and moodier than his normal persona.

He phoned Aileen on the Tuesday. She suggested they meet up on the Saturday evening for a drink. A most un-Aileen like offer and normally it would have excited him, but he wondered, 'Will I still be alive on Saturday?' George found it depressing and scary. He just wanted Friday to be over but not one way or the other, only one way. He reconciled himself to the fact that if they didn't kill Pakus and his cronies, then he, George, was certainly a goner. If you have any doubts over killing someone, the realisation that if you don't kill them, they will kill you, helps a lot.

David O'Connell confirmed he would visit Belfast later in the week. "It would be good to go out for a session. Alan. do you remember those nights with Yuri Shevlov at the Interpol Conference in Rome and the International Police Conference on Global Crime in Chicago?"

Alan remembered them well. Just remembering it caused his head to feel sore.

"Yes, Yuri introduced us to the serious drinking of very potent vodkas, including his favourite. What was it, Stolichnaya?"

"That's it," agreed David. "Yuri has kept in touch. In fact, recently I contacted him regarding this case. Tell you more when I see you."

Yuri Shevlov chummed up with the Irish men on the first day of an Interpol conference where he was an invited guest. O'Connell was a Chief Inspector and Alan a Sergeant who had passed his Inspector's exams. Yuri described himself in his line management strand as a lieutenant in the Criminal Division of the Russian Police (IPA) within the Ministry of Internal Affairs (MVD). He was seconded to the Federal Security Service (FSB) whose remit was to ensure the security of the Russian Federation.

David and Alan got lost in the labyrinth of Russian security apparatus and decided that he really worked for the KGB. Yuri pretended to be horrified and proclaimed that organisation no longer existed.

"We are a stable democracy like you, for the moment." He added mysteriously.

Yuri lost much of the gravities of his position because he was standing on a table in a Roman Bar after nine vodkas.

He came from Vologda in Northwest Russia, a city the size of Belfast. Shevlov asked lots of questions relating to issues in Ireland post 'The Troubles,' and how effectively the two police forces on the island cooperated. He mentioned to his new friends, if he wanted to advance his career, he would have to move to Moscow and be involved in specialist activities. Yuri did not specify their nature.

Chief Superintendent David O'Connell arrived in Belfast, went to lunch with senior officers, including Robertson, and then got down to business with Walker and Farrell in their cubby hole.

O'Connell advised, "According to the Garda National Economic Crime Bureau, the European drugs cartel moved here less than two years ago. They were responsible for ruthless actions, including two killings against home-grown groups who were out of their depth with a more ‘professional’ outfit. Let me reprise what I mentioned in my phone call, so we are on the same page. The leader of the European group, Lithuanian and Bulgars, is a man called Arturas Pakas, and he was the uncle of Fedor Pakas, the man killed in the Shaftsbury Square incident. The most dangerous member of the group in Ireland is a Bulgarian called Dimitar, somebody or other. We believe he carried out the Dublin killings.”

Walker and Farrell increasingly believed that the Shaftsbury Square killings were unplanned, a random act by Patrick Quinn to steal the cash Fedor brought and the drugs from Liverpool. How he hoped to get away with it was a mystery. His former comrades, the Lithuanians and the police would all search for him. As an alternative he could give the money to his colleagues. They would pay off their Liverpool suppliers and Quinn hoped to supplement his earnings over time by selling the drugs discretely. Why he thought the Lithuanians would lie down and roll over after Fedor’s death, made little sense. Intelligence from those in West Belfast drugs dealing suggested Quinn was not the sharpest tool and made a spontaneous decision which cost him his life. The whereabouts of the money and why someone else was there continued to baffle the detectives.

O’Connell shared more information.

“A much more alarming element is that the Lithuanian gang were part of a European wide larger cartel led by Andrius Pakus, brother of Arturas, who has the unlikely nickname, ‘The Fat Man.’”

“Very Philip Marlowe,” Walker suggested.

“Well, maybe Alan,” O’Connell agreed, “but when we dug around Interpol intelligence, ‘The Fat Man’ is creating viable drug industries in the South of France, Northern Italy, and Greece. Interpol has described him as a ‘dangerous and very violent person.’ It takes a lot to spook those guys, given the numbers of low life throughout the continent. He seems to have moved part of his operation to Ireland, sending his trusty lieutenant, his younger brother Arturas, to set up an Irish franchise. Dublin is a cosmopolitan European city these days with much EU interconnectedness. I suspect this deal, which culminated in the killings you are investigating, was an exploratory move to test the waters for expansion into Northern Ireland."

"Oh no," sighed Farrell, "as if we don't have enough low life of our own. Will they have considered the para-military activities of our drug gangs? They might find they have taken on more than they can chew."

O'Connell thought for a moment, "They were violent but there were only two killings of guys in medium-sized outfits in the greater Dublin area, leaving small single or two person outfits which are scattered. We have been advised a former Dublin IRA volunteer called Pol Tobin has been gathering together the displaced remnants of the other gangs to challenge the Lithuanians.

There have been a number of territorial skirmishes, but Tobin is testing the opposition. We expect next year there could be a full-scale territorial gang war in Dublin."

Walker considered this European element. "I have come across Poles, Rumanians, and Turks, but not Lithuanians. Is there any significance in that?"

"Not as far as we know," O'Connell replied, "Lithuania has its proportion of 'bad guys', but the Pakas clan are different. This is where Yuri Shevlov comes in. He ferreted about with his Russian and Baltic connections. He tells me the Pakus brothers' dad was Lithuanian, but their mother came from Russia and hailed from a criminal family in what is now St. Petersburg. The father died when the sons were young and the boys ran wild, so she brought them home to Russia to her own family. God knows what they would have picked up there given their already wild streak. They returned to Lithuania in their late teens as they were being 'leaned on' by the Russian authorities for various misdemeanours. Historically, Lithuanians and people from Yuri's home city of Vologda are at loggerheads. Remember, he described it as having similarities to Ireland, a historical conflict, and a set of distant mutual grievances."

Walker tried to absorb all this, but O'Connell continued.

"The younger brother, Arturas, moved to London and worked for London Transport. He then became a waiter, eventually ended up as a doorman at a nightclub in the East End. After that, five years ago, he moved to Liverpool. He made connections there and served an eighteen-month prison sentence for assault. He lived in England for ten years, speaks English fluently.

Yuri says that his older brother, Andrius, moved around from France, mostly Marseilles, for a while and then to Chechnya. There he became entangled in the civil war and gained a reputation for killing and torturing opponents of his then boss. Yuri said he remains a controversial figure with powerful friends and even more powerful enemies. He knows too much, also there is a personal grudge arising from the break down in his marriage. His ex-father-in-law is a dangerous character, close to top people in Moscow. It is believed Andrius might use information he has to create problems for oligarchs and politicians who have risen high. They want to forget their origins or the things they authorised in Chechnya. Andrius went off the radar for a couple of years, but recently he has been living in Romania and Bulgaria and has a major role in drug importation and distribution. Interpol, believe he has killed several rivals during his rise in the underworlds in those countries."

O' Connell paused for breath and to stretch his legs in the small office, walked over to the board with the charts, timelines, and photos. He paused at the picture of Aileen and George and the heading MI5.

"Nice looking woman. Seems familiar."

"Yes," agreed Walker, "she is the rising star of Northern Ireland politics. You will have heard of her father, Edmund Proctor..."

"Oh, of course," O'Connell cut in, "but what's this guy doing there?" he pointed at George.

Farrell did a double take. "You know George McNeill?"

"Well, not by name," the Garda replied, "but we have pictures of him with Paddy McCann. You know, top ex IRA boss."

Farrell shook his head, but Walker mused, "Paddy McCann, I am sure I have heard that name."

"He may be a little before your time, but according to RUC intelligence passed to us, he was very active in the late 1970s early 1980s. He served at least two prison sentences but was suspected of several very serious murders and bombings between 1980 and 1985. His wife and daughter were killed as a reprisal by loyalists in 1986 or 87 and he fled to Dublin with his son. We have kept him under surveillance. His boy emigrated to the US and McCann visits regularly. A colleague in intelligence worries he might bring in Irish/American money to fund the dissidents, so we follow him around for a few weeks after he returns to observe if he makes any contacts.

He has done nothing to create any suspicions, so I intended to recommend we didn't continue the surveillance. Anyway, he met 'your man there' recently in Dublin. Is he really MI5?"

"We don't know," Walker responded.

“Could Paddy be prepared to hand over information on the dissidents to MI5 or is he a go between for McNeill and whoever he really works for?” asked Farrell.

“Really unlikely from what Paddy’s files say,” hazarded O’Connell, “but I will check that out.”

“So, who is McNeill?” Walker mused,” An innocent passer-by who stole half a million euros; a banker for the West Belfast drugs gang who ended up with the money from the Shaftsbury Square incident to mind for the gang; an MI5 agent or an agent provocateur or a combination of some or all of these?” Walker was struck, as he had been throughout his career, how a big event unfolded almost by accident and yet there are no such things as coincidences.

O’Connell dropped a final bombshell

“You see your charts? I thought they rang a bell, but just seeing them brought it to mind. A photograph of all that was seen by an informant of ours. It made little sense to him, and he couldn’t make us a copy, but the gang have a photograph of what is on your wall. I am afraid you have a leak.”

Walker sighed. “This has happened before, but I understood we sorted it. So, the Lithuanians know all that information?”

“Yes, they do. I will let you know if they move North. Arturas favours a black Audi 6,” suggested O’Connell and he gave Walker the registration number.

Walker asked Farrell to check if any CCTV picked up the Audi recently, although he added,

“I know that is a long shot and they may use a different car.”

"They might already be here," said Farrell.

"I'll check." replied O'Connell.

A few days later, he confirmed Arturas was in Dublin that day, as were Vito and the Bulgarian.

Yuri Shevlov leaded against the kiosk in the Gara Bucuresti Nord. Built in the late 19th Century, it had been extended and modernised through the 20th Century. It was no longer as comfortable a place for a Russian official as it had been when Romania was in the Soviet orbit. Still, he had many clandestine meetings in his career, this one was disturbing. His instructions came from near the top but not the top, he was a foil in a game whereby he might end up on the losing side.

"You have connections with the police in Ireland have you not?"

Yuri did not look directly at the older bespeckled woman who stood beside him sideways on.

"Yes."

"There is an issue there we need you to address, here are your orders, read and destroy."

Yuri shivered turned, "But…" she was already gone.

George came home on Thursday evening to prepare himself for tomorrow's big day. He phoned Terry and when asked to speak to Melissa, Irene said she was watching a favourite TV programme, and could it not wait until he saw them on Saturday. George lost it a bit, which surprised Irene, but she persuaded her daughter to go to the phone.

"He is in a strange mood, not like himself at all, just talk to him."

Melissa chatted away, but she was shocked when George, at the end of the call, added, "love you."

Walker tried to phone George to alert him to the fact the Lithuanians may have identified him, finally getting hold of him on the Friday morning. Reasonably enough, George asked how his identification had happened.

"It is possible, "Walker reluctantly admitted, "it may be because of a leak from within the PSNI."

George's reaction amazed him. Instead of complaining and threatening to complain to the Police Ombudsman, the press, political sources, George seemed almost flat. He didn't seem alarmed, giving the impression he felt he could handle the situation. Walker wondered, for a moment, if the MI5 link was true. Maybe he is a latter-day James Bond taking it in his stride.

Walker assured him that when he was informed the gang were travelling north, he would arrange for George to receive police protection.

He then asked, "I could station a couple of men outside your house today?"

George panicked but managed to say in a normal tone.

"No, Inspector, I don't think we need to go overboard with costs to the taxpayer. If you get word, they are coming, that's fine."

George reckoned the gang would be over the border. He did not need the police nearby on the night he hoped to facilitate the execution of the gang members.

Walker made sure he recorded the offer of police protection in the file and George's negative response. 'You never know how that will turn out. The phone call finished after ten o'clock. George sat around the house, getting anxious. Martin Breen arrived at 3.00 pm.

"Where is Liam?" George enquired.

"He will be in position when he needs to be. He will leave the van further down the lane. When we have done what we will do, he will bring the van around the back lane to ensure there are no lights to alert the neighbours."

George marvelled at Martin Breen's matter of fact demeanour for the task ahead but got more anxious as the afternoon wore on.

Breen saw volunteers in the old days become panicky going into action and tried to distract George with tales of his 'operations.' They ate a sandwich lunch, though neither ate much.

Martin insisted George have a couple of whiskeys to relax him.

George's physical capabilities for the night ahead did not worry Martin, as he believed he would be incidental to what would happen.

"It will all be over in less than thirty seconds he told George. If not..."

"If not, what?" George almost wept.

"If not, we will be dead, and we will have nothing to worry us." Hardly a reassuring reply.

The minutes towards seven o'clock dragged on. Twice George felt sick and fled to the downstairs loo but couldn't bring up anything.

Martin Breen disappeared upstairs before six and he either made not a sound or had skipped. No sight nor sound of Liam.

What happened if they both cleared off with their first payment? But why would they have left, or at least why would Martin have returned if they planned to skip? They have their down payment. If Martin hoped to grab the outstanding twenty-eight thousand and leave before the Lithuanians came, he left it a bit late now. All these doubts, emotions, fears tumbled through his mind one after the other.

George had bought a cheap briefcase similar to the one he found with the euros. He filled it with books and carefully stacked the twenty-eight thousand euros across the top. At first sight, the case looked full of cash. He would show it to Arturas, but not let him check it. It would prove a useful diversion when they arrived and enable Martin and Liam to surprise the three men. They would strike four minutes after the gang arrived. This planning a gangland slaying is turning into a piece of cake, George reflected, but could not bring himself to smile at his own black humour.

There was a knocking on his front door at 6.45. George froze. If it was Gerard next door, he would be caught up in a horrific situation. He hadn't bargained on an unexpected visitor. Although his lights were on, he resolved to sit still and hope the unwelcome guest would go away, but the knocking persisted. Plan B was for him to be quite rude and drive the person away no matter who they were. He could always apologise later if there was a 'later'. His rudeness might save their lives.

He opened the door and Arturas and Vito pushed past him.

"Thought we would come early." said Arturas cheerfully.

This time, Vito did not grab him. George walked into the lounge after the two Pakuss' and was not surprised Dimitar was standing in his favourite pose, hands clasped in front of him, gazing at the wall opposite the kitchen door. George remained calm. It was starting to feel similar to the dentists. The hour before you go in is the worst part. Once you hear the drill, you are nearer the end. 'Nearer the end,' that did not sound good.

Both men sat down, Vito on the settee where George joined him, Arturas on 'his' comfortable chair.

"I see you have been decorating." commented Arturas. George adopted a conversational tone to use part of the four minutes.

"I am very impressed by your English."

This pleased Arturas, as he prided himself on speaking English with only a limited accent.

"As a young man, I worked as a waiter in London and then I became a guard on the London Tube, worked in nightclubs and after that I moved to Liverpool."

"What...?" George began, but how could you ask, 'what led you from those normal occupations to become a gangster, killer, drug dealer?' Not a straightforward conversation to continue, but Arturas anticipated him.

"What led to this life, well partly family connections. My brother is a very dominant character and, in many ways, a father to me. Partly I enjoy having a nice car, a nice home and plenty of money."

'How shallow,' thought George, 'you sound just like me,' and that was precisely how he was meant to feel.

Their only difference, George hadn't employed violence. After this night, he would be another Arturas.

Arturas looked at the briefcase.

"Ah, the money is good. There has been a change in conditions. If you give us anything less than half a million euros, Vito gets to," he paused, "play with your little friend Elena. Your children will be left alone, for now."

That explained Vito's smile when he arrived, they guessed he would be light.

George looked at his watch. Three minutes, eight seconds. He needed to keep the Lithuanians occupied for another fifty seconds. George lifted the briefcase and opened it, and Arturas nodded approvingly at the money. Vito leaned over, forty seconds to go and as he leaned over, Vito collapsed on the settee.

It wasn't only Pakus who could use the 'early' trick. Arturas looked up and then to the side as the crash of Dimitar hitting the floor distracted him. He gazed at George; his face wreathed in surprise. He rose from the chair drawing a pistol from his jacket turning towards Martin. The latter stood beside the slumped Vito. George kicked out at Arturas, and both Martin and Liam fired shots into Arturas, who tumbled onto the polythene.

George stood shocked and sickened at the sight in his front room. Thirty seconds earlier, the three men were alive. For all they were bad guys, the hopes and dreams they used to have were gone now. Their families might have loved them, depended on them, whatever. Their lives were gone.

Martin sensed his mood.

"Never forget that could have been you lying lifeless and them packaging you up to dump somewhere."

What would Terry and Melissa think or feel if George disappeared? What would Jan and Elena think or Aileen or Claire if he just disappeared.

Liam broke the contemplation.

“We need to move them quickly or it will be hellish difficult. I will bring the van around the rear. Martin, start wrapping.”

George lifted the Glock, which Martin had laid down, and put it into a drawer in the coffee table between the chair and the settee. He stood frozen as Martin covered Arturas’s body with the sheets of polythene. He spied a heavy lead pipe on the floor and asked what it was for.

“That’s for the other end of this trip,” answered Martin grimly and George realised the bodies were destined for a watery grave.

Liam came back and with even more expertise, finished wrapping Vito and Dimitar. George helped carry the bodies to the van. It was dark, cold, and raining. Nobody was around, too early in the night for people to note an engine being started. The next morning, he heard a brief snippet on the news of a van found burnt out three miles from a remote corner of Lough Neagh.

George took the men’s money from the briefcase, ensuring they could see nothing remained inside and said, not altogether convincingly,

“My guys will be impressed with what you have done.”

Martin searched Arturas’s jacket, removing, as George noted, his wallet and pocketing it. He came across keys for an Audi car. Liam went out to find the Lithuanian’s car. He located it several streets away.

Martin grinned. He gained a nice car, although the number plates would have to be changed.

"Liam and I need to move quick."

George didn't ask where they were going, and they didn't enlighten him. He hoped he would see neither one again.

Chief Superintendent O'Connell got a message to Walker to phone him urgently just before 10.00 pm.

"Alan, I have just been advised that Arturas, Vito and the Bulgarian crossed the Border this afternoon at 2.00 pm. Anything your end?"

Walker said, "Not much, we waded through the CCTV for a number of weeks and a week earlier various sightings of the Audi you mentioned were seen in West Belfast which we expected but also South and North Belfast which seems really odd, as if they were scouting those areas.

John pointed out McNeill's kids live in South Belfast and his Belgian friends in the North of the city, but we don't know for sure what they were doing. "

Farrell, after digging around, found that the house George McNeill lived in now belonged to, or once belonged to, Paddy McCann. He hesitated to mention the word 'coincidence' to his boss given the growing tension, but it was in his head. There may have been a sale of the house recently, but the paperwork had not come through from McCann's solicitor in Dublin, so that was less clear. According to the person in the records office, these matters take time.

George went to bed; exhausted at first, he couldn't sleep as his mind ran through the horrors of the evening. If you add the killings of

Paddy McCann's wife and daughter, a 'house of death'. For the first time, George contemplated selling his 'home for life.' Finally, he fell into a deep sleep that lasted through to almost ten o'clock. He got up, showered, prepared a breakfast, which he could barely eat, and reluctantly went into the lounge. It was tidy, apart from a small amount of polythene covering on the carpet and a half-painted wall.

He looked in the drawer of the coffee table. The Glock was there. Behind the settee lay a discarded briefcase full of books.

No time to linger; he needed to get to the Ormeau Park for Terry's game at eleven o'clock. For a gangland mastermind, his was a low profile on a normal weekend. He would be with his children, then coffee with Claire and finally the Tielemans for tea. Elena was coming home specially. They wanted a proper catch up about the Boxing Night event. Gosh, so much happened since then. Life was normal, well, normal bad dream as opposed to new nightmare.

George drove to Terry's game, still reeling from all that had happened. They met Melissa after the game for a Mac Donald's lunch. George was the typical single dad: watching his son's football game, taking son and daughter to MacDonald's and meeting an attractive female friend for coffee. It is the sort of thing any gangland boss who commissioned three executions might do. More and more, George felt that weekend he was starring in his own episode of the Sopranos.

George met Claire for a coffee in the city centre. He was pleased when she gave him a peck on the cheek, and he felt she was glad to see him. He resolved not to pry into the education adviser and Claire already decided she would not mention Aileen Whyte.

They stuck to their scripts.

"How are Terry and Melissa doing?"

"They are good at the moment. How is your sister and wee Karen… and of course Mandy?"

It was Mandy who told Claire Peter Donald was unhappy with his trip to London but that got too close to Aileen; so, he steered away from it. Claire's job, without mentioning Education Advisers, became the main topic of their conversation. George shared his experiences and new role in Glasgow. He accepted a job at a level he hadn't operated at before. Could it all be too much for him, she wondered? He acted friendly, interested and nice, but also distracted and she was certain it wasn't his family or that woman Whyte that troubled him. What else preoccupied him? Every so often she glimpsed a faraway, sad expression, a reflection of his soul. Something inside was deeply troubling George.

She wanted to encourage him to share it, but she wasn't sure if, deep down, that was a good idea.

Last night's killings kept intruding on George. How could they not? He made efforts to banish the thoughts and tried to sound upbeat and friendly. He realised that if Claire was part of his life, regardless of the Aileen complexity, she would be drawn into the Shaftsbury Square events. Also, last night's if they surfaced, 'no pun intended', he reprimanded himself. He was less concerned of the outcome's impact on Aileen. She would hate him for casting a cloud on her political ambitions, but she was a tougher character and being Aileen could turn it to her advantage. There would be those with influence who would assist her with that.

He knew Claire could be called to give evidence and it would lead to a media frenzy, headlines, 'gangster killer's moll' and with accompanying newspaper pictures. Also, 'the girlfriend of gangster killer George McNeill is called to give evidence today...' She did not deserve that. Mandy would have loved it.

Claire thought long and hard about George and tried to understand her feelings for him. She went out with Colin but couldn't banish George from her thoughts. She decided she liked him from the first morning. Claire liked the way he talked and how he laughed when he mentioned Mandy, never maliciously. Embarrassed at his own weakness but not brought down by it. Despite her initial reservations, she enjoyed the party at the Tielemans. Jan and Elena were lovely and so fond of George. He must be pretty worthwhile with such friends. So nice and so devoted to him.

The Charity Dinner was different. She felt she was moving to a different stage in their brief relationship, publicly his partner and then Aileen Whyte got her claws in. The night they spent together meant something, but for the first time this afternoon she caught that far away silhouette in his eyes, it grew and almost enveloped him.

George returned to Riverdale having done the grocery shopping for the weekend. Gerard was moving a garden bin to prepare to start spring pruning and called jovially

"Did you have a party last night?"

George smiled weakly, "Ah, guys from my old office were passing."

He hoped Gerard hadn't realised including Martin and Liam there were five men, an odd party and none left by the front door. There was a message flashing on his answer phone. It was Aileen.

"Hi, we didn't confirm the venue for the drink," she said brightly, "I will come over to yours later. I want to see the new house."

He looked at his watch, ten to seven. How many times had he wanted to see Aileen, and for various reasons, she couldn't make it? He occasionally fantasised she might pop in after a constituency meeting and surprise him. They would have a passionate night in his bed. Now he felt sick to his stomach. He didn't want her to see him in this state or even to be in this 'tainted' house. Now too late to cancel and Aileen arrived shortly afterwards.

"Have you eaten?" George asked and fortunately the answer was yes. He didn't feel like food.

Westminster and the girls were the main subject of their conversation, then they watched TV. George opened a bottle of wine, and Aileen surprised him by initiating physical contact. He wasn't a big wine drinker. Aileen said she could stay.

This aroused him as did the fact that she must have planned it. Eventually, they ended up making love in his bedroom. 'Isn't it funny when your dearest dream comes to pass how other events can spoil it.'

It wasn't to be the passion of their first or their second London coupling, but it was satisfying, caressing her smooth skin, kissing her passionately and her responses.

Aileen knew he was dipping in and out, one minute there. Another far away.

"There is something on your mind George. What?"

"Not really."

Aileen was rarely this involved in George's world, but she sensed his distraction and responded.

For a fraction of a second, he longed to tell her. With her connections, she might find a way out.

‘Well, just last night, down in the room we were sitting in I had these three guys shot, rolled them in polythene sheeting and ‘my gang’ disposed of their bodies, apart from that not a lot going on,’ but he knew he was kidding himself. He attempted to surmount his guilt feelings, reminding himself what would have happened if the gang hadn’t been taken out. Eventually, they both fell into a deep sleep. Aileen woke him around 7.00 am.

“I have to pick up the girls and take them to church,” Seeing the look on his face she added, “It’s expected.”

As she drove off, Aileen wondered if the Glasgow responsibility was too much for George. She pushed behind the scenes for him to have the role

Chapter 10

Death Revisits Riverdale

As February became March, George believed that the elimination of Arturas, Vito and Demitar really signalled an end to this chaotic period in his life. He phoned Aileen the week after their night in Riverdale; she was curiously distant and apologised but had to cut the call short. George felt a bit dismissed but later in the day, when he thought about it, oddly relieved, though he couldn't fathom out why.

He went up to Donegal and was irritated by the lack of progress. George felt it was time to act, and he made it clear that he would seek another builder and current bills would not be paid unless the work was done within four weeks. The laid-back Irish builder and his friends were surprised at the change in George. In true builder fashion, they had taken on a lot of work as if balancing plates and did a little here and a little there. George had seemed quite amenable to the slow pace before, but this was like a bad tempered and 'tough' twin brother had turned up. Of course, they could remind him the price and the timeline were linked and previously he had agreed with that, but after further discussion, no one felt like taking him on. It was agreed to avoid further conflict with the mad city guy work on the cottage would continue apace.

George drove off in grim humour. He had the thought that if they gave him grief, he would bring Martin and Liam up to 'lean' on them. When his anger subsided, two thoughts occurred to him. He was not angry at them, but the killings were impacting on him and, his notion to bring Martin and Liam in was the typical response of a bullying gang leader who was frustrated. Neither thought was much comfort to him. He thought of other times he had hinted at a gangster role, with

'Honest Sean' the car dealer, with Eric Grimshaw over the small house, and even with Hamish. 'What have I become?'

O'Connell phoned Walker with bad news.

"Artur Pakus has not been seen around for a while. We have heard from Interpol that they had a whisper that Andrius Pakus is concerned at not having heard from his brother recently and if there is no word in the next week, he will come over to Ireland. He came over once before to repatriate Fedor's body to Lithuania. He was irritated at the bit about you guys bringing it to the Border and then a new police involvement from there to Dublin airport. I don't think Irish history is his strong point," he chuckled, but then became very serious,

"I phoned Yuri. He didn't know about this, but he said we should not underestimate this man's propensity for violence."

'Why bring Yuri into it, he has enough intelligence?' Walker thought

Given the news from Dublin, Walker ordered surveillance on the house in Riverdale. A car stuck in the vicinity would stand out. In Belfast, a strange-looking car in a street always leads to neighbour unease and frequent calls to the security forces, especially a car with two men in it.

Fortunately, there was a solution near at hand. A member of the police support staff who lived in Riverdale worked in the Lisburn Road station; Walker had previously decided not to ask her to spy on her neighbour, but now he sent for her.

She was told there was concern for a neighbour, she could mention this to no one. She was asked if two officers could be stationed in a front upstairs room three nights a week and warily, she asked about the nature of the concern.

Truthfully, well up to a point, Walker told her the officers would be there to protect him rather than him being a major criminal target. Further, he himself posed no danger to any of the neighbours. She had to tell her husband, a teacher, so of course he complained about every aspect. Walker rolled his eyes. The world would be less complicated without teachers, a Mao Tse Tung moment. Robertson moaned about the budget, but Walker countered, "He is only in Belfast from a Thursday to a Sunday night or a Friday to a Monday night, and this is about to break. Don't forget we have two dead bodies and three foreign nationals missing on our turf."

Life in Dublin for Paddy McCann went on much as before. He contemplated improving his small flat or swopping it for a large one. He really wanted the proceeds from his house to benefit his son and grandchildren. He spent about three months a year in New Jersey, something he simply existed for. He had no other interests and only one close friend, Joseph (Joe) Higgins. He first met Higgins on an operation near the Border in the early eighties. They had to shoot their way out of an ambush by the Security Forces, relationships forged under fire. A couple of years later, the man had taken a considerable risk in attending Deirdre and Orla McCann's funerals. The two men had embraced at the graveside. They also 'starred' in a much-watched video made by the Security Forces, given the prominent IRA men who also attended. Only the presence of a very large and angry crowd prevented arrests being made.

Paddy and Joe met at least once a week for a drink, occasionally for a meal when McCann was in Ireland. He got to meet Joe's boys and grew fond of them as they got older. The eldest Joe Jnr was the image of his father. Tall, square jawed, bright blue eyes smiled a lot. He played Gaelic football, 'with more enthusiasm than skill,' his father intimated.

He had an appalling disciplinary record and was continually in trouble for fighting on and off the pitch. "Far too handy with his fists," according to his father.

Joe Jnr had completed his apprenticeship as an electrician, "I stay well in with him," said his dad. "He is the only one of us who is going to be rich."

The middle boy Rory was as quiet as his brother was verbose, 'He is the thinker in the family, the only one with brains according to his mother, apart from her of course.'

He was at college and had one year to go of his teacher training course.

"Yes, he will soon be let loose to propagate and nourish young Irish minds and take them into the 21 st century."

The youngest boy, Artie, was the apple of his mother's eye. His favoured status there protected him from chastisement from his older brothers. When he was young, "I'll tell mammy." could lead to swift retribution. Aged fourteen, he experimented with drugs, starting with glue, then various other addictive substances. Rory discovered this through the brother of a friend of Artie. He and Joe Jnr wreaked havoc on a few youngish dealers, so no one was inclined to offer Artie fixes. The parents got involved and eventually Artie was turned off substances. He currently had no settled work, but Joe brought him into the firm in a manual capacity to toughen him up.

At the Glasgow office over a period of weeks, George made a point of seeing each accountant on their own. When he told Sandy about this he groaned and said, "They will think that if they get rid of me, everything will be fine."

George encouraged the staff to chat about their work, speculate about what areas they felt the firm could branch into, what they were doing wrong, what they could do better, what they hoped the acquisition by Baileys might bring. The sum total of all this was that most thought they were unappreciated, they felt they should be paid more, they should have more annual leave and the firm should do more to improve morale.

Without using the exact words, their hope was that Baileys would get rid of Sandy Burney. Twice someone referred to him as 'Wee Burnie'. Sandy wasn't that small, but George realised much later it was a reference to a character in a Scottish TV show and it wasn't complimentary. He had to put up with a host of slights from Sandy, little digs.

"Well, you wouldn't know this but in Glasgow…" or Sandy not coming to meetings or arriving late or having to leave early to "deal with urgent firm business."

Other staff were surprised how George took this so calmly and in such an unruffled manner. Would he at least have Sandy in for a 'quiet word?'

Laura thought 'Sandy is weak and lazy and lacking interest in the firm or the staff or the clients.' She wondered if George was the same.

He left Laura until last.

"I think something big is brewing," she told her partner Cat. Glasgow was going through a period when it was cool for all females to be called 'Cat'.

"Initially, I thought he should see me first. It would save him a lot of time, but from what I hear from Belfast, our Mr McNeill might be more to reckon with than he seems."

George began his conversation with Laura a month after he first started and ran his list of questions past her. One by one she responded,

"Why do you want to know that it is not important?"

George sighed, "Well, what do you think is important?"

Laura launched into it.

"This has been a dysfunctional firm for years. The Board that you guys bought out was old and disinterested in anything except the bottom line. Sandy has run the firm, generated minimum profits keeping a weather eye on the Board. They never asked about the turnover in staff, why we had prestigious offices and antiquated IT, why we didn't win contracts we should have because Sandy isn't highly thought of. You guys coming in means a chance for a real leap forward if the dead wood is removed. Freya, for instance, who just flutters her eyes around Sandy, does the minimum of work, and carries stories back. In fact, I think..."

George interrupted; he had a sense where this line was going.

"Tell me about the contracts we should have won, tell me about our rivals, in fact could you do me a report, for my eyes only."

Laura hesitated, more work for her, but George was going to act. And said, "OK."

Laura's verbal assessment had come as a bit of a rush, but her report was succinct, appropriately detailed and while she didn't make recommendations, what she did was give George both history and substance to his own impressions. They met off site at the offices of a friend of Laura's. Meticulously, he went through her report in detail. Laura was exhausted by the end of the day.

His relationship with Sandy deteriorated. Several times, things came up Sandy hadn't bothered to tell George about. He let the first one go, but after a call from Belfast about an invoice for over eight hundred pounds, George called Sandy in.

"Look, Sandy, Accounts have been on about this invoice. I look daft because I don't know about it."

Sandy looked sullenly at the top of George's desk. "I am not used to having to go to someone else about expenditure, anything below ten thousand pounds was dealt with by me. Above that it went to the Board."

George was astounded, Baileys just didn't work that way. Sandy added,

"It's been fine that way." Implying he didn't intend to change the practice just because you are here. Sandy was pleased that he had taken a stand against George.

"Sandy, Belfast will not pay any invoice that I have not authorised. If you fail to get my approval, you can explain to the creditor, they won't get paid. That's all."

He saw the hostility in Sandy's eyes, and he bent to continue reading the file in front of him. The truce, such as it was, was over.

Laura invited George up to her flat in the West End for a meal and to meet Cat. It was a gamble on Laura's part If she hadn't been gay, he would have been suspicious as he was of Freya. The junior accountant suggested to George, "If you are fed up on your own in the flat, I could meet you for a drink after work."

George couldn't work Cat out. She seemed even more strong willed, even 'bolshier' than Laura. The conversation between George and Cat was odd, Laura thought. She wondered if they were competing for her attention like two siblings, but Cat could hardly hide her irritation. Finally, after one more 'look', Cat retired to bed and Laura and George finished the business analysis.

Later Laura asked Cat.

"Well, what did you think of him?"

"As you well know, I think all men are a total waste of whatever went into creating them," she paused, "well except my dad and my brother, sometimes. But I could cheerfully have got hold of him and throttled him. Talk about no sense of humour, no conversation, no sense of fun. I mean, do you think he has ever done anything in his life, been with anybody? What about this glamorous MP girlfriend? Is there any truth in that? I think he was kept in a cupboard for twenty years and just brought out for this," Cat stopped, exhausted.

"I think you scared the life out of him. That is the way he was when he first came to the office. He grows on you. He has two kids and I keep going back to what I now hear about him from my pal in Belfast." summarised Laura.

Baileys Partners had fallen back from their regular updates with George since not much changed on a week-by-week basis. He did a formal report at the end of March incorporating much of Laura's detail and met with them. His recommendation was clear; several people had to leave the firm, including Sandy. Baileys needed to bring their own person in and restructure the management to bring more oversight to each department. They had to consider whether the expensive City Centre offices generated enough profit to sustain. They needed also to strengthen the previously tenuous link with Baileys in Belfast. George was glad he had worked so hard on Laura's information as Cyril put him through the mill, but he was prepared. Cyril knew he was fighting for his diversification strategy. Some around the table felt that it was too much trouble. George tried to draw a parallel with the Glasgow Board of McIntyre and Matheson that neglected the business and their own investment. He said, “diversify, expand or die.” Music to Cyril’s ears.

Peter Donald thought to himself, what wasted years, if only George had been drawn out. He was much more capable than any of them realised.

Mind you, stealing astronomical sums of money and having a few folks assassinated brings out the capacity in the quieter folk.

George felt he couldn’t get too close to the staff socially. The major topic would be, “What’s happening?” and there was enough of that around the office.

They noticed how relaxed he was with Laura and Sandy was incensed about that as the relationship between them was so poor and his relationship with George was deteriorating fast. Cat had accused Laura of staying at the firm only because leaving would mean Sandy had won.

George enjoyed Glasgow. He visited the Kelvingrove museum, and he longed to go further north, even to the Islands, but the cold and the damp made it unattractive.

He went through to Edinburgh a few times. Their dad brought both Terry and Melissa over twice and for the first time since he was about two, Terry shared a bed with his dad; they were equally uncomfortable.

He arranged for one of the younger accountants, James, to take Terry to ‘Firhill for thrills’, which wasn’t quite Celtic or Rangers, but Terry enjoyed the Glasgow patter and the deprecatory way the Glaswegians viewed their team.

The deal with Melissa was endless forays into Buchanan Street. They would have lunch. His credit card was taking a bit of a hammering, but he felt his relationship with Melissa was improving.

He telephoned Claire most Tuesday nights. They hadn't met since the afternoon in Belfast, and George had not made contact for a couple of weeks afterwards. Then, on an impulse one evening in Glasgow, he phoned her for a chat. Claire was confused. She was certain George liked her and wanted a relationship, but then he would disappear for a while and when she was getting used to his having dropped out of her life, he called again. They had pleasant chats about his work, her school, family things. However, when George came over at the weekends, he did not meet with her and that rankled.

She knew it couldn't just go on like this. So, on the next call, Claire took control.

"George, I find it upsetting that you pop into my life and then disappear for weeks. It can't go on like this."

"It's just, if you had a chance of a relationship with someone less complicated than me, I wanted to step back, but then I really miss you and want to hear your voice again."

Claire considered this.

"Is your complication, Aileen Whyte?" she said softly.

It was an important moment. Previously George had been secretive, obfuscating about his relationship with the MP. This was not the moment to deflect or brush the topic away.

"I haven't seen Aileen for a while."

In making that statement, he knew he was actually telling himself there was no future for Aileen and him. How could there be? He didn't want to be in her world. She was like a desirable but unobtainable female fantasy. Aileen treated him like he treated Claire.

It was time to face up. Which was the relationship he really wanted to invest in? If he sought to develop a relationship with Claire, he was drawing her into troublesome issues he might have to confront. He decided he should share some facts so that she could make an informed choice.

"Look, we need to talk this over. Why don't you come to Glasgow for the mid-term long weekend?"

Claire had visited Edinburgh with her sister a couple of times but had been only fleetingly in Glasgow. They agreed the date and George told Terry he wouldn't be in Belfast that weekend.

George met Claire at the airport. She had a 'dinky' little overnight case, as he described it, and was genuinely pleased to see him. She needed to progress this one way or the other and she felt her uncertainty was receding the more time she was in George's company. She was sure Aileen Whyte was almost out of George's system and she felt he wasn't trying to play both women off against each other. She did briefly wonder if Aileen knew that her relationship with George was changing or about to change. She liked George's temporary home in the traditional tenement behind the Mitchell Library, very convenient to the City Centre.

They had a typical day of a couple, meals out and in, shopping, cinema and walks in Kelvingrove Park. For George, it was the most relaxed period he had ever shared with another person.

Laura invited them for a meal to her and Cat's flat in the West End. George had never been in a social situation with a single sex couple.

In fact, it had been years since he had been in any situation either as part of a couple or with another couple, except the Tielemans.

Claire laughed at him when he admitted it was ‘just like spending time with any other couple.’

It brought back memories of when he and Irene used to go out with other couples or have them to dinner when the children were young. George was so quiet everyone commented on it which made him retreat further.

He did not mention work, though Cat did before she got the ‘look.’

He knew he was developing a working relationship with Laura as a colleague, and he treated her differently from the other folk at work. At first, he tried to avoid that, but rationalised Laura was the first person who had been positive to him when he arrived.

He was already thinking through plans for her in the new scheme of things. Cat was growing on him. Even more forthright than Laura, she said what she thought immediately and with no thought to hold back or gently ‘suss’ out what was going on or might go pear-shaped. He was surprised to hear that Cat was a social worker, not what he imagined about....er social workers, lesbians, people called Cat. As for Laura and Cat, they really liked Claire but wondered, where was the MP?

When Claire went back to Belfast, he missed her around the flat, her laugh, the way she had rearranged the soft furnishings and the love they made every night and some mornings as well. He decided he had to act. Of course, being George, he put it off. She agreed to come back in two weeks. He knew he had to tell her something about what had happened since August, gosh was it only eight months.

He said that when she came back in two weeks, he would share things with her that he hoped might help explain his behaviour.

“I know what you are worried about,” He was thinking of his relationship with Aileen, “But they are small fry compared to what is actually going on in my life. “

Claire had not pressed him. She knew he had almost decided to confide, but he still had a bit of a way to travel. Sometimes she felt like shaking him. Her mind was a whirlwind of what these other things could be. If they were not about a woman, she reassured herself they can’t be important, not things she couldn’t handle. Her last guess was that George might move permanently to Scotland. Now that would be a challenge.

Whatever he told her George knew could put her in danger, or at least at risk of having to face the authorities. He needed to be very careful and say just enough to explain his mysterious side, but so little it would not make her vulnerable.

He felt tired often. The constant commute from Glasgow, the new job, and the strain of the Pakus killings led to sleepless nights and constant worry. He had previously lived his life avoiding stress. His initial good fortune had turned on its head and he knew he was not programmed to handle all the burdens that accompanied his actions. He was having doubts about his future with Claire, partly because he feared he could put her in danger, but he also he wondered if she was really interested in him. They were involved in this dance, first one came forward, then backed off and then the other repeated the pattern. He couldn’t see that her distancing was a response to the messages he was sending out. As a result, neither was taking the relationship to its next stage.

In Glasgow, matters with Sandy Burney had deteriorated further. The Scotsman could scarcely offer a civilised word to George, who understood the problem was the lack of decision making from the Baileys end coupled with uncertainty about Sandy's own future. Although at first the atmosphere was welcomed by other staff as it kept Burney out of their hair, eventually the becalmed state impacted on everyone. 'No-man's-land' is not an attractive working environment. Laura pleaded with George to get a decision from Belfast, "before we lose good people."

At the beginning of May, the Partners invited George in for one of increasingly infrequent briefings. It was in response to his incessant emailing and calls that Glasgow was at a tipping point and was 'drifting.' They had the presentation in the 'Board Room', an inner sanctum that was rarely seen by any employees except the partners and a few administrative staff who, for various reasons, had to go in.

George settled himself at the end of the table with Peter in 'the chair,' in Andrews's absence, and all the Partners in their appointed seats. He thought how odd the smell was of this musty, too infrequently used room. Typical Baileys, it was for senior people only. If a member of staff had a meeting and all the meeting rooms were booked, they had to practically crawl on their hands and knees to a Partner to get permission to use it. At the end of the meeting, which as usual appeared not to be reaching any significant conclusion, he was surprised when Cyril coughed and pronounced:

"George, we would like you to take on the role of managing the Glasgow operation. It will be a fixed term two-year contract to get it sorted out and teed up for a more permanent arrangement. We will be guided by you how that should unfold."

"Will you want me there five days a week?" George asked.

"Yes, we appreciate you have things to tie up here but four days for the first three months and five days thereafter."

George accepted the responsibility, not as well paid as his consultancy, but pretty well paid and more secure. He had no need of the Euros now. The rent from his property was also boosting his bank balance. It was increasingly apparent the Partners were accepting his analysis, but this meeting had started out similarly to many others. The appearance of an important decision at the end, with no preamble, was so 'Baileys.' George was confident he knew enough about the Glasgow end of the business and, as for the Belfast end, he was Baileys through and through.

"He was not only the best choice but probably the only one, even Cyril agrees," Peter said to the still doubting Walter Andrews.

"I don't know if he has shed a layer or added one, but he is not the same man."

The latter finally gave his assent.

"I don't doubt his loyalty or even his willingness, just his capability. I admit his report was very good. I hope he has a person with actual ability at the Glasgow end."

Andrews didn't tell Peter that Aileen Whyte had been lobbying for his appointment for a while.

By mid-May, the days were getting longer and warmer and George believed he was through the worst. He felt that a little more time between the killings, and they would recede. George was determined things should go back to how they used to be. He would rent out Riverdale and move to Glasgow. He would miss a good neighbour like Gerard but less so that woman from across the street who initially was friendly with a wave if she was driving or a cheerful "Good morning" but now seemed to look the other way when she saw him.

George could use the Donegal cottage as a bolt hole, although it would not be convenient. He needed to get Terry and Melissa used to the arrangement that occasional weekends, he would stay in Glasgow.

Breen had disappeared. He hadn't been near Riverdale for two weeks after the shootings when he did a little gardening. Even Gerard commented on his absence. George was relieved he could get another person for the garden. In fact, if he never saw Martin Breen again, it would be fine by him.

This Saturday had been quieter than usual. Jan and George had gone out for a meal to plan a visit the following weekend to Donegal where there was progress on the cottage and George wanted to show it to Jan.

He had also told David about his 'bolt hole, so much for keeping it secret and he and Moira were keen to have a week there in the Summer.

"It's a promise," said George. It was a fairly normal conversation between brothers and normality was what he craved.

George had been 'patched ' by Terry and Melissa. They had gone to Dublin for the weekend with Irene and her new 'man'. He told them in two weeks' time he was staying the weekend in Glasgow. He did not tell them about Claire coming over.

In fact, he had never mentioned her to them, although their mother had shown them a picture from the paper of George, Claire, and the Chief Constable.

His ex-wife musing, incredulously.

"Has your father got a new young girlfriend?"

Children are really put off by the thought of their parents having relationships and neither paid much attention. Elena had phoned Jan to say she had three parties that she 'had' to attend over the weekend and wouldn't be home. Jan suggested her latest boyfriend might be more serious than previous ones, so George had to counsel him through that. They went home about eight thirty pm.

About 9.00 pm, he settled down to watch television when there was a tremendous crash on the front door.

It gave George quite a start, and he heard aggressive shouting and then more blows being rained on the door. He dived into the coffee table drawer and took out the Glock 19 pistol, a 9 mm Lugar favoured by the Metropolitan police, as he had subsequently found out after the shooting of Arturas, Vito, and Dietmar. Sensibly, George removed the magazine from the pistol. He did not want an accidental shooting of whoever the party was at the door. George hoped the sight of the gun would deter them. He hurried down the hall as the blows continued on the door and he flung it open. A figure hurled himself on George, they were eyeball to eyeball, and the Glock was knocked from his hand onto the hall floor. It was Martin Breen.

Across the road, the surveillance team had come on for their usual 6.00 pm to midnight Fri to Sunday shift. The officers heard the shouting and banging and reacted immediately. They phoned Walker but couldn't reach him. They then tried Farrell and also failed to contact him. In that event, their instruction was to contact the duty inspector. They explained at least one figure they could barely see was trying violently to break into the Riverdale property.

"Is he armed?" the inspector asked.

"We can't see." the officers replied. A decision was needed.

The orders are to protect the resident, so the inspector instructed them.

"Approach the property with your weapons ready but give loud and clear warning about who you are, that you are armed and instruct those inside to come out."

Both officers hurried down the stairs, across the street, drawing their weapons.

George fell back against the wall in the struggle and Breen lifted the Glock from the floor. His eyes were wide, pupils dilated. George's initial thought was he was drunk but could not smell alcohol when they were up close, and then thought Breen was on substances. He was hysterical, demanding 'the money.' He couldn't or wouldn't explain why he was in such a state and acting so aggressively.

He ran into the lounge and George got to his feet and, without closing the door, followed him, speaking softly and in a placatory tone.

"Martin, Martin, calm down. There is no money here. What has happened?"

They faced each other in the lounge, and Breen steadied himself then said.

"I know you have money here; I need it now."

As he finished, there was a shout.

"THIS IS THE POLICE. In the house, come out with your hands up. WE ARE ARMED OFFICERS, throw any weapons out first."

“You bastard,” Breen said accusingly at George, “Working with the fucking peelers now,” and he ran back down the hall towards the open door with the pistol in his hand, swearing aggressively as he went.

George followed him, taking the magazine out of his pocket, and waving it at Breen’s back,

“There is no ammunition in the gun Martin, STOP.”

Breen was about three yards through the front door when he was instructed by Officer A at the top of his voice.

“THIS IS A FINAL WARNING, DROP THE GUN.”

Breen stopped, weapon still raised, and turned around, trying to make sense of George’s shout about the ammunition.

In his statement later to the enquiry, Officer A said.

“The gunman then turned around to shoot McNeill, so I fired twice.”

The second officer, Officer B. was side on at the door and in his statement, he recorded that he “I couldn’t see the second man but when he came out of the house, I launched myself upon him knocking him to the ground.”

As George went through the door, he saw Breen on the path in front of him turning to face him with his weapon raised, George tried to put his hand up to his face but then was knocked violently sideways. He thought it was the force of a bullet, but of course, the gun was empty except for one bullet in the mechanism’s chamber, although he didn’t know about that. As he fell down, the magazine fell from his hand onto a flower bed. Officer B instructed him to remain still on the ground.

Other cops arrived and officer B recognised George and helped him to his feet. As he was getting to his feet, George lifted the magazine up and handed it to the police officer who bagged it.

George's abiding memory, as the police took him away, was of Gerard's shocked expression as he stood in his garden, having seen the whole incident.

He had been attracted out by Martin Breen's initial violent knocking on the door and the entire event was reminiscent of a very traumatic experience almost twenty years previously.

George was taken to the Royal Victoria Hospital to be checked over. The officers said Inspector Walker wanted to see him if he felt up to it. As they waited for the Doctor and then on the way to the Police station, George wondered how he should play it. If they cautioned him, should he ask for a solicitor, if they just pretended, they wanted an informal chat again should he demand a solicitor.

He might be connected to two crimes, at least. The disappearance of the money and the deaths of the two men in Shaftsbury Square. The gun the police had, when forensically tested, would reveal it killed Fedor Pakus. They needed to complete the jigsaw by finding out how Breen fitted into the Shaftsbury Square incident. Was he in or near there on the day Fedor and Quinn died, and if so in what role? The next part of the equation was how Breen and George were linked to the three disappeared men. George felt his best tactic was to stay on the fringes and not provoke closer inspection by increasing suspicion about himself.

Later, in Lisburn Road Police station, he was interviewed by Inspector Walker and Sergeant Farrell.

“Mr McNeill,” began Walker, “we need to establish the details of the events this evening. I have a copy of your statement in front of me. Do you mind if we record this? “

George nodded his assent.

“You say your only knowledge of the deceased,” he emphasised deceased, “was that he volunteered to act as your gardener shortly after you moved into the house, and you paid him accordingly.”

George listened carefully. If they knew anything Walker would add, “and in Euros” but Walker moved on.

“You bought the house from a Paddy McCann. Had you known Mr McCann long?”

“No, I only got in contact with him through my next-door neighbour. I came across the house quite by accident.”

Walker gave Farrell a ‘check this out’ look. Farrell nodded. Both statements about the house and Breen were of course true, but in view of the subsequent incidents, neither policeman believed him.

He knew Paddy McCann had nothing to do with this and he could try to object about him being brought into it but in truth; he didn’t mind them pursuing that strategy.

It kept them away from other narratives, such as, had he hired Martin Breen to eliminate three missing European drug dealers, or had he stolen half a million Euros in a briefcase they thankfully knew nothing about. George thought about Breen. ‘Poor Martin, it had all gone so grievously wrong for him.’ He didn’t know what had triggered the drug fuelled incident, but Martin paid for it with his life. Walker cleared his throat, back to the ‘interrogation.’

George remembered Breen saying, on one of the drinks evenings, that if volunteers, whoever volunteers were, were taken in for questioning by the Security Forces to avoid giving anything away they should refuse to speak and focus on something in the interrogation room. These might range from a crack in the wall or the ceiling, a piece of equipment or furniture, anything other than engaging with their interrogators.

Almost sub-consciously he stared at a crack in the wall above Walker's head. Walker noted first the silence as George mused about 'the deceased' and then the avoidance technique. Farrell recognised it too, not MI5 then IRA, hmm.

Farrell, "So your gardener knocked loudly on your door, and you let him in. When did you notice he had a gun in his hand?"

"Only when he came into the house," that was vaguely true. Before that George had the gun.

"So why do you think he came to your house? "

"I do not know; I thought the poor guy was out of his head on drugs, but I do not know why."

"Just while we are here, Mr McNeill, if you recall many weeks ago, I warned you that a team from this Lithuanian drug cartel had identified you?"

George nodded. Walker continued.

"We know they actually came to Belfast about that time. Did you have any contact with them? Do you know where they are?"

George answered the second question.

“No, I have no idea where they are. Look, I am not aware I have done anything illegal. I am exhausted by this evening’s events and upset by them. Can I go home now?”

Walker knew it was a challenge to charge George, but with what?

Being the victim of an ex-IRA man out of his head on drugs or living in a house that attracted death. Although they knew about only two shootings, the third had still to come to the ‘surface.’

“Of course, you must be exhausted. I will have you run home, but please be aware the leader of the Lithuanian team in Ireland has a brother, Andrius. Interpol has described him as ‘a vicious and very violent criminal. His brother Arturas is the ‘less violent’ of the two. We believe Andrius is coming to Ireland. We have stationed a couple of officers outside your house. Thank you for all your cooperation.”

As George left, he could not help reflecting that the words ‘less violent’ were not what immediately jumped to mind in his experience of Arturas.

Walker went down to the incident room. ‘Mc Neill in Shaftesbury Square when the two men were killed, coincidence? McNeill buying an expensive car shortly after a large sum of money disappeared, coincidence? McNeill later buying a house, with what? A coincidence? McNeill suddenly friendly with an MP and a Government Minister? The gun that killed one of the men found in McNeill’s house, coincidence? Members of a drug cartel who are interested in McNeill disappeared near his house, coincidence? A key witness killed at McNeill’s house, coincidence? Too many coincidences and I don’t believe in coincidences.’

George was driven home. He was glad there were a couple of cops outside the house. He did not fancy a meeting with the ‘serious and violent criminal.’ His brother was bad enough.

Knowing his current run of luck, Liam would turn up too, although even Martin said he had not seen Liam since the killing of the three men and did not know where he was. He nodded at the two cops and as he went up the drive, noticed a light on in Gerard's house. On an impulse, he retraced his steps and knocked softly on Gerard's door.

Gerard came to the door. "George, is everything OK?"

He brought George in, and Grace made coffee.

"Oh, Gerard, it was awful. Martin Breen came to the house under the influence of drugs. He started to break in. You warned me about him."

Gerard nodded as if to say. 'If only you had listened to me.'

"Then, fortunately for me, there were two police officers passing,"

'I wonder, was that a coincidence,' thought George to himself.

"They tried to detain him, and he pulled a gun and was shot dead, poor man."

Gerard was horrified. He thought to himself, that house must be cursed.

"Well," said George, "I just thought I should tell you not to worry. There are a couple of cops outside the house, but I think whatever Martin Breen was doing, he was doing it on his own."

George went back to his own house, did not even undress but collapsed into a sleep interrupted by gun battles, mostly involving Arturas and Martin with a sprinkling of other characters, even Sandy Burney, thrown in.

George woke from time to time thinking of Breen, Arturas, Vito, but never Deitmar. He could not face his complicity in what had happened to them. He sought refuge in thinking it was to save those he loved, but it was a cold comfort.

Across the street an apoplectic teacher was ranting at this wife.

"You brought those police in here, the staff room will go 'ape' on Monday."

His wife looked at him coolly. Really, when he went into teacher mode at home, he could be quite irrational."

"The staff room won't say a word, and do you know why?"

Vigorous head shaking from her spouse, the concept of not telling the staff room was too difficult to bear.

"Because they won't know we have any involvement. The police will state they had the guy who broke into Mr McNeill's house under surveillance by two cops. None of the neighbours will have noticed the cops came out of our house. They will be too wound up in what happened afterwards to notice or to have retained that and you will never ever mention it to anyone. If it leaked out that you were the source of disclosing police information, you could be charged. Remember the form we signed and?" As an afterthought she added,

"I would divorce you. Now come to bed."

She held out her arms and smiled. He nodded, not convinced.

Two days later, Robertson, Walker, and Farrell reviewed the latest developments.

"There will be an investigation into this guy Breen's death. Tell me our guys are squeaky clean."

"Yes," said Walker to Robertson, "we will not reveal details of the surveillance naturally, but we will say we stationed officers nearby McNeil's residence because we had ongoing intelligence from colleagues South of the Border, he might be the target of a foreign drug gang."

Robertson again, "The two cops say in their statement that they saw him acting violently towards the property, but they did not know if he was armed. Could he have been given the gun inside the property?"

"Unlikely," interjected Farrell. "Whatever McNeill is, he is no gunman. A bookkeeper for the mob, MI5, definitely not, previously involved with the IRA, possibly."

"We saw things in our interview that alerted us." Walker added.

"Forensics have confirmed that the Glock 19 that Breen aimed firstly at our officers and then at McNeill is the same gun that killed Fedor Pakus in Shaftsbury Square in August. Breen's fingerprints were on it."

Robertson queried," Did they check if any other fingerprints were on it?"

"Not on the gun but on the magazine, there were McNeill's."

Robertson sighed, "So do we know why the magazine was not in the gun?"

"No, but remember, there was a bullet in the chamber. Mc Neill's fingerprints would be on the magazine. He found it in a flower bed and handed it to an officer, and the officer saw him lift it up from the ground. “

“Where do we go from here? Will you charge McNeill? I see you let him go?”

Walker and Farrell exchanged glances; Walker contended.

“What do we charge him with? Being attacked by an armed ex-terrorist whom he tried to help by giving him odd job work, I can just hear his solicitor?”

“Yes, but if he is squeaky clean, why would a drugs gang be interested in him?” asked Robertson.

Farrell responded: “As for being the target of an international drugs cartel, his gardener’s involvement in the Shaftsbury Square shooting may have unwittingly led the Lithuanians to think Mc Neill was Breen’s boss.”

Robertson asked incredulously: “So you think he is an innocent party, despite the car, the house... all these--- coincidences?”

Walker winced as Robertson mentioned the ‘coincidence’ word again, although more in the vein, ‘that might not be a coincidence.’

“Not at all, it is just we are not ready to bring Mr McNeill in. There are too many,” he paused, “unknowns. We think he was in Shaftsbury Square during or shortly after the shootings. We think he was involved in the money’s disappearance. He had a very plausible story about how he met Breen, but we didn’t believe it for one minute. Too much of a coincidence. “

“We don’t believe in coincidences,” opined Farrell. Walker ignored the provocation.

“Then,” Walker added, “there is the disappearance of the three men who came North. Maybe he knows the answer to that. If he doesn’t tell us, he may answer to more ruthless and violent people.”

Later Robertson made a phone call to an old and trusted acquaintance who, in turn, did the same and the third person phoned Aileen Whyte. Aileen digested the limited information she had been given. She felt it was consistent with the transformation she had seen in George from their first meeting to subsequent meetings.

‘Silly boy,’ she thought,’ well out of his depth. What was all that chasing after Sir Toby?’

She was fond of George. If she could extract him from the situation, she would, but she could not be near any crime. She was encouraging Andrews to put him in charge of the Glasgow operation. From what George said to her and what she gathered from Andrews, however reluctantly, he was well on top of that. If he moved permanently from Belfast, he could leave behind whatever he was involved in. Also, it would take the spotlight off her if he was arrested living in a different country. She would have to finish with George. She had enjoyed their relationship, but recently she began to think it was an interval, a distraction from all the good and bad things going on in her life.

She needed to draft a statement........ just in case.

The weekend press did not get hold of the details of the shooting but reported that an armed man was shot dead in Riverdale Drive Belfast by police officers after failing to surrender when requested to do so. He was believed to be under the influence of drugs. Police enquiries were ongoing.

Farrell called on Irene. He assumed that anything he told her might be relayed to her ex-husband. He told of the incident leading to

Breen's death. Irene remembered strange phone calls recently from George. She felt all this was tied in with his new car and house regardless of the new job, however; she said nothing. At the end of Farrell's questions, he added one more.

"Is your husband now or has he ever been a member of the Provisional IRA?"

At this, Irene burst out laughing. It was a genuine reaction.

"I knew my husband from school until we split up. I saw him every day. He is a very quiet, even nervous individual who has never had any involvement in politics of any kind. In fact, he wouldn't have been comfortable in the Boys Brigade, never mind the IRA."

Farrell thought about the Special Branch information on George's overnight visits to Aileen in London.

He said nothing, but he wondered if Irene really knew George as well as she thought. His visit to David McNeill yielded similar results, although David, unlike Irene, found nothing funny in the question about para-military involvement. Unwisely, he acknowledged he felt his brother was acting out of character for the past six months or more. He realised he had said too much and clammed up. Farrell reported back to Walker.

"I am pretty sure they are both decent enough people and that prior to six to eight months ago our Mr McNeill was a model citizen."

Walker was clear. "We need to tie McNeill into the Shaftsbury Square incident

Chapter 11

The Fat Man Comes

George, as always, when facing something truly unpleasant, put the tragic Breen incident out of his mind. He returned to Glasgow. It was as if being in a different city absolved him of any responsibility for events in Belfast. He wondered why he had run to tell Breen about the magazine, but the entire episode happened so quickly and was so fraught. He knew he hadn't deliberately engineered it. That said, Breen's demise made George feel safer. Apart from the elusive Liam, the link with Arturas, Vito, and Dietmar was gone. He wasn't at the point where he was comfortable, but he was close.

Another Monday, an early rise, parked his car at Belfast International airport and then a quick 35-minute hop to Glasgow. He picked up a taxi to the office, bought a coffee and a bagel, and walked into the foyer, getting the lift to McIntyre and Matheson's floor. The receptionist smiled at him. She didn't know him, but she got the message jobs were under review. Emboldened by the Board's confidence in him, it was time to act in Glasgow and inform the staff of the future management arrangements. Laura came in to speak to him, ostensibly to ask a question. A decision from him was needed, bur she was really interested to learn if 'Belfast' had yet come to a decision. Every week he was conscious of the looks of expectations from every quarter for the first hour he was in the office. He should tell Laura of his plan, but accepted Sandy was entitled to hear first.

He sat down in his office composing himself and asked a member of staff from the General Office to tell Sandy Burney he wished to see him.

Sandy wandered up the corridor as slowly as possible. 'So, he is summoning me and using someone else? I know what this means.' He walked into George's office. No knock, no "Good Morning," a sullen face and "You wanted to speak to me?"

"Sit down Sandy please," George was nervous. A more experienced manager would have handled it differently. He betrayed his inexperience and his lack of appetite for the task ahead, making it worse.

"Sandy, the Partners have agreed to allow you to move on. They want a new broom in to drive the company forward."

"Oh yes, and who might that be?"

George went on the front foot. "Me," he replied.

Sandy half sniggered; half winced.

"You do not know Scotland, you have no contacts, you have no managerial experience." Laura wasn't the only one to make enquiries.

"The place will be gone in six months. You were always out to grab my job. Nobody here saw what you put in the reports to Belfast, no consultation, no involvement of anyone else." he subsided.

This was not the time to tell him at least another of his colleagues was involved.

George thought, 'I cannot be bothered by this man's snide comments.'

"The Partners asked me to stay on, your departure was certain when we acquired the firm, look at the turnover; this place is moribund. “Sandy interrupted, “And you are going to turn it around?” he asked sarcastically.

“I believe so; but, if not me, someone else will.”

Sandy stood up and stepped forward, so his body pressing on the desk, and then lowered himself, staring straight into George’s eyes.

“You had a hit list from day one and I am on top of it. You go and fuck yourself. See you in court.”

George’s recent run in with Arturas emboldened him. He took his time and rose slowly to his feet and stared straight at Sandy. For a moment, as he stared into George’s eyes, he panicked, ‘ Was this guy more than he appeared? Could he have underestimated him?’ he stepped back. McNeill would have an input into his severance. He informed his wife the first week George arrived in Glasgow he was out; he just lost his temper.

As he stood there, George raised his voice again.

“Garden, leave for your period of notice. Baileys HR people will be in touch about your package. Clear your desk by lunchtime. You can go.” he waved his hand airily in dismissal.

What neither was aware of was how much this conversation was conducted at the top of their voices. Many people were listening or relaying the contents to colleagues. To an extent George was aware of this but allowed it to happen. He wanted people to realise it was crunch time, there would be casualties, and their priority should be to ensure they were not on the list.

An older accountant, Angus, aware of what was coming, was next. Sandy revealed to him a year before that the organisation would let him go. A busy Summer with Freya forever on the ‘sick’ followed by the Baileys takeover delayed it. He smiled, agreed he would contact HR in Belfast, shook hands,

"If it's all the same to you, I would like to leave now and not work my notice?"

George agreed.

Next in was an already tearful Freya. She begged, she pleaded, she cried, she muttered threats claimed she was bullied, harassed, all the usual nonsense of the incompetent. He waited for the waterworks to be turned off, then spoke.

"Freya, you don't like this job. Your heart isn't in it, nor is any other part of you. Your sick leave record is poor. Two years ago, a better manager would've let you go."

Well, he would if you weren't sleeping with him. The last bit was left unsaid.

"You and Sandy were close; everyone knows you were close ......"

Freya interrupted,

Is that what it's all about? George was thinking.

"Those bitches, jealous because we were good friends. I bet that major witch Laura is behind all this."

'She isn't jealous of your relationship with Sandy for sure.'

"It works like this, I want you to finish today, before lunch, if you can hand over all your files, correspondence, emails to Laura."

Freya scowled at that mere mention of Laura, but George didn't know who else would have the appetite to find out how much 'live' work she sat on.

"I will contact HR about your severance. You will remember from your contract how your work has to be kept up to date and subject to the oversight of a senior member of staff."

She didn't recall that or any other detail of her contract.

"Laura is a senior accountant. She is not management, only Sandy is," then she subsided.

"Freya, Burney is gone. I am the Chief Operating Officer.

He didn't allow Freya time to work all this out but sent her to her office to prepare her workload, reminding her that her severance would depend on the state of her work.

He called in Laura. She was a little concerned.

"Right Laura to business."

"That was some show. Nobody has moved in the office for the past half hour. We heard you both shouting. We heard Freya crying, but we didn't hear Angus. He just came out smiling, as always."

George rose and stuck out his hand. "Congratulations Laura, I am the Chief Operating Officer, and you are to be my deputy.

Freya and Angus won't be replaced due to the savings required. You and I will take the slack from Burney and the other two and your existing workload.

Later we will determine how it is shared. Your title is odd, Bailey hates titles. They pretend they are dissenters opposed to any formal hierarchy, but no organisation operates power more stringently for all their free-thinking reformist mantra. They didn't want a Chief Executive or a Managing Director. In their desire to avoid a hierarchical structure, they have come up with a more cumbersome arrangement."

He sighed and shrugged his shoulders. On a more practical level, he explained her new salary band:

"You will start at the bottom, of course; it is based on Baileys tiers."

She supressed a smile as he mentioned the figures. 'Cat will love this. '

"There is a price to be paid for the savings."

A price George remembered he was not prepared to pay when career opportunities came up in Baileys over the years.

"We have two priorities: settle this place down and get more business. You know, the Scottish or the Glasgow scene I bring the parent company clout. "

She was full of ideas and links to help expand the business, and her ideas interested him. They had to 'sell' the firm. Sandy's departure would prove positive for existing and potential clients.

"You have to discover what Freya has and get it from her."

Laura shrugged. "Don't think that will be time-consuming."

He outlined his next actions.

"I will see each staff group and explain what is happening, put it in writing to each and phone HR in Belfast to prepare them for Sandy, Angus, and Freya's contact with them."

It was a busy week in McIntyre and Matheson as George made changes. He acted on Laura's suggestion, removing irritations that Sandy never tackled. They were small, according to Laura, but meant the staff would see the organisation was listening to them. He sat down with each member of staff to ask what issues the 'new' management team required to address. Laura was miffed, after all she held all the answers. George pointed out that even if they repeated points, she made they would have a greater sense of ownership if they could articulate them to him. He suggested to Laura that she was entering a honeymoon period. Colleagues who were delighted she took over day-to-day management could resent her role or at least test her. George experienced it often at Baileys' when someone came in or moved up a level and took responsibility for former peers.

On Friday night, he drove to the airport to pick up Claire. This was to be the weekend that he would confide in her. He also recognised that his 'secret' needed to be shared, it was too high a burden. Too much information would expose Claire to either the Authorities or those who had a claim on the euros. They went out for dinner to an Italian restaurant and enjoyed a passionate night back in the flat. On Saturday, they got up late, ate breakfast, and George suggested they explore the Necropolis. This is the large Victorian cemetery near Glasgow Cathedral. It was a warm sunny day, and the Necropolis lacked the gloomy Gothic like persona it often presented.

They sat for a while in silence: "Claire, I don't wish to say overly much, the more I tell you, the more likely the information could create difficulties for you." he began.

Claire couldn't prevent an audible intake of breath; this was not what she expected.

"Also, please do not, under any circumstances, reveal anything I tell you to anyone else unless failing to do so would make you unsafe. Last Summer, I discovered something, and I benefited from it, but my actions angered people. It is unlikely that the problem will return, but it is possible."

"Was it at work? You didn't steal from a client's account, did you or the firm?"

"No, nothing to do with work," he replied, not responding to the stealing issue.

"What I found I should have handed in to the Authorities. The men who used to own it had no further use for it. My mistake was keeping it." He stopped.

"If the people who used to own it have no more use for it, what is the problem? I mean, you could at least be entitled to a finder's fee?" Claire persisted.

"The people who owned it are dead."

"You didn't kill them, did you?" asked Claire.

George turned around to her in horror, but Claire laughed nervously.

"I mean you killing people, don't be silly."

"I have decisions to make." he concluded. "I need to tell the authorities everything to clear the slate and make full restitution." He sounded definitive.

“I am sure you will do the right thing,” responded Claire, not at all sure he would. The worst was over, no other woman, especially no Aileen Whyte.

Sunday was less carefree somehow, but for both of them it passed too quickly, and yesterday’s revelation was not mentioned.

As she flew back to Belfast, far from satisfying Claire over his strange behaviour, George only deepened the mystery. She guessed he took something that wasn’t his, despite his protestations. Is this why he toyed with her, protecting her from his crime by keeping her at arm’s length.? Could she forgive? And another question she could not answer. Why did she care for him? Their time in Glasgow was happy, but---

Should she go to the police, “My boyfriend,” --- (were she and George too old to be boyfriend/girlfriend.?) ...., my partner, he wasn’t her partner, the person I am sleeping with every other weekend), ‘may have acted wrongly.’

“Really, madam, ‘may have,’ what is the nature of this wrongdoing?”

“I am not sure; I think he found something and ...”

Claire wasn’t sure how she should play it. Was it even down to her? In a process that George would have been proud of, her conclusion was to wait for his “decisions.” George hinted over the weekend that he would like her to move to Glasgow. That was more concrete but a big step and one she wasn’t ready to take. The mystery added to her uncertainty. She struggled to explain the attraction he held for her. After the drama with ‘thingy’, she wanted a settled and secure life. In Scotland, she was relaxed, warm and secure with George. In Belfast he came over as less reliable, preoccupied. If they were to have a future, it might be in Scotland. The big car and that nice but soulless house meant little. She could not explain the attraction, even to herself, but after Glasgow she accepted it was real, and it was important to her.

The Fat Man arrived in Dublin in mid-June. He was comfortable with his nick name; indeed, he encouraged it. There were parts of the Balkan states where the mere utterance of it created fear. His reputation for brutality in Chechnya, his alleged links with the Russian security services together with his imposing stature, he was 6 feet three and must have weighed 270 maybe 280 lbs, all complemented the fear factor. He had an almost permanent smile devoid of warmth and a rasping accented voice that added to his menace.

He called a Council of War, gathering together the remnants of his brother's associates, including several local men who had gone 'over' to the Lithuanian gang. David O'Connell now considered them as a Russian gang.

"It is simple," Andrius began, "I intend to find out what happened to my brother and my nephew also if the same people were involved in my son's death——, and I want our half million Euros back."

He surveyed the table. He spoke quietly. People leaned forward to catch his words, but nobody looked him in the eyes. He was rumoured to possess a fearful temper and capable of killing on a whim.

"So, what have we got?"

Jim McGrillen was close to Arturas, and Andrius met him when his son's coffin was transported south to be repatriated. He produced the photograph from the PSNI incident room.

"The guy with the blond girl is called George McNeill. Arturas met with him in Belfast and was returning to meet him, but then disappeared. We think he is the likeliest source of information."

Andrius rasped, "Do you think he could have killed any of my family?" and, remembering, "Dietmar. Dietmar is trained and not an easy person to kill."

Jim shrugged. "McNeill was not on our radar when we did a deal with the 'Northerners', the deal that went pear-shaped."

Andrius growled.

"Go on, what do you mean Northerners, like Scandinavians?"

Jim tried to explain.

"This is one island but divided into two politically. The north-eastern corner is British, the rest is Irish."

"British, Irish, is this like Ukraine or Georgia and Russia?"

As far as Jim knew, Georgia was in the United States and renowned for peanut farming, but wisely did not display his ignorance of post-Soviet politics.

"So," mused Andrius," the northeast corner is English."

He was interrupted by another Irishmen, Mark Frawley, a ruddy faced Kerry man, trying to be helpful.

"Not so much English as British."

Andrius suppressed his rage. These Irish bastards were trying to make a fool of him. If I shot one, especially the red-faced one, the others would see sense.

Instead, he tried again.

“My son’s coffin was escorted to the border by English police,” aware of the rising tension neither Irishman contradicted him, “then the Irish police met the cortege, right?”

Both Irishmen nodded vigorously, and Andrius relaxed.

“Different jurisdictions,” pursued Frawley unnecessarily.

Andrius glared at him, thinking, ‘Ah Ha like Armenia and Azerbaijan because of the religious element. He had heard they fought over religious sensitivities, more like Serbia and Kosovo. ‘

“Do the police shoot at each other?” he asked, he remembered a gunfight between Georgian and Russian police that broke out at a border crossing.

The Irishmen shook their heads.

“They are as thick as thieves,”

Frawley grunted, then remembered the company he was in and subsided.

Andrius turned to one of his own men and spoke in Russian.

“Why did we come to this godforsaken island?

His comrade, unwisely, reminded him.

“You suggested it was the easiest bit of the EU to transport drugs into because of the lax security and also the local competition was low level and disorganised.”

He had said too much and went quiet as Andrius glared at him

“So, who is McNeill? Is he someone who should concern us? “

Jim looked at the photograph and pointed to the Chief Constable.

“That is the head of policing in the North. The woman here is his wife, who also was a senior detective in England.” He shouldn’t have brought England into it again.

“Hah,” grunted Andrius, “so I was right.” Nobody contradicted him.

“Is the blond woman McNeill’s girlfriend?”

“Well,” answered Jim, “One of them.” He pointed over to the picture of Aileen Whyte.

“She is also his girlfriend. According to those small handwritten notes, they may have lived together, briefly, in London.”

Again, Andrius was filled with triumph.

“London, capital of England. I was right all along. The blond girl is pretty, but this woman has a real presence. I would like to meet her.”

Jim elaborated, “She is the rising star of, er... Northern Irish politics, tipped to take the top job someday.”

“I wonder how she will eliminate her rivals?” added Andrius. “She might benefit from my talents and experience.”

“There is also reference to a British Government Minister at the Home Office being associated with McNeill and MI5,” added McGrillen.

“So, is McNeill a drug dealer?” he flashed a smile at the Irishmen, ‘I catch on quick.’

McGrillen waited for a minute, hoping a fellow countryman would chip in, but they realised the less they said, the better. Eventually McGrillen responded, “The cops don’t seem certain. Under McNeill’s photo there was typed on a line; ‘drug dealer, in brackets ‘banker for the mob’, below it on another line ‘MI5,’ and reference to the Home Office minister, below that ‘IRA terrorist. At the risk of creating further complications, “he explained,” They are a local terrorist organisation.” McGrillen was a member, active in his youth, he gulped on the word ‘terrorist.’

“Finally, the last line says, ‘innocent passer-by.’ That refers to the shooting in which your son died.”

Andrius was then subjected to another history lesson on organisations in Ireland and the fact that although there was a Peace Agreement, not accepted by everyone, others drifted into supplying and dealing in drugs. Frawley delivered the lecture ponderously and Andrius grew to hate him. He wanted to make an example, impose his will. He grew restive at the volume of information. The niceties of the various elements in Ireland interested him not a whit, but he recognised the words ‘MI5’ which interested him.

“This McNeill, according to the photograph, is either a terrorist or he is in the secret police. He has powerful friends like the Chief of Police and Interior Minister. He has two mistresses, the politician and er.... the other one. Do we know where he lives?” There was no response.

“McNeill must be a serious gangster. He will have worked his way up, but he will have done his share of killing. We need more information, so who do we bribe, the guy who photographed this?” pointing at the ‘map’ from Walker’s office wall?

“He has gone quiet and is suspended from the police force.” McGrillen stated.

At last, another Irishmen spoke.

“I have been delving around looking up property records. McNeill lives alone in a house sold to him by an IRA man or ex IRA commander called Paddy McCann who lives in Dublin. I have traced a couple of bars he drinks in.”

Andrius considered this, then spoke. “McNeill must be the Big Man and dangerous, yet he lives alone, unprotected, in a small house, so his gang must live in the adjoining houses. How do we get to him?”

McGrillen interjected dubiously.

“There are addresses here of his family, girlfriends, and an associate. From what your brother stated, he has children at this address. He lives across the city. Also, he has a friend with a daughter in the city’s north and a girlfriend in the east and another on the south side.”

Andrius nodded.

“Right, a lot to choose from, but if we get a person, he is close to, he will sing like a canary. Where is the politician in all this?” Andrius ventured. He was keen to meet her.

“Don’t go there,” said McGrillen. “She may have a police escort, any attempt to grab her will bring a lot of grief. We should play this low key.”

Andrius surveyed McGrillen, this guy was trusted by Arturas, but he is too cautious.

"Listen," he said to McGrillen. "I have been making my own way since I was sixteen. All I had to concern me was my brother. Sure, I have a wife, but we are no longer together, we have a son."

He paused for a moment then went on,

"We do not get on, but she lives in Russia under the protection of her father. He is a very influential man, there is no love lost," again a pause and McGrillen was sure Andrius was contemplating what he would like to do to his father-in-law.

"If things change as they might, who knows what might happen. "

He finished his personal reflection.

"Now my brother is missing, and I don't care who has to die for me to learn what has happened to him.

After more discussion, it was agreed to pick up Paddy McCann and find out how much he was involved and if he was a part of McNeill's 'gang.' Andrius ordered McGrillen and Frawley to do this but to take it easy on McCann.

"See if he is prepared to answer our questions. Drop in the money and see if he bites. McNeill must not be alerted to how high the stakes are. If he has the money, he knows we will come for it, and he will do a deal. The family business can come later." He added grimly.

The next night, Paddy and Joe left the pub. They did not see a car approaching, but a man jumped out and waved a gun in Paddy's face and 'invited' him into the back seat. Joe moved forward, and the man cracked him on the head with the gun. They drove off to a secluded place.

McGrillen began: "Our boss, he is a foreigner, and has had a sum of money, half a million euros, stolen in Belfast."

McCann did not recognise either man, but the handgun focussed his mind.

"I have not been involved in anything there in twenty years."

"The boss believes you are friendly with the leader of the gang, who stole the money. George McNeill."

Both men stared at Paddy McCann intently.

Paddy showed no flicker of recognition at the name." Never heard of him." he replied.

Paddy was older now. In the past he expected he could be picked up by the RUC, the army, a loyalist organisation, UVF, UFF, UDA, Red Hand Commando, or a rival Republican group. Each dictated a unique response. Would he be detained for a few hours, days, years, or be killed? This was so unexpected, coming from nowhere. He weighed it up, old skills die hard.

Whoever these people were, he was sure he could take the weapon, kill the gunman and the driver, and stroll off. However, that would have repercussions. Who did they represent and why they were interested in him? If issues were kicking off, he did not want to be involved. If he could reassure these guys, they might go away, then again, they might not.

"Well, you 'sold' him a house, so you know him." McGrillen asserted.

Paddy hesitated, thinking 'the guy who bought his house in Riverdale.' "Ah," said Paddy, "him."

"Yes, him." McGrillen muttered crossly, "don't fuck with us," and he hit Paddy with the gun on his face, drawing blood. Paddy licked the blood at the side of his mouth, tasting the salty liquid but made not a sound.

"Careful," cautioned Frawley, and Paddy realised it was aimed at the guy beside him, not him.

'So, they haven't been told to rough me up, this guy just lost it.'

Paddy had been 'roughed up' by a selection of the groups mentioned above. By their standards, this was tame stuff.... so far.

"I remember him. I didn't connect him to the theft of stolen money from," he hesitated," guys like you."

"What do you know about him?" the next question posed.

"He came across a house I owned by accident. A friend of mine who lives next door told me he is a regular guy, works as an accountant, a friendly neighbour, unassuming, lives alone, likes a nice garden, that's all."

"That's all?"

"Yes, that's all." The conversation was ending. Of McNeill they knew nothing. and he hardly added to that. An extra tidbit would satisfy them.

"One other thing, I only met him twice and had a phone call with him, but he insisted on paying cash. That was unusual."

McGrillen thought, 'Yes, that is odd. Criminal gangs use friendly lawyers and accountants to handle their affairs.'

"Aye, he paid me in euros." replied McCann. As spoke, he and McGrillen became aware, at the same time, that was the stolen money, but Paddy's face remained impassive.

"You can go." ordered McGrillen.

Paddy got out of the car. He turned to look at McGrillen. If he apologised for the blow with the butt of the pistol, Paddy might not kill him, although he might.

McGrillen snapped.

"WHAT?" Paddy smiled at him and vanished into the rural Dublin gloom.

"I don't like that bastard," McGrillen muttered to his mate.

"Did you see his smile? Reminded me of Andrius's smile?" Frawley replied,

McGrillen shrugged but was uneasy. They reported to Pakus, who instructed, "It's Sunday. Let's go North and get McNeill. He has the answers and the euros."

"I wouldn't do that," declared Frawley.

Andrius paused, smiled, and turned round.

"Why?"

Frawley began.

"You must scout out the situation a bit…"

He didn't get any further because the 'Fat Man' shot him in the forehead.

"Get rid of that." ordered Andrius pointing at Frawley's body.

After the killing, Andrius had calmed down, his blood lust satisfied. The 'Fat Man' was a long way from home, Andrius intended to get his reputation across, and he did that.

At O'Connell's instruction, a Garda undercover unit placed both Andrius and McCann under surveillance. They thought they saw a weapon as McCann was put in the car but were instructed to hold back until they were certain. An officer, who knew McCann, he was involved in the surveillance team after his trips to the United States, radioed this information to control.

They followed McGrillen and his associate as near as possible to the secluded place where they parked. They could not get closer without betraying their presence and once again sought instructions. When O'Connell was contacted, he instructed them to intervene in case McCann was to be assassinated.

The car with the two men drove past them. The officers were ordered to find McCann and get medical help, assuming he was still alive. By the time they got to the place Frawley had parked, Paddy McCann came sauntering along in the dark without a care in the world. O'Connell instructed he should be brought in for questioning. For the second time that evening, Paddy was put into a car by armed men who did not identify themselves. They were police.

'*You can fucking smell them*,' he muttered to himself.

The Garda officers remained in the front seats. Paddy guessed this was not a formal arrest, but it was a lift to the city.

“Nice taxi service you guys offer driving around deserted country lanes, offering lifts to stray pedestrians.” Paddy said in conversational tones.

“Our boss wants a wee chat with you, “a cop said brusquely.

‘*Yeah,*’ thought Paddy, ‘*everybody’s boss wants a piece of me.*’

O’Connell introduced himself affably to Paddy.

Right.’ thought Paddy, ‘Good cop, bad cop, so where is the bad one?’ O’Connell was a senior officer, something big was going down for sure. O’Connell got to the point. “You were picked you by two members of the Pakus Lithuanian drug gang. What did they want from you?”

“The who gang? “replied Paddy, “Never heard of them.”

“Hmm, you are on their radar; Paddy and these boys play for keeps. Tell you what, let’s swop information, you tell me, and I will tell you what I know?”

Paddy knew it was unlikely O’Connell would tell him anything, but he played along.

“A cup of hot coffee might help me remember,”

O’Connell nodded at one detective, who left for the canteen.

“Me first because I don’t know a damn thing. These two Neds, who are Irish by the way, pick me up, one pulls a gun and starts going on about stolen money. Cheeky bastard slaps me with the gun. Stealing money is not my bag and I don’t buy or deal with drugs. Now, what are you going to tell me?”

O' Connell sighed. He rather thought the McNeill case would get messy for him. There were elements which might become politically sensitive. If you factor in a drug element, the shooting of an EU national living in Dublin albeit in Northern Ireland, a British Government Minister, and a well-connected Northern Ireland politician, who is associated with a possible perpetrator, there was much to engage the press. Add in the disappearance of three other EU nationals living in Dublin missing presumed dead, fortunately again in the North. A lot of 'maybe's in there.

A joint Garda/PSNI operation like this left fertile ground for political mischief from politicians and the media. O'Connell was two months off retirement. His responsibility for combating drug crime in the Dublin metropolitan area brought him plenty of media attention. Enough campaigners out there looking for a scalp, any scalp. The most voluble originated from a big Dublin crime family associated with a couple of politicians whom they used to attack the Garda and O'Connell. One of its denizens was working to build up the indigenous drug operations threatened by the Lithuanian group. O'Connell phoned Yuri Shevlov regularly, the latter acting as a mentor in this.

"Am I detained with a view to being charged?" asked Paddy.

"Oh no, Mr McCann, you are helping us with our enquiries into crimes, none of which we believe you have any direct involvement. We would prefer not to charge you. If we did that, we might have to make the United States Immigration authorities, or the US Department of Homeland Security, aware you are a person of interest to us. That would make future trips to the United States problematic for you, and we don't want that, do we?"

Paddy's heart sank, his most vulnerable point. 'Not even good cop, bad cop just cop shows nasty side.'

"I am concerned this foreign drug gang might believe you have an involvement, and your life could be at risk."

Paddy said nothing. Whoever sent the two guys who picked him up might kill him if they saw him as a 'loose end.'

"I think it would be in your interest if we kept an eye on you," O'Connell finished.

Paddy shrugged and was allowed to leave.

He phoned Joe and advised him of his night's experiences. The crack on the head already made Joe furious. "That doesn't sit well with me, Paddy. There will be a pay back." He suggested they find out where the Lithuanians were based and strike first.

Paddy paused. "We should take our time. I could travel to Belfast and see McNeill or wait for an event and we could act then."

"An event?" said Joe querulously. "What do you mean by an 'event.' "

Paddy paused.

"It is coming to the boil; we should let that happen. Then, when the two sides get into each other, the ones we want taken out will have their eye off us and we can catch them unawares. Also, the cops will watch me for a while, but when it kicks off, they will have more important fish to fry."

Joe suggested dubiously.

"It's your call Paddy," he wanted to crack a few heads because of tonight's events.

Meanwhile, George remained ensconced at home, blissfully unaware of events south of the Border. He took a week's holiday from Glasgow, leaving Laura in charge, intending to go up to Donegal and bring stuff that was needed for the cottage. On Saturday, he treated Terry and Melissa to a meal.

When he got home, he phoned Claire; no reply, but he left a message. He intended to call and catch up with Jan, but his phone rang. It was Aileen.

"Can you come over and meet me after 7.00 pm tomorrow?"

Once George would have been excited by an invitation, and his imagination was full of the possibilities. His heart sank, but he agreed, although he had moved on, or matured. George wanted his relationship with Claire to develop if he could keep her safe. There were no such worries for Aileen. He reckoned she and Abbi could see off any gang of foreign criminals. He drove up the Malone Road driveway, parked his car, and rang the bell. Of course, it was Abbi who let him in. 'Well Abbi, you have won this one.'

"Why, Mr McNeill, what a pleasant surprise."

Yes, 'like root cannel treatment,' not said, but the tone implied it. George didn't wish to fight with Abbi. They were leaving each other's lives with no regret on either side.

"Please follow me."

As they went into the formal dining room, Rosemary gave a friendly wave from the top of the stairs. She was on her mobile. He smiled and waved back; their unspoken alliance still intact. Abbi's frown deepened at this brief exchange, which she was clearly meant to see. Aileen was seated in an easy chair and did not stand up to greet him when he entered. For an instant, he wondered to himself, 'Dear God, is Abbi part of this?'

'My mother and I want to discuss your future involvement or rather non-involvement with the family.' Surely not. He remembered when he called to pick Aileen up for dinner and Abbi and her grandmother almost interviewed him. 'Are your intentions for my daughter /mother honourable?' 'Of course not.'

Aileen nodded to Abbi, who turned and left the room.

"George," she declared, assured, and taking control. "Let me get straight to the point. I have enjoyed our relationship. It helped take me out of my dark place. I enjoyed every aspect," she stated, looking meaningfully at him.

"When I first met you, you were so kind and..."

"Biddable?" interjected George

"No, no, you changed. I was under massive stress from Campbell and the election and how he might influence it."

George;" But..."

"No, let me finish. I was weaker., sadder, I leant on you. You were sorting out issues I couldn't influence. Ever since I was a teenager, I dreamed of a political career. My father and I talked about it all the time, planned for it. Then I met Thomas and fell head over heels in love. It wasn't a wise decision. Is love ever wise?" she mused. Then she continued.

"I lost my political career, my marriage deteriorated and now I can recapture my original dream, nothing will stand in the way of that, NOTHING. We don't have a future together. I am being honest with you; We have no future together. I have commitments with the girls, my constituency, the party. I have no room for a partner."

Family and career come first, no surprise there. Aileen planned to lead up to it more softly, but in the end, her instinct took control. She said what needed saying and what must happen. There was no negotiation, such as allowing for perhaps a few nights over the next months in London and a gradual lessening of ties. Finite, this relationship ends here.

George gazed at her. She looked lovely even in this serious, non-negotiating command mood. It was ironic, the old George might have lasted, albeit as an appendage. He always knew this moment might arrive. No tears, no pleading, no 'it's been fun or fulfilling or I hope you find happiness Aileen.' He smiled, bowed his head ever so slightly, left the room, the house, and her life. Aileen stood at her favourite spot, watching him stride out to his car.

Aileen thought, 'it should have ended better. I should have been more grateful or affectionate, a quick peck on the cheek.'

From him, she got nothing. Was he sad, angry, relieved? She was relieved, but a bit nonplussed by his lack of reaction. Still, he had the nice wee blond in his life. Aileen felt an odd pang, 'steady Aileen, you wanted to finish it, you had to finish it, you can't allow jealousy to rekindle old feelings and after all George might be in serious trouble.' She resolved to help him, if she could, from the background, she owed him that.

He drove off, met up with Jan, they had a number of drinks. George had never mentioned Aileen and would not talk about her now. As far as Jan knew, and hoped, Claire was to be the woman in his friend's life. After a few drinks, George lowered his voice.

"Look, Jan, I did a stupid thing last summer. It is hard to explain and there are a lot of reasons, best if you don't know the details."

Jan knew the car, and the house had come out of the blue and he hoped George had won the blasted lottery or maybe an inheritance, although he thought it strange; he never mentioned anything. They got a taxi to Jan's house and, after more drinks, collapsed onto their respective beds.

George woke early on Monday morning with a sore head. He went downstairs. Jan made no sound; he headed home for a shower. He scribbled Jan a note, 'Long time since we had a night like that, we never got around to mentioning Elena. Next time, eh? Eh see you soon, G.'

When Jan read the note he went, 'Dammit, I meant to explain about Elena. Oh well I can phone him tonight.'

The cops reported that McNeill returned home on Monday morning.

The previous night, O'Connell got a message to Walker to suggest they should speak urgently. Walker returned the call. If O'Connell phoned him on a Sunday night, it was on the verge of kicking off:

"The Fat Man has crossed the Border," said O'Connell. "We can assume he is heading for Belfast to get McNeill."

"Right," said Walker, "I have cops outside McNeill's house and others in a car in the vicinity."

The Fat Man's team headed for Riverdale Avenue. They 'clocked' two police officers outside. McGrillen sent a man to scout McNeill's house. He didn't get too close, but no lights were on in the house and no vehicle parked in the driveway. The cops looked bored. All this he reported back.

"Why are the police there? Could he have been tipped off we were coming?" posed Andrius to his group.

"There was an item on the BBC NI news concerning a shooting in the street two weeks ago. It might be a coincidence; McNeill might not be involved." McGrillen replied.

McGrillen was becoming more and more anxious. He knew Andrius's reputation and Arturas 'bigged' his brother up as a man to be feared and a major player in European crime circles. His dark record in Chechnya and active links with Russian crime circles were a worry.

On first meeting, Andrius, when his son's body was being brought home, he spoke little. His physical presence was imposing, but Arturas did most of his talking for him, at first McGrillen wondered if Andrius spoke English.

The cold-blooded way he disposed of the unlamented Frawley, suggested he wanted the Irishmen in the group to receive two messages. First, do it my way and second, don't bring me bad news. But no thinking through, getting intelligence, assessing opponents. He didn't either understand Ireland or its links with armed and ruthless para-military groups.

McGrillen mentioned to Andrius they were crossing the Border and was met with a blank stare. It wasn't impressive by Balkan standards, no armed police, no security check, Was it advisable to pick up McCann, when they got so little of information from him and then released him.

How would McCann handle that? Would he go to ex-colleagues or go to the Garda. In fact, the latter came to him. It was all too loose.

McGrillen suspected Andrius wasn't that interested in the cash, just a way to keep his local men sweet, his brother's disappearance and his son's death were what concerned him. The real Andrius would come out when he learned the facts and when he took revenge. Still, it was all too careless for McGrillen's liking.

The group was expecting George to live among members of his gang. How were the four of them going to confront and resolve that? They should also have sought intelligence about police activity in the area and if the shooting in Riverdale was linked with McNeill. They went on to McNeill's children's' house. It appeared full of people. Irene, her partner, her parents, Melissa, and two friends, and Terry were there. The group from Dublin was not sure who these people were, they could see the house was full, they couldn't snatch someone. Could they get to Elena, but she was a student and unlikely to be home. They had to get a person close to McNeill, but who?

Chapter 12

There Are Coincidences After All

George spent Monday shopping for essentials; buying household duplicates for his home and the cottage including cleaning products, tins of coffee, kitchen implements, brushes and a pan, all quite normal. Then there was another moment of massive change in his life. Around 6 'o'clock, his phone rang.

"McNeill."

"This is George McNeill?"

"You don't know me, but I know you." The voice had a heavy accent and George's stomach was sinking.

"McNeill, you have my money, you know what became of my brother. We need to meet. I have something precious of yours."

Then the line went dead. The caller hung up. George collapsed on his chair. They had come for him. They possessed something precious of his.

In a trance, he contacted Irene. Melissa answered,

"Mum is at a parent teacher evening."

"Is Terry OK? I mean, is he there?"

"No dad, he left for the pub with his mates twenty minutes ago. There is a game on TV. He actually made me tea. What do you think of that?"

George relaxed, "Well done that boy, OK? I mean I must go, bye."

"Bye Dad." Melissa hung up. She was concerned. 'Her mother was right; Dad is losing it.'

He then rang Jan, what a normal, reassuring voice from his friend.

"Jan, ---- Elena......."

Jan cut him short.

"George, I meant to tell you last night, Bebbie is ill, she has been in hospital. I was going to go over, but she was discharged from hospital, and I have the business to manage. Elena wanted to be with her aunt and is in Brussels."

"Are you sure?" asked George.

The drink must still be affecting his friend. "Yes, of course. I am just off the phone with her. "

"Right, look Jan, I must go."

Jan was nonplussed. "George is there anything wrong?" he asked.

"No, no.... it's just a matter has come up. Speak later, bye."

George was shaking with the tension. Arturas's brother had growled, 'We need to meet, I have something precious of yours.'

When he hung up, George was seriously rattled What "something?" He didn't want to "meet" the psycho, 'a dangerous and violent criminal.' His brother was bad enough, the 'less violent,' according to Alan Walker. As he sat there, shocked, the phone rang again.

"Now McNeill, you have had a few minutes to think, and I believe you have not rung the police, which is what a law-biding citizen would do. It is because you have much to hide from them and much to tell me. Let us see what your 'precious' thinks, shall we? "

A voice 'tinny', broken, came on the phone, "George, oh George" the tears could be heard through the abject pleading in the tone. George guessed it would be Claire, though how they traced her he was not sure, presumably through the leak from the Detectives.

"Claire, I am coming over," he declared, but it was now Andrius on the line.

"Of course, you are. Get here quick. My guys are getting bored, and the only thing to entertain them is this woman."

George felt sick. He remembered Arturas's threat to Melissa and Elena. They knew how to get a reaction, one with a disabling effect. Thank goodness he hadn't said anything trite to Claire like 'Don't worry,' because there was a lot to worry about.

As ever, he could not find a parking space outside Claire's house. In fact, he was forced to park a couple of streets away. A mobile surveillance unit was not able to contact Walker but followed George from Riverdale and parked nearby. They observed him leaving his car but did not follow him.

George hurried up Claire's garden path, not noticing the twitching curtains of her next-door neighbour. The front door was ajar. He went straight down the hall, turned right into the sitting room. Claire was sitting on a chair, head hung down, sobbing gently. He could see the remnants of the tears, and a bruise on her cheek. Her blouse was torn at the shoulder. Her nominally two-person settee filled by a large figure who smiled to welcome George. He resembled his brother except for the large reddish-brown scar running down one cheek. There were three other men standing in the room, adding to its crowded appearance. One reminded him of the late unlamented Dietmar, as he stood staring into middle distance with his hands clasped in front of him.

Another man suggested to the figure on the couch.

"We have been here too long already. Time to leave."

The big man nodded. Then everything went black. Then pain in his head as he tumbled into an abyss of darkness. The last thing he heard was a muffled cry from Claire.

Meantime, Alan Walker caught up with his mobile patrol.

"Any sign of him or anyone else in the house?"

"House, what house? We are parked near his car." The cop gave the name of the street.

"That isn't where he is. Get round to .... someone get me Claire Turner's address NOW!"

Precious time was being wasted and by the time the officers arrived at Claire's house, all they discovered was a parking space next to her door. The house was unlocked, and the officers ran in, weapons drawn. There was blood on the floor and signs of a struggle. They knocked on neighbours' doors and she of the 'twitching curtains' informed them four men went into Claire's door an hour and a half to two hours earlier, then another man ran in from the street and fifteen minutes previously they all left.

"One man appeared ill; two others were supporting him."

"Did they all get into the car?"

"I am not sure because of the hydrangeas. They are doing well, don't you think?"

"Never mind the bushes. Was Claire Turner with them?"

Twitching curtains sniffed at the dismissive tone of the officer, who was conscious Walker was furious with them.

"Claire, I assume so. There was a smaller person with a---" pause, "big man."

All this was relayed to Walker. "We have lost half an hour at least; can we stop them on the M1?"

He phoned O'Connell to alert him

Meanwhile, McGrillen assumed the police might track McNeill, and he suggested they drive over the Border by back roads near Newry and avoid the motorway.

Down in Dublin, O'Connell moved quickly. Would the gang take McNeill to their usual haunts? He had no information of anywhere else they might use, but there was a person who might. He ordered Pol Tobin; a local gangster trying to breathe life into the local Dublin drug cartel, to be picked up. Initially, Tobin was not prepared to co-operate but then guessed the Garda moving against the Lithuanians would be in his interest. He revealed they used a small farm building near Bettystown, thirty miles from Dublin. His guys followed two

Lithuanians to it months earlier. David already advised Walker and Farrell to come to Dublin immediately as the entire business was going to kick off. A Garda patrol car met Walker and Farrell at the Border and drove them south, 'blues and twos' in operation.

George came to. He was in total darkness but could hear loud noises below and in front of him. He lifted his head and banged it. He was in the boot of a car and the noise was the engine combined with the sound of the wheels on the road. He was unsure how long he lay in the dark. It seemed hours but was only an hour and a half. Could they have let Claire go? There would have been no point in keeping her. They must know he would do whatever they wanted. The gang showed their power, their intent, their capacity to be ruthless. After a while, the road became rougher for ten minutes or so, then the vehicle stopped. The boot was opened and, though it was getting dark, George blinked at the unaccustomed light. Two of the men grabbed him and marched him into a large barn.

He could see Claire just in front of him, stumbling a little, a man had a firm grip on her neck with the palm of his hand. George and Claire were tied to chairs facing each other. Both had been allowed to go to the toilet on the way in. A guy stood with each, to Claire's embarrassment. At first, George couldn't relieve himself, then the emotional energy hit him, and he did. The man with him spoke in his southern brogue, "Scared, eh, you have good reason, tell him everything he wants to know and give him everything he asks for and you still might get out of this alive." They both knew that was unlikely.

O'Connell's problem was that: if he located George and Claire and went in heavy-handed and either hostage died, the media and politicians would blame him. If the Garda stayed secure and the gang killed the hostages, he would be blamed or if the hostages survived but a Garda officer was killed, again, he would be blamed. They could surround the building and try to persuade those inside to surrender, wait them out. The 'Fat man' was not the surrendering type of that he was certain. He had his own reasons for not wanting that. In consultation with his own senior officers, it was agreed there would be serious consequences for the hostages if they pussy footed around.

David reckoned volunteers were needed to move in first and eliminate these guys, then the Garda could be the cavalry riding to the rescue in the last reel. He was going to have to call in favours from the Special Tactics Command to bring armed officers; an idea was forming in his mind.

He dialled an old pal.

“Barney, I am dealing with a tricky situation. Foreigners, armed drug dealers, according to the PSNI, a British MI5 officer (he closed his eyes) and hostages. I need Armed Support but guys who will obey rather than ask questions?”

His colleague whistled.

“MI5, hostages, drugs, ... shit man, I wouldn’t be in your shoes. Are you sure you have got this right?”

The correct answer would have been, ‘Of course not, I am having a ‘breenge’. It may all go tits up.’ What he actually said was: “Barney, I am all over this. Trust me, it will be fine. I will ensure your officers are as safe as they can be, but they need to be tooled up, body armour and all. “

“Do you require any spare body armour?”

“No, just for your guys. “

“OK, I will get it organised, rather you than me.” Barney then made a careful note of the conversation.

David O'Connell hoped to retire as an Assistant Commissioner. It would have made a difference to his pension. The combination of hostility from the media and politicians was a barrier. A Promotion panel rejected him a year previously, although he was next in line. He was told it didn't operate that way anymore, besides his cavalier attitude, his failure to have the press on his side and his contempt for some politicians made him too risky an appointment.

Minding their own business, Joe Higgins and Paddy McCann were sipping their pints in a local pub when a figure in a raincoat sidled up to their table and sat down beside them.

Higgins glared at him. "YES?" The man nodded to McCann.

"O'Connell wants you clowns at headquarters?"

McCann put his glass down and looked the stranger in the eye. "Are we under arrest then and, if so, for what? Drinking pints? "

"You don't like cops, do you McCann?" To 'ingratiate' himself further, he added.

"As far as I am concerned, I would shoot you fuckers and dump you in the Liffey, but the boss wants you and what the boss wants, the boss gets."

Higgins made as if he would make a fight of it, but Paddy put a hand on his arm.

"Steady, Joe, let us go along with our new friend," New Jersey was on his mind.

O'Connell was all bluster and superficial charm.

"Thank you for coming in gentlemen. I need your help."

He outlined the hostage situation to both. He was brief and to the point. An armed gang needed to be neutralised and the hostages freed.

"So, what do you want us to do? You are the cops. Go in and rescue those people?" asked Paddy.

"We will, but there are issues for you. They have already picked you up once, Paddy. They don't leave loose ends."

"What?" exclaimed Joe, "are you seriously suggesting you wish us to go in first while you lot sit on their fucking arses as usual? We take all the flack, maybe get ourselves killed. In the name of God, man, why would we? You couldn't make this up, "turning despairingly towards Paddy?

Paddy was thinking, this sounds like 'the event.'

"We need time to discuss this on our own," Paddy replied crisply.

"OK." responded O'Connell.

Paddy turned on music on his mobile phone.

"Those bastards will try to listen in. Joe, there is nothing in this for you. McNeill means nothing to me. I have sympathy for the girl, but it was McNeil who got her into this. Mind you, I would like to pay back the bastard who cracked me with his gun. He is right, I am exposed "

The gang might prefer to eliminate him. He didn't fancy looking over his shoulder for the rest of his life.

When he got out of their car, he knew he hadn't seen the last of them.

"Is this also about New Jersey?" Higgins asked. "

Paddy shrugged.

"New Jersey is the deal breaker, but also it concerns the bastard hitting me on the face, that doesn't sit well with me."

Joe made the connection between the guys who picked Paddy up, the one who gave him a crack on the head, and these guys. He was increasingly attracted to the idea of giving them a doing.

" I don't care for drug dealers. My youngest, Artie, he got onto glue when he was young, then graduated to harder stuff. Me and his brothers found out who was dealing and ... let us say, baseball bats and acute hospital care transpired. Thanks to his older brothers, we got him out of it. I hate drug dealers, especially foreign drug dealers, especially those who crack me or a mate of mine on the head, "He paused, "Besides, it would be like the old days."

Paddy grinned, "I suppose it would. We need people we can trust."

"My boys will want involved."

"Ok, but no guns for them. They can bring the bats."

They summoned David back in. "OK, we are up for it. I have your assurance t the US Authorities will hear nothing from the Garda Siochana?"

"Agreed."

"It's just I live for my visits. If they were stopped, I would have a terrible rage, no boundaries to it." Paddy added convincingly.

O'Connell was not easily scared, but if he backtracked on his commitment, he was certain Paddy would have him.

"We will transport you and provide arms. What do you need?"

"Three automatic pistols, one with a silencer, two magazines each, will be enough. Joe's boys will have their own weapons."

O'Connell was explicit:

"Right, you go in when I say, you come out when I say, and you stop when I say. I cannot guarantee what line the media will take at the end of this."

Neither Paddy nor Joe was certain what he meant, but they agreed.

Shortly afterwards, Walker and Farrell arrived. O'Connell told them of the plan. Walker appealed to him.

"David man, this has the portents of a disaster. You cannot use civilians in a situation like this. If any of the hostages are killed, you will be hung out to dry, pension and all."

Just then, a sergeant came in and handed O'Connell a message. He turned to the group:

"It's started. An associate of the Lithuanians, a guy called Frawley, has been fished out of the Liffey with a bullet in his forehead. They will be out for revenge."

Farrell remembered the more gung-ho days of the RUC. Then 'cavaliers' took a few risks, primarily to protect their own officers, but confident enquiries would be limited if 'bad guys' were taken out. It was fine in those days, but twenty years later, various victim groups and people with political agendas demanded full blooded enquiries.

O'Connell's plan could be made to work, in Farrell's opinion, but was reliant on McCann's discretion, plus that of any other survivors. He wasn't absolutely sure O'Connell wanted any survivors, not the 'civilian' group, the drug gang, or maybe the hostages? 'Keep thinking like this John and maybe you and Alan, as potential witnesses, won't return to the North alive.' Farrell was also angry at McNeill, who created all this mayhem, with more loss of life.

"If it wasn't for the girl, for two pins I'd let him stew in there." he suggested to Walker.

The teams arrived almost three hundred yards from the deserted farm buildings. Five Garda officers were already in place.

The Inspector in charge reported:

"There are three guys outside the buildings, one of whom is armed and the other two have hurleys to crack heads. We think there are four others inside the barn and the hostages.

They were all inside before we arrived, but Gard Timmoney climbed up to the hayloft, he didn't go inside but he observed two people tied to chairs, a big man sitting on an old settee and two men near the front door and, he wasn't sure, possibly another below a hay loft. "

"Good work." responded O'Connell.

Coupled with the Armed Support Unit, plus Paddy, Joe and the boys, Walker, Farrell, and O'Connell, there were twenty gathered in the dark. They moved forward to two hundred yards from the buildings. Instruction were issues 'No torches.' It was near 8.00 pm, still not dusk. O'Connell withdrew the Inspector and the five officers who had staked out the farm buildings originally and instructed them to put a roadblock half a mile up the dirt track leading to the buildings.

"You won't be seen from the main road, but I don't want anyone. I repeat anyone straying up here. If anyone comes and doesn't obey your instructions, arrest them. "

"Are you expecting the gang to have reinforcements coming, Sir?"

It wasn't a casual enquiry. What the Inspector was saying was, if more armed gangsters were coming, he wanted weapons.

"No, I very much doubt it." responded his chief.

As the five officers prepared to withdraw, he reconsidered the concern. He whispered to the Inspector,

"This will be done and dusted 30 minutes from now, don't use torches down there either. If anyone does come and you are worried, text me."

Paddy took command of his group. He sat in a huddle with the Higgins' and gestured to the Police support unit.

"We have to be careful. I don't seriously think they will take us out, but if shooting starts, as likely enough, they will get trigger-happy. We need to get inside and eliminate the opposition.

Rory Higgins shivered.

"Are we to take prisoners?"

The response from Paddy was direct.

"I want all opponents eliminated."

But as this level of violence was new to the boys, adopting a more conciliatory tone.

"You guys will be outside 'interviewing', sentries with the hurleys. They are your problem. I want to approach the armed guy. I have a silencer on this pistol, though not on the other one. I'd better fire the right gun." he added cheerfully/

Joe laughed; the boys collectively drew in their breaths. McCann then issued orders.

"Now, this has to happen exactly as I say. Artie climbs into the hayloft and checks exactly how many people are there, the whereabouts of the hostages, and also how many are armed and reports back? Then, Joe Jnr and Rory are to inch their way across the ground and use their baseball bats to dispense with the men armed with hurleys. At a signal from your Da, you are to attack, I will dispose of the Lithuanian on the door with this silencer. None of this will take place until Artie's return with the floor plan of the inside."

Paddy ordered Artie to head to the hayloft. Joe was queasy. Paddy was in command mode, but it was Joe's son and Joe's wife. He could go and one of the older boys could take his gun, but he didn't want one of his sons to shoot someone. How well would Artie do against an older guy in the 'baseball bat v hurleys' free for all? All this took seconds by the time he decided Artie had disappeared. Higgins was to look on the next ten minutes as the longest period of his life. Joe Jnr sensed what his dad was feeling and squeezed his shoulder. Paddy was oblivious. He possessed little regard for life and death at the best of times.

As ten minutes became fifteen, Artie returned.

" I climbed right inside. There is a load of old junk, reins, straps, and an old metal bucket up there. I had to be careful. There was a guy below me. He held an automatic gun, larger than a pistol. Opposite him, at the door, are two others, both had guns in their belts. Then there was a big man on a sofa, he was talking to two people tied to chairs. They were at right angles to each other. I'd say they were more than halfway between the guys at the door and the guy under the loft, but closer to the ones on the door."

Artie would not be involved in the fight. He would return to the hayloft. After precisely ten minutes, he would drop the bucket and any other things in the loft on the gunman below. This would cause a distraction and allow Paddy and Joe to burst into the barn and deal with the men just inside the door and their boss. Before this, Joe Jnr, Rory, and Paddy would have 'taken out' the guards outside the buildings.

The 'Fat Man' was comfortable on the old settee. This out of the way spot was safe, so he didn't mind the Irish men outside not being properly armed. McGrillen was armed, as was his mate, but Andrius told the other Lithuanian to keep an eye on the Irishmen. He no longer trusted McGrillen.

He let George and Claire just sit there tied. Experience taught him the longer captives had to think, the more scared they got and the more likely they were to spill the beans. He told George and Claire of his younger days growing up in Lithuania and later in Russia. He wanted them close together. It emphasised to George how much Claire's predicament was his responsibility. Andrius took particular pleasure in detailing his gruesome activities in Chechnya. Even a hardened criminal like McGrillen was sickened, not only by the detail, but by the pleasure Andrius took recounting it. McGrillen was also getting irritated at the time being taken. He understood the police North and South of the Border would run a major operation. Time to draw all this to a close.

When they were first tied up, George tried to manoeuvre his hand, keeping his wrists slightly apart, but the Lithuanian saw what he was doing and slapped him across the face. Claire gave a moan, but the man tied George's hands extra tight, which was painful.

Andrius nodded approvingly but counselled:" Make sure the blood circulates. I wish him conscious for the next bit."

George's feet were tied first as the man tying it was distracted by Andrius. George was more successful in keeping his feet just a little separate, so there was a small gap. As unobtrusively as possible, George worked at slackening the bonds on his feet, finally succeeding in slipping off the back of his shoe. He could kick it off and have his legs free. When Andrius began a monologue trying to both sicken and terrify Claire, George, though feeling equally repulsed, was tempted to charge chair and all at Andrius. He gave up on the idea, it would have little impact.

Meanwhile, outside, Paddy ran through the timeline. Watches were synchronised, and Artie set off first for his hayloft. It was getting darker, and Joe Jnr and Rory watched a noisy dispute develop between the Irish men and the Lithuanian with the gun. They kept reducing the perimeter of their patrol so they could spend more time chatting, as they were bored. The Lithuanian was conscious of this and yelled at them to split up and take a wider radius. Unfortunately, his English was limited, and the Irishmen called insulting comments about him to each other in low voices.

Artie made his way up the ladder and disappeared into the Barn. Joe Jnr and Rory crawled over towards the Irish sentries. They split up. The plan was their dad would signal when they should attack.

The best plans rarely survive first contact with the enemy. The boys could not see each other or tell Paddy what was going on. Conscious that Artie could be exposed, Joe Jnr launched himself at one of the Irish guys who was having a quiet smoke leaning against a fence.

His task was made easier by the fact the smoker laid his hurley stick down to light the cigarette. Rory couldn't see all this, but he and the other Irish man heard the sound of wood on bone and the man's muffled cries as he was rendered unconscious.

The second man rushed in the tumult's direction but had to pass Rory to get to it, a task which proved beyond him as a baseball bat splattered his nose and then did considerable damage to his cranium. The Lithuanian, alerted by the noise, should have gone inside to alert his compatriots but stood for a moment and then announced to the Irishman approaching him out of the dusk words to the effect, "Vat the fuck is going on with your mate?" Unfortunately, the figure approaching him was Paddy. and he dispensed with the usual niceties and shot him twice using the gun with the silencer.

"On one hand, he experienced less pain than the two Irish guys, on the other...... he was dead." Paddy said later.

Paddy and Joe crept inside. As they did so, the bucket hit the ground from the hayloft. They were in a small anteroom but went straight through the door to the main part of the barn.

Andrius leaned forwards fumbling for a cigarette and putting a hand on Claire's thigh. He winked at her, and Claire thought, "If he unties me to do something to me, I will scratch his eyes out." She was past fear now and was at an angry stage. As that happened, there was a sound of what proved to be a bucket and a load of heavy tackle falling on the Lithuanian underneath. He fired his machine pistol, mostly upwards, as he struggled to rise to his feet simultaneously, trying to disentangle himself.

McGrillen and his mate looked over at the hayloft, this allowed Paddy and Joe to come through the door. Paddy and McGrillen recognised each other in an instant and, as McGrillen drew his weapon, Paddy shot him twice. Joe grabbed the mate and tried to take the gun in the guy's hand. When he couldn't, he shot the fellow. It was later estimated at least four times. Andrius turned away from the hayloft as Paddy and Joe stormed in, dropping his lighter and drawing his pistol. He turned towards George and aimed the gun at him, then he smiled at George and turned the gun towards Claire. Claire stared in horror at him, unable to believe she was going to be shot.

The shooting was a signal for O' Connell and the Armed support unit to rush the building. In the quiet still air, the shooting carried out over the local area. Coupled with the large amount of vehicular traffic, it led to a number of calls to the Police control, in Central Dublin,

O'Connell's inspector, who was with the five guards near the main road, was detailed to monitor any local emergency calls. He intervened with a call to Central Control.

"This is Inspector Ryan; I am on an operation with Chief Superintendent O'Connell just outside Bettystown. We have a situation under surveillance relating to a gun battle between two drugs gangs; we will intervene. We have armed support officers on side."

The reply from the duty inspector at Central Control was, "OK, let us know if you require further back up."

George did not hesitate. As soon as the Fat Man turned towards Claire, he kicked off his shoe and moved forward, though his hands were still tied to the chair. He got between Claire and the gang leader, butting Andrius in the face just as the latter fired two shots. The Lithuanian was then further distracted by a bullet which penetrated his cheek, fired by an onrushing Paddy McCann.

George fell down, still strapped to his chair; he had been shot twice in the chest. Paddy reached the sofa and shot the Fat Man again, this time in the neck. The big man rolled sideways, Paddy applied his gun to just behind his ear and fired again. The Fat Man's lifeless body lay sprawled across the settee.

Meanwhile, Joe ran over to the Lithuanian still trying to disentangle himself from the material Artie dropped, intending to be involved in the fight. As he moved closer, Joe noticed blood on the top of his head, but was falling on him from above.

"Artie son are you alright?" he shouted.

"I think so." came from Artie in a voice not at all sounding as if he was alright. "I've been shot." And then silence.

Joe was livid and shot the unfortunate man, still caught up in harnesses, before scrambling up the ladder. The older brothers came through the door, and both ran up the ladder to their dad and Artie.

Paddy, meantime, untied Claire. Initially, she was silent. He then bent over George and undid the remains of his bindings. Claire gathered herself and also knelt beside George.

"Is he alive?" she asked Paddy.

"Yes, but he has lost a lot of blood. If they get him to hospital and if those bullets haven't destroyed vital organs, he might make it."

Paddy got up; he had lost interest in George.

"How is the boy?" he shouted up to Joe.

"He has lost blood, but as far as we can see, it is a flesh wound."

Just then, O'Connell and his Armed Support Unit poured into the barn, followed by Walker and Farrell. "Give me a status report." O'Connell instructed the Sergeant in charge of the Unit. He also contacted Ryan and told him to send for three ambulances. Two of the Armed Support Officers were qualified First Aiders; one went up the ladder and bandaged Artie, who was carried down to the ground floor by his brothers. The other went to George and sought to stem the blood flow. He was unsure if there was serious internal bleeding.

Claire stood. She was fed up sitting, anyway the only seat was the chair she had been tied to and was not going near it. Walker spoke to her. She was strangely calm, shocked. Farrell was standing beside Paddy McCann, eying him suspiciously. He read in a briefing report McCann was a 'cold-blooded 'killer. He had met similar in his police service, but never in these kinds of circumstances. Neither man spoke to the other. The silence was broken by the Sergeant's report to O'Connell.

"Sir, one-man dead outside from gunshot wounds, two seriously injured. They reminded me of a head-on motorway smash when I was in 'traffic.' Inside, three men dead, one seriously wounded, unlikely to make it and one lad with a flesh wound. A hostage shocked but physically OK. Another with two gunshot wounds, too early to say if he will make it. First ambulance due in twelve minutes."

The Chief Superintendent considered the likely questions he would face. Why were ambulances not on site or nearby? Concern over a breach of security was the best answer. He stood beside the body of Andrius Pakus. To his sergeant's and Walker's astonishment, he took out his mobile phone and took pictures of Andrius's lifeless corpse. He turned to them both.

"The photographs are not souvenirs. The Minister will prefer to be certain this man is dead. There may be international implications."

To Walker, this was odd. The Forensic people would arrive soon. There would be photographs galore of the scene and the casualties.

O'Connell and McCann huddled together.

"We're all done here." grunted David.

McCann spoke.

“I take it nothing will be said now or any time in the future?”

O’Connell nodded, “All done.” He didn’t thank McCann or the Higgins’ for the risks they took. The latter wanted Artie checked out medically.

Paddy suggested to Joe. “I can come with you guys.”

“No,” replied Joe, “if you ever want an evening meal or your breakfast at our house again, be best to let the storm pass.” McCann nodded and hitched a lift back to Dublin with a couple of Gards.

The ambulances arrived with police escorts, but there were no doctors on board. George was in one with two Gards accompanying him. Claire went in another with a female Garda officer, the wounded Lithuanian from below the hayloft and the Irish ‘sentries’ were in a third. The Lithuanian was declared dead upon arrival at the hospital. The other two guys went straight to Intensive Care.

Artie was taken by his brothers to an A&E unit. He was bandaged and all the Higgins’ went home to face potentially the most dangerous experiences of the night, Joe’s wife’s reaction to Artie’s shooting. After a doing, fortunately interrupted by Artie being forced to bed despite his protestations, his older brothers and their dad retired to the sitting room with two bottles of whiskey and relived the night’s happenings.

The Irish media, acting on a press statement from Garda headquarters, headlined, “Four men shot dead, one seriously wounded, two seriously injured, one less seriously wounded, in drug gang war in a Bettystown farm.”

Later editions corrected 'five shot dead.' They quoted Chief Superintendent David O'Connell, "We received intelligence an incident involving armed men was likely to go down at a specific location. Unfortunately, by the time we arrived, we could not intervene to prevent the fighting. Suspects have been apprehended. I am pleased no officers or civilians were seriously hurt in the incident. Three men are detained in hospital, two with serious head injuries and one with gunshot wounds, whose prognosis is unknown."

O'Connell spoke to Inspector Ryan and the sergeant in charge of the response unit. He began by saying,

"Do any of your men enjoy a drink?"

"Oh, that's very kind of you Sir." replied the unwitting sergeant. The inspector said nothing.

O'Connell glared at the sergeant.

"The Commissioner wants a particular line to come out covering this incident. He doesn't want any mention of the people from the North or McCann's outfit after a few jars, CLEAR.?"

"Perfectly," chorused both officers.

"If it comes out, I have ways of knowing who leaked it and I'll have their pension, clear."

The officers nodded.

"One other thing," he paused," you and your cops did well there, this will be made explicit in my report, and it will be on each officer's record."

“Thank you, Sir, “again in unison, walking away. When they were out of his hearing the Inspector said, “He’s from Cork.”

“Of course, he is.” agreed the sergeant.

Once over the Border and in their own car, Farrell asked: “What do you make of your pal, O’Connell? I mean, what was all that about? You consider him unconventional, but those risks were just plain mad.”

“Yes,” agreed, Alan, “I tried to talk him out of it. I can’t understand why he made those decisions; it is a puzzle.

He will have his reasons but there is being professional and there is being cavalier, which is way off the Richter scale.”

“It’s just,” Farrell said quietly, “I got a distinct impression he didn’t intend the ‘Fat Man’ to come out of it alive.”

Walker nodded; he had had the same impression.

George got time to think in his hospital bed. He phoned Peter Donald and said he was in an accident in Dublin and was in hospital. He explained he was currently on a week’s leave. The accident meant he couldn’t go to Glasgow the following week, and Laura would benefit from support. Donald was shocked and sympathetic.

George said he “I will only remain in hospital for another two or three days on a precautionary basis.

He should have said, ‘I was knocked out, driven from Belfast to near Dublin in the boot of a car, tied to a chair for two hours, punched in the face and then shot twice, apart from that my day was fine, how was yours?’

Instead, he advised Peter to phone Laura, she could handle the Glasgow office for a couple of weeks, and he would phone her at the end of the week. Peter wanted to talk more, but George was weak from the exertion of the phone call and shut it down as quickly as he could.

A solicitor called Malachy Drinan came to see him. He told George the Garda contacted him and described George as a person the police were going to interview and charge with serious crimes. There was also an extradition issue with the UK (Northern Ireland) authorities.

He motioned to the-armed Gards at the ward door.

"You must be a big fish," he announced cheerfully. "All to do with the drug war shootout?"

What an odd way to describe it. How much should he share with Drinan, who would brief a barrister, maybe two, on his behalf, one for the courts in the North and to one for the courts in the South? He told Drinan about Paddy McCann being at the buildings where he was shot. He had wrestled with an explanation for his decisions since the first afternoon in his office and at the Barrows and he was no nearer finding faintly plausible explanations a defence barrister could use in court. How could he explain why meek, mild George McNeill ended up having to be rescued from a drug cartel and was helping with police enquiries into ten violent deaths and the disappearance of half a million Euros? What was the moment of change? How could he tell others the reason if he couldn't explain it to himself? He continued to reflect on all this.

Three days into his hospital stay, O'Connell and Walker, were permitted to interview George under caution. Malachy Drinan was present. O'Connell indicated he intended to caution George.

Malachy launched forth:

“Chief Superintended can you clarify if my client is going to be charged with any offences that occurred in the Republic of Ireland?”

David hesitated. He muttered, “The whereabouts of half a million Euros needs established,” and the “disappearance of three foreign nationals’ resident in the Republic of Ireland for at least a year prior to them going off the grid.”

“Well Chief Superintendent, is there any evidence these matters took place in the Republic of Ireland’s jurisdiction? I think Chief Inspector Walker will agree they both occurred in Belfast, or are you claiming jurisdiction for crimes in Belfast?”

Both were aware Drinan was firing a warning shot over the political sensitivities that abounded in the whole drama.

O’Connell was irritated but fought back.

“I expect to receive an extradition request from the authorities in Northern Ireland concerning both issues......” He then petered out.

Drinan again.

“My client is unsafe in the North, witness the fact he was abducted and subject to considerable violence, as was Miss Turner. I wonder what arguments the Northern Ireland authorities would bring against that in a Dublin court.”

It was Walker’s turn, and he began gamely.

“We wish to identify whether your client has information pertaining to the missing half million euros and the shooting of Fedor Pakus and Patrick Quinn in Shaftsbury Square last August. Further, were the missing Euros used to purchase property in West Belfast?

In addition, we wish to know what became of Arturas Pakus, his son, Vito. and his associate Dietmar? Finally, we want to know what his relationship with Paddy McCann is, a convicted former IRA terrorist."

"My client has no information concerning any of the matters pertaining to the missing foreign nationals. Regarding Mr McCann, your colleague Chief Superintendent O'Connell can help. He has a working relationship with Mr McCann."

Walker cursed David inwardly for his reckless and inexplicable use of McCann and his cohorts, but he said nothing.

Drinan again:

"What my client, who has been severely wounded because of police, particularly PSNI, negligence, wants to know is how he was abducted under the noses of PSNI officers who were supposed to be keeping him under protective surveillance. Need I also remind you, Chief Inspector, my client and, Miss Turner, were identified by these gangsters through a leak at your Police station. A photographic leak that included a British Home Office Minister, the Northern Ireland Chief Constable, and a prominent MP, all of whose lives could have been put at risk."

He had taken a flier here, but the prospect of this coming out in court and the subsequent media coverage proved a powerful weapon.

Walker could only imagine what Billy Robertson would say. Drinan had played all his cards, his strategy was to persuade the cops they achieved the dismemberment of a serious and ruthless gang in the South and one likely to spread its tentacles North, hostages were rescued, and George McNeill suffered enough. The money was still outstanding, and one final card needed to be played. George asked to see David O'Connell on his own.

As he walked by Geroge, Walker leaned forward.

"I don't know if you consider yourself an unlucky person who stumbled into someone else's nightmare or a clever sod who is extracting himself from a series of crimes but think on this. Because of your actions eight men are dead. If you had done the right thing in Shaftsbury Square most of them, including your gardener likely wouldn't be. Just remember that when you think of the last few months."

Walker left the ward with Drinan incensed by the latter's smug attitude but reminded himself no court case against McNeill would survive a PSNI Chief Inspector thumping the defence solicitor no matter how much he wanted to. He stood glowering and ignoring Drinan's prattling.

Inside George went straight to the point: "Chief Superintendent, would you agree I have committed no offences in the Republic of Ireland? Further, would you accept I have been a victim of a shooting an enquiry might suggest could have been avoided if the Garda had not let matters play out?"

O'Connell had his own reasons for that, but George was right. The gang could have been apprehended earlier. He neither agreed nor disagreed with George's claim. It was conjecture, however; the truth mattered less than what your enemies make out of the entire business and O'Connell guessed they would have a field day.

He expected he would have to do a deal with McNeill. It was a pity Alan didn't recognise that, the Ulsterman could be a bit tight arsed, always acting by the book. Even when they met up with their old pal Andri Shevlov, Walker limited his drinking while Shevlov and O'Connell got rat arsed; at least Alan stayed sober enough to see them safely to their hotel.

George, “If a portion of the money could be returned, would that close the business as far as you are concerned?”

“It would help,” agreed O’Connell. “But there is the matter of the disappearance of three foreign nationals.”

George, “Believe me I genuinely have no idea where they are.”

O’Connell, “How much money are you talking about? We have a strong policy dealing with the proceeds of crime”

George nodded, “Approximately 240,000 Euros.”

“The difficulty is,” O’Connell surmised, “The authorities in the North would have to agree so the money could come down from Belfast.”

George laughed. “What if I told you the money was in the Republic of Ireland? Would that change things?”

David could imagine the headlines. ‘Retiring Dublin Garda Chief brings down foreign drug cartel and delivers a quarter of a million Euros into the Criminal Assets Bureau’s coffers. After thirty years of crime fighting, Chief Superintendent O’Connell, who is shortly to retire, described his latest crime fighting bust as his best.’

He would retire with a further decoration, no Assistant Commissioner’s pension, which rankled most of all, but his opponents in the media and the political establishment would hate having to credit him with it. They came to an agreement and George agreed to take O’Connell’s officers to the Donegal cottage before returning home.

Drinan and Walker were invited back in. O’Connell said.

“Sorry Alan, but Mr McNeill can facilitate the return of a fair proportion of the lost money. He will face no charges here.”

Walker stormed back up North. He said to Farrell. “It’s above our pay grade. It is up to Robertson.”

They demanded a formal minuted meeting with their Chief.

“Who is minuting this?” Walker asked in Robertson’s office.

“I am,” was his boss’s terse reply.

“This was not a turf war. The Garda got mercenaries in to eliminate the foreign gang.” began Walker.

“Arranged by your pal.” Robertson observed. “What was the outcome? Bad guys taken out, hostages returned safely, all outside our jurisdiction. Could brothers have fallen out, maybe the ‘disappeared’ returned to take out the others?”

Walker stared incredulously and Robertson was conscious he had pushed the boundaries too far.

“As for McNeill, the money issue is sort of resolved and there is no evidence linking him to the disappearance of Arturas, Vito and Dietmar.”

Walker and Farrell were furious, but neither could see a way forward unless evidence turned up.

The only person who might help was one of Martin Breen’s associates, a Liam McVeigh, whom they could not trace. He was, according to sister, living somewhere in Spain. If they did find him, there was no evidence to seek his extradition.

"This did not happen on our turf; it has nothing to do with us." Robertson finally ruled.

Later Robertson made a call. "I have put it to bed. It's not our bag, no scandal." He confided to the old man he was speaking to.

Claire was taken from Dublin, through a change of police cars at the Border, to her sister's house. She was upset when she saw Liz, who appeared pale and drawn as she pretended to the family all was well and dealt with Claire's abduction. The entire incident had only lasted twelve hours, but it felt more like a few lifetimes.

Claire ate toast, sipped tea, and relayed what occurred to a horrified Liz. After she "told all" she brightened up.

"Did you tell Mammy, or Kev?"

"No to Mammy, yes to Kev." replied Liz. "What happens now? Will you be OK to go to work, should you take a break?"

"Work would be a port in a storm right now, but can I stay here for a bit?"

"I imagine your house must feel like the house of horrors."

"Actually no, I don't feel that way. It is simply the neighbours; I know they will be all over me and I am not supposed to disclose details of what took place. I am exhausted. Can I go to bed?"

"Yes, your room is ready, but Karen wants a hug. She knows nothing, but she senses all is not well with you."

"Right, I'll pop in on my way to bed."

Claire wanted to sleep but then the tears came. 'They all think I have done so well. What with the breakup with 'thingy, 'coming home, getting a job and my own house, and not throwing myself into a relationship that was safe but not for me? George made her feel different, relaxed. It wasn't easy. At times he acted so distant, he had secrets, now I see why. But a lot of the distance was to protect me. Anytime we were together, I was.... content, happy, once we got Aileen Whyte out of the way. I wanted him in my life. I am not prepared to write this relationship off yet.'

Claire returned to school the following week. Liz insisted she have an appointment with her GP, which she duly did. She described to him elements of her traumatic experience, but it was enough to convince him to persuade her to see a Counsellor who specialised in Post-Traumatic Stress Disorder. The female police officer who accompanied her on the drive up from the Border stayed in touch and also suggested she seek counselling. That fizzled out, Mandy was on hand with her less professionally based counselling.

"What is the future for you and George? You only told me bits and pieces, but it must have been exciting. Is he the one, would he," she paused for a minute, then said dramatically, "take a bullet for you?"

'Two actually,' Claire said inwardly.

George also returned to Belfast and rested at Riverdale. Gerard and Grace were neighbourly in their usual way and Peter Donald came over to see him. George had the impression Peter was aware of a little of what happened. He was solicitous and encouraged George to take another week off. He promised he would go over to Glasgow and help Laura. This proved the last straw. There was no way Laura could cope with Peter in Glasgow, or Peter cope with Glasgow. He declared firmly after his week off; he would return to Glasgow.

Terry and Melissa were dropped off by their mother and on Saturday night Jan drove George to his house where he and Elena cooked a meal.

"You should stay here for a while, George. I can nurse you. I did it for my auntie last week."

Elena's gentle caring almost made George feel he would like to play the sick card to its limits.

"You look so pale, you have lost weight, you hardly ate anything and carry yourself so gingerly as if you have more than just bruised ribs." Elena protested.

He agreed to stay the night but insisted on going back home the next day. George wanted to phone Claire but, as after the 'row' at New Year, he put it off. She could dismiss him from her life, which would be sensible, any remaining hope would be gone.

Eventually, he dialled her mobile, but it was switched off. He phoned her house, but the phone rang out. Finally, as he had Liz's number from the Christmas/New Year period, he phoned it. He was not surprised to receive a cool response from Liz. Then he heard Claire's voice in the background and the voices became muffled as Liz's hand was over the phone. He held on and finally Claire came on.

"Hello George, how are you?"

"Claire, I am truly sorry for all I put you through."

There was a moment's silence, then Claire answered.

"George, I had enough drama and misery with my ex-husband, but I know if it wasn't for you, I would be dead."

Even mentioning this made George wince. He could feel the pain in his chest where the two bullets hit.

"Another way to put it is saying if it wasn't for me, you would not have been abducted and assaulted in the first place."

"I cannot explain my feelings for you even to myself. As a woman all I ever sought was a calm, secure life, that sounds predictable even boring. I know you tried to prevent me from becoming part of your life because it would put me at risk. I am not sure you tried hard.

George winced, accepting the blow.

"First I need space, I need a commitment from you that drug gangs, police, money schemes will not be part of any future we may have/"

Hope rose, emboldened, he went on; "I want us to be together."

Claire responded, "Let us meet and talk and think and....... take time, then decide."

Because of the number of deaths at the Bettystown incident, an Assistant Garda Commissioner (AC) began an investigation into what on the surface was a gang dispute. He was disturbed to hear rumours the senior officer present held discussions with one gang before the incident. No one would confirm this, nor could they explain why none of the second gang was detained. O'Connell's report suggested they fled just after his officers arrived, having eliminated their opponents. His priority was to secure the hostage and the crime scene. The AC had Pol Tobin brought in for questioning.

He confirmed, as O'Connell's report stated, he pin-pointed the Bettystown site regarding the European gang. No other Dublin gang was involved, Tobin claimed. That left a possible Northern gang or paramilitaries from either side of the Border.

The Assistant Commissionaire contacted the PSNI. He was advised the PSNI believed there was no Northern involvement of any kind apart from the two hostages. He could not speak to Walker or Farrell, but a hint was dropped over there being "political sensitivities" as far as the authorities in the North were concerned. The AC recommended his report was embargoed for thirty years. The political classes and the media were so enthralled by the elimination of the foreign drug gang, they did not probe further.

July in Dublin was hot and dry. David O'Connell was settling into his retirement. No more late-night calls or anxiety creating newspaper headlines, bliss. Milltown Golf course was a fine parkland challenge built on the banks of the Dodder. David wasn't a member, but he was playing at a retired police officer's charity fundraiser.

"Young O'Connell," he was greeted by a grizzled ex-inspector he remembered terrifying him as young Gard. The man was eighty years old, and twenty-five years retired.

'I hope I get twenty-five years.' mused David. He stayed for the presentation of the prizes but declined a drink.

"I have the car and I am under orders from the good Mrs O'Connell to be home early." he explained, and he was the first away.

But he did not go straight home. He drove over to Orwell Road, parked his car, and walked down to a gate between two grey pillars and spoke into an intercom. The gate opened, and he was met by an official of the Russian Embassy who conducted him inside after some security measures.

He was allowed to keep both his mobile phones. He waited in an anteroom, sipping a coffee. A youngish man, Pavel Mendov, entered. They had never met and had spoken only twice on the phone.

"How is our mutual friend Yuri Shevlov?" enquired David.

"He is fine, just finishing a posting in Syria, but he hopes to be attached to the London Embassy next year and he looks forward to finally visiting Dublin," Pavel replied.

David nodded and took out one of his phones, opened up the photos and showed Mendov the pictures he took of the "Fat Man" lying dead on the old sofa in the Bettystown barn. He handed the phone to Mendov.

"That will be a source of relief to individuals in Moscow," said Mendov.

He rang a buzzer, and another official came in with an attaché case. Pavel handed it to David. Neither man said another word. They shook hands and David left the Embassy and returned to his car.

David couldn't restrain himself and peeked inside the case, wondering what a quarter of million Euros in cash looked like. He whistled to himself, 'It will make a fairly comfortable retirement more comfortable,' he drove home. Who could he approach to obtain advice on how to invest or spend such a large cash sum, George?

Chapter 13

Maybes Aye Maybes Naw

George and Claire moved to Glasgow together. They stayed initially in a flat in the West End near Laura and Cat before buying an old semi in Lenzie in the north of the city. When Claire became pregnant, they married. A low-key celebration with a few friends and family. George became a partner in Baileys although still managing the expanding Glasgow business. Claire worked in a private nursery in the city.

She did the cooking, but noted how he rushed to set the table, or clear the dishes and stack the dishwasher, determined to show he took nothing for granted. Perhaps most of all were the affectionate little touches on her neck, her shoulder, or the way he put his arms around her waist.

Every so often, an event triggered a dark mood in George. She recognised it; he became uncommunicative with a faraway expression. His eyes fell. Usually, they were kind but, in this situation, troubled. They were never angry; she remembered angry eyes from her marriage to 'thingy. 'At first Claire avoided it but later insisted he talk about it. More and more of the events from the Shaftsbury Square 'incident' emerged. George warned her.

"You know too much; you are now an accessory."

"Right, but the more we talk, you become relaxed after all your experiences."

“I paid most of my debt and as for the rest....... what I did, I did for self-preservation and to protect those I love. You were the only one I failed.”

There comes a time when putting the truth out is no longer worth it. People have died or moved on. You have additional responsibilities now.” ‘

George wondered, ‘What if there were more brothers, or the ‘disappeared’ came back? He could never forget Walker’s tirade in his hospital ward, ‘If he doe the right thing, eight men would not be dead.’

Five years later, fishermen made a disturbing discovery in Lough Neagh. The local Area Commander Chief Inspector John Farrell went to the scene. Later, he contacted PSNI headquarters in Belfast and spoke with Detective Chief Superintendent Alan Walker.

“One of our missing Europeans may have turned up. Forensics are on it as we speak.”

“I was about to contact you, John. Liam McVeigh died in Spain 3 months ago. Interpol eventually sent us a document from him in which he claimed he and a close friend killed three foreigners in Belfast. He said in it that he was only revealing this because the friend was dead, and he was seriously ill, and it was on his conscience.

Walker and Farrell met at Police Headquarters.

“Do we just let this go, John? Time has passed---.”

“Never.” said Farrell resolutely. “You always taught me we must do the proper thing without fear or favour. Forensics located carpet threads on the body or what remains of it. If we can match this to a carpet in McNeill’s house. We can tie him into knowing one of these guys who disappeared.”

"McNeill sold the house 4 years ago. The carpet may have been replaced."

"OK, but McNeill does not know we did not take a sample when Breen was killed."

"If you look at the big picture, a sizable proportion of the money went to the right place as proceeds of crime and a drugs gang was wiped out."

"But replaced by a local, even more dangerous mob. "Farrell countered.

"We knew McVeigh was a pal of Breen's. As such he was always a suspect, although we had no evidence. The document leaves McNeill in the clear. McNeill nearly lost his life, and the life of the woman he married. He has not got off Scot free."

"Is there any new evidence to suggest we should interview McNeill again?"

"Boss, if one body has appeared, so will the others. There might be more forensic information to link the killings to McNeill.

"One thing for sure, John, he was no mister 'big', no MI5 agent, no accountant for the Belfast mob, nor part of the IRA.

"What do you think, Alan? Was he an innocent passer-by?"

"Not that innocent. He stole money and benefitted from that theft. He did not commit a crime before or since. Let us wait and see what else surfaces."

"McNeill is living respectably and quietly near Glasgow."

“Are we going to let him get away with it?”

“In Scotland they have a phrase for this sort of dilemma, ‘Maybes Aye, Maybes Naw,’ Let’s leave it at that for the time being.”

In a park in Glasgow, Terry McNeill kicked a football with his wee stepbrother, Jan.

David O’Connell relaxed by the poolside of his villa in Naples, Florida.

BBC Northern Ireland news confirmed Aileen Whyte would become the First Minister. She recently left Westminster and successfully contested the NI Assembly seat of a colleague who stood down.

Printed in Great Britain
by Amazon

31950331R00185